Vinyl Wonderland

A NOVEL

Mark Rigney

CASTLE BRIDGE MEDIA
DENVER, COLORADO, USA

CASTLE BRIDGE MEDIA
Denver, Colorado

Cover photo by Immo Wegmann/Unsplash,
Scott Evans/Unsplash.
These photos have been modified.

VINYL WONDERLAND
©2024 Mark Rigney

ISBN: 979-8-9895934-5-3

"You can't always get what you want" – The Rolling Stones

Chapter One

ON THE DAY THAT KARL handed over the keys to Vinyl Wonderland, he scrawled four hard-and-fast rules in red ink on a torn sheet of college-ruled note paper.

1) Don't steal.
2) Wash your hands before you touch the actual records, unless it's disco, then do what you want.
3) Show up on time and lock up at closing.
4) If you value your life, do not ever, in any way, mess with the Elvis door.

I'd never heard Karl use the term "the Elvis door," but when he shoved that paper into my hand, I knew right away what he meant. At the back of the shop, immediately adjacent to the fire exit, Karl kept a life-size Elvis Presley standee, and behind that, camouflaged by the King and slightly recessed, was a door that I had always assumed went to a closet. Unlike the gray-painted fire exit door, the door that Elvis guarded was the color of reddish mulch. It even had a shaggy, mulchy look to it, as if it were made of actual sphagnum, compressed and shaped (who knows how) into a door. The handle looked like something lost explorers might find in a Medieval castle.

As for the standee, it showed Elvis in his jewel-studded leisure-suit days, sunglasses on, a mic in one hand. I thought he looked like he was auditioning for John Travolta's role in *Saturday Night Fever*, a movie I wasn't allowed to like because it glorified disco music, and believe you me, if there was one way for an athletic, rock-and-roll kid not to be cool in 1984, it was to ally yourself in any way with disco.

The primary reason that I had, up until then, paid zero attention to the Elvis door was that once I got inside Vinyl Wonderland, all I wanted to do was sort through the records. What else does anyone want out of a used record shop? Sift through enough old LPs, and time takes a hike. The mind drops into a whole new space, one made up of songs you can't quite hear—not yet, not until you get home and place your new treasures carefully onto your turntable. On top of all that, flipping through used record albums is fantastically tactile. After you've worked your way through a few bins of barely organized albums, your fingers come away dry and coated in a fine, powdery dust.

Basically, see, the entire experience is magic. The way a high school education is supposed to be, and mostly isn't.

Anyway, I read those four inviolate rules as Karl and I stood on the front porch of his mother's Clintonville bungalow. It was eight-forty in the morning in early December, and the weather was frosty. I was all bundled up, layered like a badly made wedding cake, but Karl was dressed in thin pajamas, very faded, with a motif of elephants linked trunk to tail and running the length of his stubby legs. The poor guy had been outdoors for all of two minutes, and he was already shivering, but he didn't seem to be in any hurry to get back inside.

"Not kidding about the door," he said, when he was sure I'd finished reading. "You let that alone."

Now, it's a fact that I was an official high school drop-out, but my brain was in excellent working order, and I had fond memories of how Mrs. Felsen, my favorite teacher, had marched us through the story of Bluebeard in tenth grade English, and I remembered how Bluebeard had given just one order to his clever new wife, and that was to never, ever open the door at the end of the hall. Which, of course, she did, because human beings suck at dealing with the tension between "no" and "opportunity."

To Karl, I said, "I like the name. 'The Elvis door.'"

Karl grunted as if I'd managed to seriously disappoint him. He said, "Brendan, I'm pretty sure you're a decent guy, so I'm not worried about the till, or you hosting some kind of wild after-hours party, and this'll only be full-time for a few days, but that door? I have never been more serious about anything. Your number one job, starting now, is to pretend it doesn't exist."

A word about Karl Wickett. The first time I really talked to the guy was when we were both in Vinyl Wonderland and he got annoyed with the *American Graffiti* soundtrack, featuring "Why Do Fools Fall in Love?" and switched it for Spirit's *Twelve Dreams of Dr. Sardonicus*. Pretty much the second that the needle on the counter-top turntable hit the record, my senses were on high alert. The first song began harmlessly enough, and the lyrics were more plaintive than earth-shattering—"You have the world at your fingertips"—but then a host of new instruments crashed the party, kind of like a rock band tumbling headlong into an orchestra pit, and the singer yelled, "Wake up!"

Well. I felt like that record was talking directly to me, and I forgot all about the AC/DC records I'd been fingering, and my head snapped up and I looked from the wall-mounted speakers to Karl and I said, "What on earth is *this*?"

Man, did he laugh. "Kid," he said, "you got a lot to learn."

Then he motioned me over—kind of like Santa, with a twist of his head—and he showed me the album cover, which portrayed the band members from Spirit in a fun-house mirror, warped beyond recognition, and twenty minutes later, it was like I'd known Karl all my life. Which I hadn't. In fact, up until that day, all that I knew about Karl was what I could see. He was in his late forties, he was shaped like a pear, and he wore the thickest, dorkiest glasses I'd ever seen outside of a Mr. Magoo cartoon. When he needed to read the small print on an album sleeve, he'd lean in close like a mole trying to puzzle out sunlight.

Thanks to Karl's extraordinary glasses, it was kind of hard most days to tell exactly what he was looking at, but when we met at his mother's bungalow, it was one hundred percent clear that I had his full attention. He fixed me with a steady stare, and then he lifted a hand as if he were about to give a toast at a wedding and he needed the room to quiet.

"One last thing. You're gonna get some customers who ask about that door. They'll get pushy. Some of them, they'll even tell you, 'It's okay, I've been through there before.' But if I'm not around? The answer is no."

I said, "Not a problem," and I made it sound cool and casual, but what I was back to thinking about was Bluebeard's wife, and how Mrs. Felsen was always and forever referencing that woman's dilemma, as if her life, or maybe ours, was a constant replay of the Bluebeard scenario. The only thing Mrs. Felsen loved better than Bluebeard's wife were unreliable narrators. "When reading fiction," she liked to say, "you must remain vigilant. Otherwise, you'll be fleeced, scammed, and flummoxed. Any questions?"

We had dozens, including how to spell "flummoxed," but right at that moment, all my questions were centered on Karl, and his sudden, unnerving intensity. Even though I'd just promised to keep the world away from his precious extra door, he was still staring me down as if, instead of agreeing, I'd just contradicted him.

"Repeat that back," he said. "Tell me exactly what I said about that door."

"Sure. I'm not allowed to go anywhere near the Elvis door, and neither is anybody else, even if they beg."

"That's right. Not even if they bribe you."

"Karl, nobody's gonna bribe me to open a door."

He leaned closer, as if I were the flip side of an especially interesting record jacket and he was trying to work out whether I was the stereo or the mono edition. "Brendan," he said, "when people want something bad enough, they will offer just about anything."

I took a half step back. "Look, I swear by whatever you want, this is a non-issue. I don't know what else I'm supposed to say."

He closed the gap between us and said, very deliberately, "Swear on your mother's grave."

Now that freaked me out. I was ninety-nine percent sure that I'd never mentioned my mom, and I was one hundred percent sure he hadn't asked, see, which meant that he didn't have any idea that my mother was lying right that very minute under a headstone in Union Cemetery.

Swear on your mother's grave.

It's just a phrase, right? Common enough. Harmless. Meant for emphasis. No problem, then. I was a big boy. And if that was what he wanted, then I could do it.

"Fine," I said, although my voice wasn't as steady as I would have liked. "I swear on my mother's grave, I'll leave the door alone. And I can't open it even if I wanted to, right? You're the one with the key."

He nodded at this, waddled backward a step or so, and shivered again. He said, "And let's both remember, I won't be out long. Just four or five days at most. Just until the worst is over."

By "worst," Karl meant his mother's rehab, which was the whole reason I'd been offered the Vinyl Wonderland job in the first place. Karl's mother had broken her hip, and now that she was home from the hospital, she needed full-time care—at least for the first few days. Did middle-aged Karl still live with his mother? He did indeed, three hundred and sixty-five days a year.

"That front door key," he said, "it sticks sometimes in cold weather, but don't let it beat you. You're in charge, not that little stick of metal."

"Gotcha. Boss."

He grinned as if I'd just paid him a real tickler of a compliment. "I could get used to that. Never had an employee before."

"Never?"

"Not part of how this place is supposed to work."

"If you say so."

He grinned again, but he looked embarrassed, too, as if he'd just been caught wearing mismatched socks. He said, "I think if it's just for a few days, she won't mind."

In the moment, I assumed that by "she," Karl meant his mother, and it was only many days later that I realized he'd been referring to someone much more dangerous.

Twenty minutes later, right on time, there I was: the new sole proprietor of Vinyl Wonderland. I knew my job was small potatoes—although Karl had hired me on at five dollars an hour, which handily beat the federal minimum of the day, $3.35—but even so, when I settled into the chair-backed barstool behind the counter, I felt like I'd won the lottery.

I'm pretty sure I felt like that for the whole first day and most of the next. Then Celine DeLapp walked in, and everything went to hell.

Chapter Two

WHEN THE WOMAN WHO TURNED out to be Celine DeLapp pushed her way out of a snowstorm and into Vinyl Wonderland, it was just after seven in the evening, less than an hour until closing, and I was cleaning fingerprints off the discs in Karl's most recently purchased record collection, so the whole shop was drowning in a stink of ammonia. Between discs, I was working my way through a fifth of cheap-skate bourbon that I'd taken to storing in easy reach under the counter. I had Grand Funk Railroad's "I'm Your Captain" on the turntable, and I was trying to decide if I loved or hated what I was hearing—perhaps it was possible to ride both those waves at once? The bourbon seemed to be saying yes, absolutely, and while we're having this little chat, why not down another swig?

"Where," demanded Celine, "is Karl?"

Now, I'll admit that she startled me, but the context is crucial. Customers at Vinyl Wonderland were sporadic even by day and downright rare after dark, and on top of that, the bass guitar line in "I'm Your Captain," really did deserve my full attention, so. The point is that I rallied, or tried to, and after waging a valiant war for control of my tongue, I managed to say the most obvious thing in the world, which was, "Karl is not here."

"Who the hell are you?"

That was a much tougher question, and instead of answering, I stared at the snow that had blown in behind Celine's military surplus boots, and then I stared at her ripped-to-shreds cargo pants, and after that, I stared at her heavy leather bomber jacket (easily one size too big for her skinny shoulders), and at last I found myself staring into her defiant, cat-green eyes. Her blonde hair was cut super-short, except for the bangs, and she had a knife-edge Hollywood jawline, the kind that makes its owner stick out in any crowd, anywhere.

Since I still hadn't responded, Celine gave up on me, marched to the middle of the store, and shot a look into the back corner. She said, sounding hopeful and mournful all at once, "He's really not here?"

"Out sick."

Which was more or less true. Have I mentioned yet that back then, the truth and I, we had a pretty tenuous relationship?

Celine swung around and took a long look at me, and that made me so nervous that I held up the nearest greasy forty-five—by which I mean a record, not a gun. Forty-fives are what the recording industry used to call a "single." The A-side was the hit, and the B-side was whatever the producers had lying around that they thought wouldn't do their shiny new star too much damage. The disc I was holding right then was Lou Christie, that "Lightning Strikes" song, and Celine had me so far off my game that I was waving it around like a maraca.

"You," she said, "look like an imbecile."

No record in history ever got put down faster. Grand Funk Railroad played a final note, and then the stylus worked its way to the center of the record, emitting light scratches all the way, *tk-tk, tk-tk, tk-tk,* before lifting away and returning to its resting place. This was an awkward bit of timing, since now the only thing between me and Celine was silence.

"Sorry," I said. "Can I help you?"

"Did Karl tell you I'd be coming?"

I did my best to look ignorant, which, let's face it, didn't take much. I said, "And you are…?"

She introduced herself, first name first, last name second, then added, as if she were putting on a suit of armor, "DeLapp is my married name."

Married? She looked to be all of twenty, maybe twenty-two, but either way, not much older than me. True, I knew a couple kids who'd been a few years ahead of me in school, and the day after graduation, they got hitched.

Sweethearts since the age of sixteen, married at eighteen. My mother used to tell me she had bunches of girlfriends who were married—"married off"—right out of high school.

That thought, I put away in a hurry. Dwelling on my mother was something I avoided at the best of times, and fretting about her when faced with a girl like Celine? That would be a recipe for disaster.

Not that Celine was a girl. If she was married, she'd definitely jumped ship on girlhood. I wasn't too sure how or when the transition to being a grown-up happened for most girls, but marriage seemed like a pretty clear Maginot Line. It also meant that I needed to stop thinking ("Right now, Brendan Purcell!") about how pretty she was. Celine DeLapp was absolutely not available.

For a basically corrupt kid, I really was kind of jaw-droppingly innocent.

Outside, a snowplow thundered past, and a spray of salt and slush spattered the Vinyl Wonderland window. Celine and I both glanced toward the noise, then got back to the business of locking horns.

"The fact is," she said, "I need the key."

"The key?"

"The key, dummy. To the door behind Elvis."

Now, Vinyl Wonderland had four doors total, exactly like that freaky Moody Blues song, "House of Four Doors." Just like any place of business, the shop had a front door, mostly glass, the kind that in warm weather got propped open with the help of several bricks that Karl kept piled in the outside vestibule for exactly that purpose. Anyone exiting through the front door wound up on North High Street, a four-lane artery where you could catch a bus north to upscale Worthington or south to campus, and then downtown.

The shop itself was set partway along a row of adjoining brick-fronted buildings, two stories high. I never did find out who or what occupied Vinyl Wonderland's second floor, but I do know that next door on the left was a State Farm insurance office, and on the right was a tiny, cramped shoe repair place where this ninety-year-old cobbler would fix sandals, shoes, or boots for so little money, it's a wonder he didn't starve.

Inside Vinyl Wonderland, the main room had an L-shaped floor plan, with its back end bending around behind the cobbler's shop. When you walked in, the first thing you'd see was Karl (or me) behind the counter, probably peering at an old album cover and hoping to ring up a sale on what must have been the world's ugliest cash register. (It looked a lot like my 7th grade Texas Instruments calculator, only bulkier.)

Past the front counter were all the record bins, row after row, carefully divided by genre: Jazz, Gospel, Rock, Classical, you name it, pretty much everything except for Rap and Hip-Hop. Karl, who played six instruments in three bands, had nothing against rap, but in 1984, that whole genre was too new to have trickled down in large numbers into the second-hand shops, which Vinyl Wonderland most definitely was. Some days, we'd have a Sugarhill Gang record in stock, or maybe Grandmaster Flash, and if we did, well, we just filed it under Soul or Blues.

Wedged way back in the most distant corner, completely invisible from the street, but in easy view of Karl's perch at the counter, was the rear entrance, Door Two, which led to a grimy restroom with a flickering fluorescent light, and, next to that a storage closet. If you went to the end of that short little hallway, you'd get to Door Three, and the alley out back: trash cans, parking for Karl's beat-up Ford Pinto, and the kind of broken pavement that held puddles for days after a rain.

Door Number Four, as I believe I've mentioned, hid behind the King.

"Hey," said Celine. "Earth to Cash Register Kid. I need the key."

I blinked at her. "That's a key I don't have. And Karl was real clear."

"About?"

"That door. He said, don't let anyone go through there. Which I can't do even if I wanted to, since, like I just said, I don't have the key."

Celine's eyes had narrowed down the way movie actors do when they want to convince you they're being really intense, except that with Celine, she wasn't acting. In fact, I was pretty sure that this girl—woman—whatever—was seriously intense most of the time.

She said, putting careful emphasis on each word, "I have been in there before."

In? In where? I'd been assuming the door went pretty much nowhere, except perhaps to something electrical. Old plumbing.

"Great," I said, because what else could I say?

For a moment, Celine stuck her hands on her hips, the pose of someone who's rethinking their strategy. Sure enough, in another moment she was headed my way, with those heavy boots in the lead, clumping like someone twice her size across the floor. In different clothes, maybe she could have sashayed, or glided, or even just plain walked, but with those boots, plus the century-old floorboards at Vinyl Wonderland? She might have looked like a punk-girl pixie, but with that footgear on, she moved like a tank.

"Listen," she hissed, as she placed both hands on the counter, fingers splayed, "I *need* to get in there. And you are the one on duty, so you clearly know the score."

Her sports metaphor slid me right back in my comfort zone. Until dropping out of school, I'd been a useful cog for the Whetstone High soccer team (go Braves), and I had a mixed-up, totally incoherent idea that someday soon, I'd be playing for them again—that the coaches would actually go out of their way to track me down, recruit me, get me back in the fold. Part of me knew that would never happen, but even so, it was pure pleasure to spin that scenario out in a daydream—to deny, as it were, the score.

"Hey," said Celine, and she reached up and snapped her fingers in my face. "Are you even listening?"

"Look," I said, "my name's Brendan."

"I don't care."

"Okay, I just thought—"

"No, don't think. Just shut up and gimme the key."

"I don't have any key!"

Well, I guess I must have really shouted that last part, because Celine reared back as if I were a snake and I'd just struck at her. She pushed off from the counter, took a full step away from me, and brushed her bangs out of her eyes with a fierce little gesture, as if telling herself that she was above being frightened.

"Let me get this straight," she said. "Karl left a kid in charge, and he didn't explain."

Now, it's a fact, see, that hardly anybody likes feeling stupid. Related to that, people appreciate feeling informed (it makes them feel powerful) and

I'm no exception. The truth is, I probably like information more than most. Back then especially, information, to me, was a sea-worthy raft capable of surviving the enormous ocean of Real Life, the one where I continually found myself lost and adrift. That's a metaphor I first learned in fifth grade, and I knew it wasn't original, even then, but it made visceral sense to me, and it led to a long line of half-assed art projects—me, bobbing along in lonely boats—that even my mother couldn't bring herself to coo over.

Anyway, when it came to information, I didn't necessarily know what to do with it once I got it, but (as Celine had so helpfully put it) I liked to know the score.

With that in mind, I stood up to my full height, which was a little over six feet, and I loomed over pesky Celine DeLapp like some latter-day Bela Lugosi, and I said, making no attempt to disguise my annoyance, "This is a record shop. I sell records. That's what Karl is paying me to do, so. Is there something I can help you find?"

Celine bit down on the side of her lower lip, looked at me as if I was the most useless thing since broken crockery, and said, "You know what? I'm gonna go pay Karl a visit."

"What, at home?"

"You think I don't know where he lives?"

I dropped back into my seat and said, "I really hadn't given it a lot of thought."

To my surprise, she laughed. "All right," she said. "I'm sorry. Friends, okay? Let's be friends. I just—I was expecting Karl, I found you, and we got off on the wrong foot. So, I'll get out of your hair, and we'll start fresh another time, okay?"

Mute, I nodded.

But she didn't leave, not quite. At the door, she turned back. "I'm serious," she said. "The world's a tough place. Let's be friends."

"Sure," I said. Not because I was feeling it, not because I wanted anything to do with this lunatic girl—woman—person—no matter how pretty she was, but because it seemed like the quickest way to get rid of her.

Celine pushed at the door, and a whirligig of snowflakes flew in. "Friends," she said, as she leaned on the door and zipped up that tough-asnails leather jacket. "It is definitely possible to have too many record albums, and you can sure as hell have too much snow. But you can't ever have too many friends."

And with that, she was gone.

Not long after, the day rolled even further downhill. A guy came in—white, early forties—and he stank. No exaggeration, the man reeked from ten yards' distance. He hadn't shaved in who knows how long, and he hadn't washed in at least a week. To call his clothes shabby would have been a kindness, and he was missing a prominent top tooth.

"So, hey," he said, in a high, sandpapery voice. "Roger sent me."

"Roger?"

He smirked and pulled out a pack of Marlboros. "Yeah. Roger. But. Pretty sure you're not who I'm here for."

That voice. It was like the man's vocal chords had been scored with broken glass.

I said, "You can't smoke in here."

"Sure, I can. It's a free country."

I shook my head. Karl hadn't added a "No Smoking" policy to his list of rules, but there were prominent "No Smoking" signs mixed into the many posters and promo pieces that covered just about every square inch of the shop's walls. My customer had even passed one on the way in, set at eye level on the front door, and no wonder. Album covers are nothing but paper, which I explained to the man with the missing tooth. "Plus," I said, "vinyl melts fast. This place is a firetrap. You want a smoke, step outside."

The man with the missing tooth smirked. "You gonna make me?"

I could have taken on the role of bouncer if I'd wanted to, and I knew it. I was younger than this guy, probably faster, and I most definitely outweighed him. However, he looked so far gone that I figured he might have a knife or a shiv, so I just reached for the phone, lifted the receiver, and hovered my finger over the number nine.

"On this block," I said, making it up as I went along, "the cops usually respond in about a minute flat."

The man with the missing tooth sighed and slipped his cigarette back into its packet. "All right, all right. Roger's an idiot, anyways."

And with that, he turned tail and left.

A little while later, at about the moment when the body odor from the man with the missing tooth finally cleared the shop, I did get one last troop of customers, a trio of high school girls, all teased hair and stonewashed jeans. To my surprise, instead of looking to see if we had any Madonna or Hall & Oates, the leader of that little pack came up to the counter with a double LP of piano works by Schubert, proof positive that you really can't judge a book by its cover.

Those three were my last customers of the night, and I closed up ten minutes early, left my bottle where it was, and headed for home, on foot, in the snow. Why was I walking almost two miles, when I could have enjoyed the mediocre comforts of my dad's mediocre Oldsmobile (a vinyl-brown Cutlass, barely two years old)? It was certainly available, since my father hardly ever left the house.

I'll get to that. I promise. The important thing is that I made it home, slept the night, woke up, added whiskey to my coffee, and walked right back to Vinyl Wonderland. I opened up, flicked on the lights, and got the till organized for the day.

And that's when the mayor barged in.

Chapter Three

MAYOR TONY ACCARDI ARRIVED IN a cloud of steamy hot breath and frosty, bone-chilling air, and before speaking a word, he stamped snow off his dress shoes, shucked off his gloves, stuffed them in his pockets, and blew on his hands. He wore a dark suit under a black wool overcoat, open enough to show off his red, white, and blue tie.

When at last he spoke, he said, "You're not Karl."

Oh, man, I thought. Here we go again.

Sure enough, before I could wrangle a useful reply, the mayor said, "Where *is* Karl? Don't tell me the deal's off. Don't tell me this dump has changed hands."

A quick word about Mayor Accardi since there was no question that that's who I was dealing with. His face was constantly splashed across the news. He liked baseball and beer, and he loved making sure that everyone who heard him speak understood that he was just like them, a regular guy, except that he had an M.B.A. and a career (on hold for now) as a consultant for several firms, the kind that pay major salaries and don't mind a break in the chain for a few years of "public service."

My dad met him once, at some sort of civic function, and when I'd asked him afterward what the mayor was like, he thought it over for a second, then said, "Intimidating and ethnic."

I really wished, even then, that he hadn't said that last part. In those days, and in that part of the world, "ethnic" was code used by white people and leveled not so much at Blacks or Asians as it was at other white people who were, well, darker. "Too ethnic" was how pale folks from Northern Europe talked about swarthier folks from Southern Europe, which was surely where Tony Accardi's forbears hailed from. I'm pretty sure my mother never spoke or thought in those terms, but sometimes I wonder. She was of her time, after all. Isn't everybody?

Anyway, I had just picked up a store-bought powdered donut (breakfast, though definitely not the breakfast of champions), and I was holding it very gingerly because of all that dry, frankly nasty sugar, and I'm pretty sure my mouth was hanging open, partly because I was ready to chomp on the donut, and partly because I was so surprised to be holding a personal audience with the most powerful man in the city. The bottom line? I looked like a dweeb.

Mayor Accardi evidently thought the same. He shook his head as if I could not possibly have been more of a disappointment, and then he headed to the back of the shop. As he went, he said, "If your tongue and your brain ever get re-connected, do let me know."

After a quick bit of re-connecting, I said, "The door's locked, and I don't have the key!"

The mayor swung around, looking profoundly suspicious. "Did I mention a door?"

"Um, no, I guess maybe you didn't."

"Kid, here's a Sunday dinner's worth of free advice. Never guess. Now, when exactly will Karl be back?"

I spread my hands in an "I don't know" gesture, dropping a mist of powdered sugar onto the counter as I did so.

Mayor Accardi started to say something, then apparently thought better of it. "Kid," he said at last, "I wasn't ever here. Are we clear on that?"

It seemed like the best thing to do was nod, so that's what I did.

"Also, you need to understand..." This time, his hesitation seemed not to come from his head, but from somewhere deep in his chest. For a second, I thought he was about to start crying, but then he blew out a breath, collected himself, and said, "I love this city. People can say what they want about my style, or my politics, but I love this place, and I always have. And that's why..."

Again, he trailed off, and this time, it seemed as if he might never start again.

"Okay," I said—like the guy needed my blessing, or my permission for whatever it was he was feeling. At this point, I was kind of hoping he really would start bawling. Thanks to my father, I was perfectly used to seeing grown men cry, and this guy clearly had the weight of the world (or something) on his shoulders. Let it all out, was what I wanted to tell him. Cut yourself some slack.

The mayor did the opposite. He gave himself a quick shake, like a wet dog spraying water, and he shot me the kind of look that hurls physical daggers and sticks them in some poor schmuck's face.

"Remember," he growled. "I was never here."

Ten seconds later, he wasn't, and the snow he'd tracked inside had melted into dirty, drippy puddles that I had to mop up quick before whoever came in next slipped and wound up suing Karl to cover their hospital bills.

By noon, I'd sold enough records to justify (at least temporarily) my continued employment, which made me feel so useful that for a while, I actually forgot about that nagging bottle of bourbon, and then, just about the moment I remembered it was there, the phone rang.

Now, the forty-year-old rotary phone in Vinyl Wonderland worked fine, see, but it didn't ring all that often. Used record shops draw the same basic clientele as a good library, the kind that I like to browse. So, I could maybe be forgiven for jumping a little when that call came in, partly because it wasn't a sound I was expecting to hear, and partly because I was, at that moment, balancing on the rickety wooden Vinyl Wonderland stepladder, trying to reach way up high to the molding strip that ran the length of the wall, on which lived our most expensive, rarest offerings: items like a still-sealed copy of The Beatles' *Yesterday and Today* (the one with the dead babies on the cover), plus the soundtrack to *Valley of the Dolls*, and a first pressing of *Piper at the Gates of Dawn* (from Germany, no less), and so on.

See, part of what had made the morning such a financial success was that I'd sold our copy of Albert Collins's *There's Gotta Be a Change* from up on that display, and now I was filling the gap, this time with *Little Bit of Soul* from the Music Explosion, a band that, as it turns out, were from right up the road, in Mansfield. That disc had a thirty-dollar price tag on the plastic sleeve protector, and the Collins LP had brought in forty. Maybe that doesn't sound like much, but remember: in 1984, a copy of *There's Gotta Be a Change* cost more than a day's pay for an awful lot of people.

Anyway, I clambered down the ladder, turned the volume low on the receiver (I had the Supremes on the turntable, a little pep for that freezing cold day), and then I grabbed the jangling phone and said, in my most professional voice, "Vinyl Wonderland, how can I help you?"

"I'm coming in," said Karl, on the other end. "Should be there in about twenty minutes."

I felt like a mutt that's been caught chewing up a favorite pair of shoes. The thing of it was, I had no idea what I'd done wrong, what I was supposed to feel guilty about.

"Brendan," he said. "You there?"

"Yeah, I'm here. Just surprised is all."

"I know. Not your fault. And you can be back in tomorrow. Or even later today. But this afternoon, there's some store business I gotta take care of, and, well. I'm the owner, y'know?"

"Sure. Okay."

"Brendan," he said, at last, "you're not fired."

I eyed the bottle of bourbon, half full, and said, "Okay."

"Just be cool, all right? I'll see you in twenty."

Thing is, Karl never made it. I waited for twenty minutes, then thirty, then forty. An hour went by, and still no Karl.

I didn't want to call him, not with his mother laid up and him so freaked out about keeping her comfortable and undisturbed, but I was frankly worried. Karl was what my mother, back when she was among the living, would have called salt of the earth. Eccentric, sure, and compulsive when it came to music, but steady. He was a guy who made a plan—hiring me, for example—and stuck to it. Nobody gets to be in three working bar bands (two rock, one jazz) without being dependable. Talent matters in the music world, sure, but rule number one, as Karl himself loved to tell me? Show up and show up on time. And here was Karl, not showing up. At all.

I took to checking out the front window every few minutes, to see if he was heading in—which was ridiculous, of course. He drove to work, see, and he parked in the back alley. So, me checking out the front window, where I had a great view of a whole lot of rapidly graying slush and a slow creep of traffic, was pure fantasy. Optimism of the highest, something's-gone-wrong order.

So, of course I had no luck at all spotting Karl, but I did get a good look, for the second time that day, at Mayor Accardi, who was parked in a snazzy sports car across the street, engine idling, and keeping a close eye on the front door of Vinyl Wonderland. I was pretty sure he couldn't see me—the window on the outside was spattered with salt and snow spray, half the glass on the inside was papered over with posters, ads, and fliers, and besides that, it was a whole lot darker inside than out—but it frankly gave me the willies, having the mayor of the whole damn city spending his time, on a work day, no less, watching my store. Watching *me*. What the hell did he think he was doing out there?

And then it hit me. He was waiting for Karl.

And his vigil had something to do with the Elvis door.

I glanced at the back of the shop. I had two customers at that particular moment. One was a regular, a long-haired guy who did a lot of shopping in order to find one or two three-dollar purchases, and the other was an older dude I'd never seen before, and as I looked over at the door, he looked down, fast, and sort of studied his hands as he worked his way through the Big Band section. I did a private little double take. He'd been staring at the Elvis door, too.

Nothing about this tracked, so I did what any good subordinate should do when they're out of their depth: I picked up the phone and called for help. Unfortunately, nobody answered at Karl's place, not him, not his mother, not no one. I let it ring twenty times easy before I gave up, and as I set the handset back on the cradle, the mayor drove off. It was good that he was gone, but his absence didn't change any of the facts, and fact number one was that I was starting to feel like I'd taken a job in a tub full of quicksand.

"It's the Peter Principle," my dad used to say, back when he could tick the boxes of happy, married, employed, and sober. "You rise to the level of your own incompetence. And the really subversive part is that almost no one sees it coming."

For a little while, the shop was busy enough that I didn't have time to fret too much about Karl, the mayor, or the stupid Elvis door, but eventually everybody cleared out, and I was left on my own, with time to think. Or so I hoped. Instead, I got about ten seconds of peace and quiet before the door opened again, and in with the latest blast of cold air came none other than Celine DeLapp.

"Relax," she said, when she saw my expression. "I may be trouble, but I'm not your trouble."

I wasn't too sure about that, but I didn't say so. I just let her know that Karl, again, wasn't on the premises.

Celine took a long look around. "I thought maybe he would be."

"You talked to him?"

"Yeah." She held my gaze as she said this. "I did."

"Was he okay?"

"Right as rain. Paid him a visit last night. He said he'd be in this afternoon."

Well, since I was getting more confused by the moment, I made a very conscious decision not to tell Celine that Karl had been AWOL for hours, or that she was right: he had indeed had every intention of showing up to work. I told her that it sounded like she knew more than I did and left it at that.

Celine threw up her hands and spun in a tight circle, the living picture of frustration. "This is great," she said. "Just great."

Meaning, it wasn't.

"How about this," I said. "You give me your number, and when I see him, I'll have him call you."

Those words were hardly out of my mouth before she'd fixed me with a stare so dismissive, it was all I could do not to back up. "No way," she said, "am I giving you my number."

"Okay, better idea. Leave him a message. Seal it up if you like. I've got paper, envelopes. I'll make sure he gets it."

"Envelopes," she said, darkly, "can be opened. On the sly."

"Not by me." This was true. I was good with my feet (hence the soccer), but my fingers were on the clumsy side. My ninth-grade art teacher called me, with what I like to think was some affection, "Hammer Hands."

After sizing me up all over again, Celine shook her head. She walked past the rows of forty-fives until she got herself a good view of Elvis, and the door he guarded. Still showing me her back, she said, "You really don't know, do you?"

"What is it I'm s'posed to know?"

She didn't say a word, which left me staring at her leather jacket, the one that said, clear as you please, *I'm the cool girl. I've got the best clothes. I know it, you know it. Oh, and while we're talking? Back off.*

Next thing I knew that jacket was headed toward Elvis, and Celine picked him up in two hands, lifted him, and set him in the corner. Now there was nothing between her and that mulch-red door.

With a quick glance my way, the kind that almost but not quite asked for permission, she said, "Can't hurt to try, right?"

I scooted out from behind the counter, protesting as I went—babbling, really—but it was too little, too late. Celine reached out, put her hand on the corroded antique doorknob, and tried to give it at turn.

It didn't budge.

"C'mon," I said. "It's storage or something. There's nothing back there you need."

Celine stepped away from the door and let out a high, nervous cackle. "Need?" she repeated. "Nothing in there that I *need*? That's a good one. That's rich."

The last time I'd been this confused was during Spanish class, trying to conjugate irregular verbs.

"Look," I said, "next time I see Karl, I'll ask about the door, I promise. I can mention or not mention you, your choice, but right now, this is like the definition of an impasse, right? So, how about you put Elvis back where he belongs, and leave the poor door alone."

She glanced from me to the Elvis standee. "Where Elvis belongs," she said, and she sounded seriously depressed, but she picked him up, and set him back in his original position. "I think he'd have liked this door. The real Elvis, I mean. I realize that doesn't make any sense to you, but Elvis, especially towards the end, he had his share of regrets."

At that point in my life, I knew precious little about Elvis Presley, except that my dad had a copy of the King's "Golden Hits" somewhere in a bin near the living room console, and that he never played it. As for regrets, well, I was starting to regret taking this job. Big Bear Groceries, where I'd worked before, was looking more attractive by the moment.

"Fine," said Celine. "I'll get out of your hair."

That, I'd heard before. From her. Word for word.

But she left, without so much as a "'Bye," and then I picked up the phone and I called Karl's house—again.

Karl didn't answer, but his mother did, and once she figured out where I was calling from, and who I was, she did her best to explain.

"There's been a—well, not an accident," she said. "He was just leaving to meet you at the shop, and he—well, the doctors say Karl had a stroke."

Chapter Four

SINCE I WASN'T FAMILY, I wasn't allowed to visit Karl in the hospital. I would have; I was perfectly willing. The thing is, see, it probably wouldn't have done much good. Karl had suffered a "significant" stroke, and he'd woken up, but he couldn't talk. Not much, anyway. Everything was slurred. Even so, his mother seemed certain that Karl was trying his level best to cover at least four specific topics: me, keys, some sort of door, and Elvis Presley.

"The Elvis part worries me most," she said. "Karl never did think too highly of Elvis, so why he's suddenly so intent on the man, I simply do not know."

None of this was exactly music to my ears. Karl's fixation with keys might mean taking my keys (and my job) away. As for the Elvis door, it seemed possible that he wanted to explain why so many people were obsessed with it. Whatever it was that he intended, he was newly incapable of delivering that message.

Karl's mother and I had a long chat over the phone, and she swerved from chipper to weepy several times in the course of our five-minute conversation. Just when I thought we were done, she insisted that I stop by the house to get a single key—a key that Karl, she supposed, had been getting set to deliver to me at the shop.

"An extra set, I guess," she told me. Her voice sounded tinny, very distant, over the old rotary's receiver. "He had it in a padded envelope, and he was headed out the door to meet you at the shop. Next thing I knew, he was leaning sideways against the sofa, and the envelope was on the floor. I knew that wasn't good. I called 9-1-1."

I asked her if she needed any help herself, and she said that she'd already organized a rotation from three household's worth of neighbors, and that while I was very sweet for asking, she expected she'd be well taken care of.

"Drop by tonight if you can," she said, before hanging up. "I'm not going anywhere, as you can imagine, and Karl seemed to think this key was pretty important."

Karl and his mother lived reasonably close, but in the opposite direction of my home, and the prospect of hoofing it both ways was too much, so once I locked up at Vinyl Wonderland, I headed to my house first. On foot.

See, now? I promised I'd get back to this topic, and sure enough, here we are. I walked to work pretty much every day, even though it was nearly two miles. In theory, I could have driven any old time, since my dad wasn't using the car, but even, then, I had a firm policy: if I was going to hit the bottle, fine, but in the aftermath, I would absolutely not get behind the wheel.

And, since in those days I usually had a first nip at breakfast, that meant pretty much no driving at all.

Now, you might think that this whole policy was some logical outgrowth of my mother having died. You might toss in a guess that she kicked the bucket in a car accident, that she was taken out by a drunk driver with a blood alcohol content that could have pickled ginger. But, while that theory would fit like a puzzle piece, the truth is—well, for now, let's just say that alcohol had nothing to do with my mother's death. No, my choice to be a car-free drunk was entirely due to a chance meeting with the one and only Jonesy Davis.

Jonesy and I would never have crossed paths if my soccer coach hadn't signed our whole team up for a day of community service, trash pick-up in and around the Park of Roses. So, there we were, twenty testosterone-driven high school athletes, each one outfitted with gardening gloves and a twenty-gallon black plastic trash bag. Duties aside, we felt like we'd been turned loose on the world, and sweet Jesus, were we ever rowdy. You might not guess it, but I was the worst offender. I know, I seem quiet, and people who met me at Big Bear or Vinyl Wonderland would have assumed I was a responsible, balanced sort of kid. I wish. In groups, I was a whole different animal, and soccer brought out the worst of my many faults—or at least, it brought out what your average adult would consider the worst.

In terms of a team dynamic, see, I was the instigator in that group. The foul-mouthed, sex-on-the-brain, ultra-crass village idiot. Name a dare, I'd try it. Name a drink, I'd claim I'd sampled it, and if actual drink happened to be available (under the bleachers, or in somebody's locker), I'd down it on the spot. I knew more dirty jokes than anyone else, and I told them whether my buddies wanted to hear them or not, especially if I was already three sheets to the wind, which I often was.

The truth, in retrospect? Half that team hated me—and I'm talking serious, gut-level dislike. The other half were afraid of me, even the ones who professed to be my friends. Which they pretty much proved not to be, just as soon as I got kicked off the team. Or dropped out, whichever. In those days, it was frankly difficult to remember which of those was the more accurate description.

Anyway, on that particular May morning, beautiful but far too early, there we were, picking up litter and surrounded by a formal rose garden about the size of, well, a soccer field. I was working my way through forty-seven different Helen Keller jokes, and I'd probably picked up all of one piece of trash, when I realized I'd meandered close to this really old white guy, short with a bent back and wire-rim glasses, and wearing suspenders, no less. Instead of picking up litter, he was quietly pruning one of the rose bushes.

Well, I had no fear whatsoever of making myself into a public spectacle, so I started in on my nastiest possible Helen Keller joke (the one about how she lost her virginity), and then I turned to the guy, this perfect stranger, and all but laughed in his face. "Too much, right?" I crowed. "Betcha don't want to hear the answer!"

Instead of shrinking away from my hyperactive teen energy, the old guy smiled, shy and diffident, as if I were the nicest person on the planet. With a regretful half-smile, he said, "Last I heard tell, Helen Keller lost her virginity when somebody left the plunger in the toilet."

These days, people call that a "mic drop," and for about half a second, there was dead silence, and then we just fell over ourselves laughing. I'd been one-upped big time, but for once I didn't mind, and before I knew which way was up, the rest of my cohort had moved on to fresher, more trash-filled pastures, and I was having a private heart-to-heart with Jonesy Davis.

He had a soft voice, with a cadence that reminded me of our then-president, Ronald Reagan, and after he was done introducing himself, he made sure I'd never underestimate him again.

"Don't want you to panic," he said, "but I can smell it on your breath."

I stiffened. Even a dyed-in-the-wool troublemaker like me doesn't enjoy getting busted, unless it's expected. When it's expected, it's acceptable, because going down in a blaze of glory is part of the buy-in for making trouble in the first place.

Jonesy smiled beneficently, as if I were on death row and he'd come to deliver my last meal. "Relax," he said. "If you've got some on you, I wouldn't mind a toke."

Sure enough, I had a flask in my sweatpants pocket, so after checking the immediate vicinity for my coaches, I pulled it out, and Jonesy took a swig and beamed. I mean, seriously, that guy had the sweetest, most cherubic smile in the whole damn world.

"'Preciate it," he said. "Now, how about you give an old man a hand. We got a late start this year, and these roses could use our help."

I told him I was supposed to be picking up garbage.

"And you're doing a lousy job," Jonesy replied, and he turned his rheumy eyes back to the nearest rose bush. "So why not changes horses?" he said. "I've got an extra pair of clippers, and you've already got gloves. Which you will definitely want. Roses, you know, they're a lot like life. Thorn after thorn after thorn."

The last thing I wanted was to admit to the truth of this metaphor, especially since it was all of five weeks since my mother had died, so I fell back on what I hoped would be a sure-fire escape hatch. "Mister," I said, "I don't know how to prune a rose bush."

"But I do. And if you shut up long enough to listen, I can teach you."

Just like that, and without once raising his voice, Jonesy had me eating out of his hand. It was like he was the lion tamer and I was the lion, but he never bothered with a whip. In the end, we wound up working over those roses for at least half an hour, and I got in hot water for it later, of course––"Brendan. Your trash bag is *empty*."––but it's hard for me, even now, to think of a half hour better spent. Not only did I learn about roses, but I got a mild, soft-spoken lecture on how to drink without putting anyone else at risk. This, he explained, involved several specific life choices. The first was living alone and avoiding any sort of long-term commitments. The second was refusing to participate in "car culture," which meant that he now got around by public transportation, a bike, or his feet.

"I'm a member of Mothers Against Drunk Driving," he said, as he stole another pull from my flask. "Lifetime."

He also told me that I should stop drinking, cold turkey, and never go back.

"Yeah, right," I said. "You're one to talk."

He smiled. Of course, he smiled. That's how he responded to pretty much everything, because the world in all its glory and all its ugliness somehow filled Jonesy Davis with magnanimous joy.

"You should quit," he said, "because drinking doesn't make you happy. In fact, I'm thinking it brings out the bear in you. Me, I'm the opposite. I'm a happy drunk. I'm at my best when I've had a few. I'm funnier, more social, less awkward. Drink," he went on, as he snipped another stem, "is my personal pair of rose-colored glasses. Pun intended."

Normally, I would have taken offense at his double-standard. Typical grown-up behavior, right? Do as I say, and not as I do. But with Jonesy, my reflexive anger, a brand of armor I wore pretty much daily, didn't work. Stranger still, I found I didn't mind.

By the time I left, I had Jonsey's phone number scribbled on a scrap of paper and jammed into my pocket, right next to the flask. I promised I'd call him next time we had a home game, so he could wobble over on his truly ancient bicycle and cheer me on from the stands. I didn't think he'd ever make an appearance, especially because soccer was a fall sport, so we didn't have a match scheduled until September, but when fall finally came around (this was before I left the team, obviously), I gave the guy a call, and he promised he'd show. And he did, too. I spotted him up in the bleachers for the rest of the season, wearing suspenders, a bow tie, and sipping Coke through a straw—a Coke I'm one hundred percent positive he'd spiked with rum brought on the sly from home.

He made an impression, that guy. The notion that I had a right to mess myself up with drinking, but that I had no right to screw around with the lives of others, struck a latent ethical chord. From that day on, I avoided using the car whenever possible.

So, there I was, trudging home with several inches of white stuff on the ground, and resolving to let the cold sober me up, with a hot meal after to finish the job. Sometimes my dad remembered to cook, so I was hopeful that I'd shiver my way in the door and find meatloaf or maybe lasagna. That night? No such luck. To my dad's credit, he'd tried to rustle up some enchiladas, but he'd left them in the oven too long, and now they were so toasty black that he couldn't scrape them off the pan. Every room in the house smelled like oven grease and burnt tortillas.

"Sorry," my dad said, still jabbing the enchilada pan with a spatula. I'm pretty sure that if he'd sounded any more disconsolate, he would have melted away, like the Wicked Witch of the West. It occurred to me, not for the first time, that if my father had done a better job of pushing past my mother's death, he wouldn't have taken up drinking as a second career, in which case, the bills would have been properly paid and I wouldn't have had to drop out of high school and pick up that first full-time gig at Big Bear. Cause and effect, action versus reaction; but was the through-line really that clean?

I peeled off my coat and the rest of my winter gear and let it all drop to the floor next to the coat closet, a slob's choice that my mother would have hated. I said, "So, frozen chicken dinner?"

My dad said, "You know what I really want?"

I was already rifling the freezer for a couple of boxes of Swanson's. "No idea, man. What do you want?"

"I want to get the pool filled again."

That sounded great to me. During the previous summer, thanks to mom dying in the spring, he hadn't had the energy to do anything with the pool.

As I got the first of the two dinners out of its box and into the microwave, my father said, "I want the pool filled, and I want to spend all day, every day, in a floating lounge chair in the middle of the deep end."

"Okay," I said. "Sounds great."

Which it didn't. Having Dad as a blitzed, depressed, round-the-clock pool ornament would deep-six any chance I had at hosting rocking summertime pool parties.

"Hang on," I said. "You're not talking about filling the pool now, right? You do know it's December."

Instead of replying, my father kept facing down the enchiladas. The smell really was foul. I made a conscious decision not to ask if he'd done anything that day to look for work. I made a definite choice not to inquire about how much longer he could handle the mortgage. I mean, we had a decent house in a late-fifties development, but in-ground pools and a basement rec room (with wall-to-wall shag carpet, no less) don't come for free. Neither did the extra room we'd added on at the back, where my mother had given clarinet lessons, mostly to kids, sometimes to adults. So far as I knew, the loan my parents had taken out to build that room, with its nearly kinda-sorta sound-proof doors, was nowhere near paid off, and the life insurance policy that had kicked in after Mom's death was fast running out. As for my Vinyl Wonderland employment, well, that was the kind of job that could defray a few costs, but in no way would it cover our expenses. Big Bear would have managed that if I'd stayed. If I hadn't been fired.

Given all this, who can blame me when I say that as soon as I was done eating, I was out the door and gone. I didn't bother asking for the keys to the car. I just took them.

The lights were still on at Karl's mother's house—in fact, it looked as if someone had turned on every switch possible, so in the dark, glinting off the packed snow, the house looked like some sort of beacon, like it was trying to summon extra-terrestrials from *Close Encounters*. On the plus side, all that light meant I didn't have to be shy about knocking, and sure enough, a neighbor-lady answered, someone I'd never seen before, and she told me that Karl's mother wasn't able to get to the door ("The poor dear"), but that she'd left a padded envelope for me, if I was the nice young man who was helping out at the record shop.

I assured her that all of those things were true, especially the "nice" part, and then I raced back to Vinyl Wonderland, parked in Karl's usual space in the alley, and let myself in. I didn't turn on the main lights, just the switch for the back hall. I don't know why I felt so furtive, given that I had every right to be there—in Karl's absence, I was the shop's sole proprietor, after all—but I just couldn't face having the whole place lit up like a fishbowl. I mean, who knew who might be watching through the High Street glass? Celine DeLapp, maybe. The city mayor.

From inside the padded envelope, I fished out a single corroded skeleton key and I marched over to the Elvis door.

"Sorry, King," I said to the standee, as I lifted it out of my way. "I need the room."

Elvis, in response, said nothing.

Still bundled up in my puffy winter coat, I faced the door. The door faced me. The keyhole, set beneath the knob, had my full attention.

So much for swearing on my mother's grave.

"All right," I said, to no one, and with that, I inserted the key. It fit. I gave it a turn. The lock mechanism grated, shifted, and let out a solid little *thunk*. I withdrew the key, shoved it in my jeans pocket, and reached out a tentative hand to grip the doorknob. To be honest, I was hoping it wouldn't turn.

I should have hoped harder.

Chapter Five

THE DOOR OPENED. I REALLY hadn't expected anything more than a supplies closet, possibly stuffed with some sort of contraband—drugs, maybe, wicked little stacks of prescription pill bottles—but instead I found myself facing a corridor that led straight away for ten yards, then hooked a sharp right. The ceiling was high and vaulted, and underfoot, the tongue-and-groove floorboards of Vinyl Wonderland quickly gave way to rough, irregular cobblestones.

There weren't any lights, so the corridor was dim, but from around the corner, I thought I detected a faint glow, a corona that suggested that I wouldn't need to bring my own light source. That was good enough for me. In I went, leaving Elvis to guard the open door.

Sure enough, when I rounded the corner, I had more than enough light to keep going. The odd thing was that the corridor continued on a good deal farther than I thought the building would strictly allow, then turned left again, resuming its original course. From around this next bend, still a fair distance away, daylight was spilling in, bright and blinding and desert-yellow—which made less than zero sense.

I proceeded slowly, trailing a finger along the walls as if being in contact with something solid would anchor me to Vinyl Wonderland, and so it was my finger, well before my eyes, that noticed that I'd left the brickwork behind and moved into a rough sort of passage bored from solid rock. Which was absurd, of course. My city has its share of bedrock, but mostly it's pretty far down, with crumbling layers of shale on top. Whatever this rock was, it was all of a piece, and it was gritty, with residual grains clinging to my fingertip as I continued to trace the walls. It was like I'd transitioned from a corridor to a tunnel, or even a mine shaft. Ancient timbers and brace-work had been set in place to hold up the ceiling, and they reminded me of bones, ribs from a Halloween skeleton, complete with dust and tattered cobwebs.

I rounded the second turn. Just ahead of me, the passageway ended, opening out into a brilliant midday landscape. The air was hot and dry, backed with a light but steady breeze. The land around was flat, or nearly so, with multiple graveled pathways leading away to every possible compass point, and mounded between these radiating spokes were inordinate heaps of—well, garbage. Junk. Piles of it, some of them no taller than my waist, but others rose higher, like low, lumpy hills.

What, I thought, had happened to winter?

And how had I gotten behind and past the back alley of Vinyl Wonderland?

Directly ahead of me, maybe twenty yards distant, stood an enormous wooden desk, the antique kind that would have made a typical office feel immediately cramped. On top of the desk lay various stacks of loose papers and folders, all weighted down by polished river stones, presumably to prevent them from taking flight in that steady, eye-drying breeze. There was also a rotary telephone, a mate to the one on Karl's Vinyl Wonderland countertop, except that this one didn't come with a telephone cord. Next to the desk was an office chair, metal-framed, lacking wheels, and to the side stood an entirely superfluous floor lamp. The overhead sun was so bright that I couldn't decide if the lamp was switched on or off.

Opposite the floor lamp, a woman leaned against the desk, reading a terribly yellowed newspaper. As I took in all these surroundings—the work of a split second—I must have let out a gasp, because the woman startled, then whipped around to get a look at me. Still not satisfied, she got a clearer look by pushing her wraparound sunglasses up to her hairline and said, "Who in hell are you?"

I fumbled my name like it was a loose football, but she waved me off. "Forget your name, how'd you get in here?"

I held up the key.

"Nobody called. Karl didn't call."

"Karl's sick. He had a stroke."

"Well, someone's supposed to call. I need warning."

"I'm sorry. I didn't know."

"If you don't call ahead," the woman said, sounding peeved, "how am I supposed to help?"

As she spoke, she dropped her sunglasses back into place, and then she let out a prodigious sigh, the kind that suggests the world has long since gone to hell in a handbasket, and now the basket is on fire.

"Um, would you mind," I began, then couldn't quite decide what to ask. "Where, exactly…?"

The woman I was squaring off with was lean and slender, with skin the color of homemade fudge and hair that had been straightened to within an inch of its life. She would have looked glamorous, like a fashion model straight out of *Ebony*, but she was wearing long-sleeve navy blue coveralls, the kind you might find on an auto mechanic or maybe a prisoner, which pretty much destroyed the effect. Her presence was bizarre on any number of levels—this whole place was bizarre—but doubly so because back in those days, I really didn't have any interactions with Black people. It pains me to say that, but let's remember that 1984 was, well, 1984. My parents didn't have Black friends. I had precisely one Black teacher, Mrs. Felsen (and she was excellent, as I've already said), but in general, moment to moment, my school was functionally segregated, with the Black kids tracked into different classes, eating at different tables in the cafeteria, and herded into different sports. Was there a single Black kid on my soccer team? No. Our squad was lily white, and so were most all the teams we played. Black kids played football or basketball, or maybe ran track. That was it.

Was any of this cause for concern? In the day-to-day terms of my life then, absolutely not. As most of my teachers were always quick to point out (with the notable exception of Mrs. Felsen), all the salient Civil Rights issues had been solved back in the sixties, and, as every teenager on the planet instinctively knew, the sixties were ancient history.

Being around Vinyl Wonderland had knocked some fresh holes in the notion that I lived in a perfect and racially balanced world, but it sure took me a while to notice. Basically, from the time I first started browsing there, I never saw anyone in that shop who would qualify as what we now call a Person of Color. But why should this have been the case? I don't think anyone will seriously argue with the notion that music is universal, and Vinyl Wonderland had a deep selection of discs recorded by Black artists—and I do mean that term, "artist," in the most serious, respectful sense. Sure, back in those days, I still thought REO Speedwagon was the height of cool, but thanks to Vinyl Wonderland, I was also beginning to get a handle on Duke Ellington and Lady Soul (among others). The great saga of American musical history was starting to unfurl, like a banner.

Anyway, being on the far side of the Elvis door had me plenty off-balance already, and now here was this woman, also unexpected, and she was headed my way with a determined stride that suggested that she had every intention of pushing me bodily back into the corridor, or maybe even grabbing me hard by the ear and hauling me all the way through to the record shop.

"Talk," she said, as she closed the gap. "Where'd you get the key? And what happened to Karl? Where's my damn custodian?"

I backed up into the tunnel and spread my hands in a gesture of surrender. "It's Karl's key! He gave it to me!"

"Lies," she said, as she reached the lip of tunnel, but she stopped there, as if she'd come up against a boundary that she either couldn't or didn't wish to cross. Not that this put her in a better temper; if anything, her proximity to the tunnel made her angrier. "Karl," she growled, "would never 'give' you that key, not without talking to me, first."

In that moment, however, I had overwritten recent history so completely that I firmly believed that Karl had willingly given me his Elvis door key— or at least, that was what he'd intended to do. The notion that what he'd really set out to do, before he was side-tracked by a stroke, was to get me as far away from the Elvis door as possible, no longer cohered. I had the key, and I'd received it (more or less) from Karl.

"Listen," I said, "that hallway back there is way too long for the building, and this place—this is like summertime. But it's winter!"

"Oh, is poor baby dressed for the wrong season?"

Sarcasm aside, she had a point. Inside my bulky winter layers, the heat in this place had me sweating like a pig.

The woman said, "Listen. You're not supposed to be here, and more importantly—trust me on this—you don't want to be here. Get rid of that key, and then go home, go to sleep, and when you wake up, spend the day convincing yourself this was a dream. If you can't manage that, then move. I'm talking cross-country, or maybe a whole different continent. Mars. Start a new life and forget that this place ever got in your path."

The more she spoke, the more preposterous she sounded, but since it was clear that I wasn't going to get a speck of information out of her, I did the one thing I could think of shy of physical violence, and that was to give up and give in.

"Okay," I said. "I get it, I hear you. Just shut up, all right?"

She glared and said, as if I were a wayward pet in need of encouragement, "Go on, now. Back the way you came. Turn the corner and keep going."

I stole one last look at the landscape beyond—that crazy, impossible vista—and then I did as she asked. I followed the tunnel back the way I'd come until it transitioned once again into a corridor, and then I turned left and walked myself back into Vinyl Wonderland, where normalcy ruled, and where everything, so far as I could tell, was exactly as I'd left it.

After a long pause, an aftermath moment that involved several deep breaths, I said, to the Elvis standee and the store in general, "That? Was nuts."

Neither the King nor the store disagreed, which was good. I sure as hell didn't want to deal with talking cardboard or talking records.

By that point, it was late, so I took care to lock the Elvis door behind me, and I put the King back in his spot, and then I headed for home, taking the all-important skeleton key with me. In fact, I added it to my actual key ring for safekeeping, and not only was it easily three times the length of every other key I owned, but it weighed more than the rest combined, so while it didn't sit well in my pocket, at least I knew it was there, so it would be that much harder to lose or misplace it, and that felt pretty crucial.

But the thing is, see, the human mind is one seriously erratic playground, and the main thing I thought about on the drive home wasn't Vinyl Wonderland, or the tunnel, or the desert trash pile where I had, against all logic, wound up. It's also true that I didn't fixate on the woman in the jumpsuit coveralls, or her middle-of-nowhere desk. Nor did I spin my wheels perseverating on all the junk and cast-offs that I hadn't had a chance to inspect. Instead, I shunted that whole shebang into some out-of-the-way mental cubby hole, because in the end, see, in the final analysis, I was still a teenage boy, and what all those adventures ultimately left me focused on was sex.

To be clear, at that stage of my life, I didn't have a girlfriend, which was part of the trouble. I even understood, deep down, that I didn't have a girlfriend because I repelled girls. I mean this as a compliment to the many teen girls I knew who wanted nothing to do with me. They understood very clearly that I didn't have anything serious to offer. They grasped, long before I ever did, that a relationship with me would be like dating a long string of firecrackers connected by an uncertain fuse, which in human terms translated to extended periods of depression and boredom, after which, every so often, I'd blow a gasket.

Despite this, I had it on good authority that almost every girl I knew thought of me as cute, and "cute," in the eighties, translates today into "hot." So, I'd had no trouble coaxing a few girls who wouldn't be caught dead with me in public into my car, or their car, or a quiet stairwell at school, or a back bedroom at somebody else's party. We'd make out; we'd suck face. (What a term.) Depending on the girl, I'd get to first base, or second, or maybe even a quick brush with third. And then, once we were done rounding whatever bases were on offer, it was my job—my mission, even—to go out and boast about what I'd experienced to as many boys as possible, beginning but by no means ending with my teammates at soccer.

One thing I learned early, though, was to leave out the name of the girl, even if that meant that my audience didn't always believe me. Most boys my age hadn't processed that part of the program, the humane part, but I'd learned that lesson early after kissing Chrissie Keener in sixth grade, and then broadcasting that blessed event, blow by blow, to an entire school bus full of kids come Monday morning. Chrissie was so mortified that she went home sick and didn't come back for a week. I felt genuinely bad about that but didn't know how to fix it. Kids are mean. How was I supposed to make them less mean? How was I supposed to turn off the spigot of gossip that now insisted that Chrissie Keener, age twelve, was a professional wanton slut?

The really sad part was that there was a good reason that Chrissie and I had kissed in the first place. A simple reason, too. We'd honestly liked each other. In fact, we'd been drawn to each other for years, long before kissing was something either of us were thinking about. But after we actually did lock lips, and I spilled the beans? The castle drawbridge got pulled up tight, and friendship got marooned on the far side of the moat.

Sixth grade, of course, was long gone. By the time I dropped out of high school, I'd burned up most of my social capital by boasting about pretty much every sexcapade I could dream up, half of them real, the other half completely imagined. The savvier boys had long since caught on that I was more bark than bite, and really, my total lack of a social life once I left school was all the proof I needed that I didn't have any actual friends, much less girlfriends. As for the girls themselves—well, as I pretty much said, they'd understood for years that I was a very limited menu. Most of them wisely ate elsewhere.

So, driving home that night, and having just had the most inexplicable experience of my life, I was definitely a case of all worked up but no place to go. There was an outside possibility that I could call up Lani Bell, whom I'd worked with at Big Bear. She was nineteen and out on her own, and she and I had fooled around at work a few times. I'd even been to her apartment, twice, so she was one of just three girls total I'd actually had sex with, but she'd never encouraged me to stay the night. In fact, she'd been seriously pissed off at me both times, as if I'd done something hopelessly wrong— which, from her point of view, I had, because when I got into bed with her (or any other girl, for that matter), pretty much everything was over and done so, so quickly. And for that? I felt more shame—daily, hourly, still—than I'd ever believed was possible.

Vinyl Wonderland made it worse, as did the radio, and for the exact same reason. Rock songs, see, not to mention blues and soul, laid it all out for anyone who cared to listen: sex was supposed to last, if not for a lifetime, then at the very least all night long. On that point, Bad Company, Muddy Waters, and Led Zeppelin were in full agreement. Sex was a marathon, and staying power was the sole path to winning love or medals.

Unfortunately for me, all the action I'd ever gotten had taken place in the wake of my mother's death. Maybe that wouldn't have mattered; maybe it wasn't even related. But one thing I know, and Lani had learned it too: sex for me proceeded according to the David Bowie gospel of wham, bam, thank you ma'am.

Honestly, that wasn't what I wanted or intended (Bowie wasn't recommending it, either, although I only figured that out many years later), but quick and dirty was the only thing I knew how to provide, and once I'd gotten off, my interest flagged. The sad fact was that I didn't actually like Lani Bell, certainly not the way I'd genuinely appreciated Chrissie. Sure, Lani could make me laugh, and I didn't *dis*like her. On the job, she was decent company. But I absolutely did not want to spend the requisite time in bed—her bed or any other—making her body reach for the stars. I mean, in theory sure. I would have loved to make her that happy, but in practice? No matter what the Gods of Rock demanded, I just couldn't work up the enthusiasm.

So, there I was, headed home. Desperate and dateless. But then, unwanted and uninvited, Celine DeLapp's face flashed into my head, and as I pulled into the driveway and cut the engine, it was Celine's hostile, vulnerable eyes, not to mention those incredible bangs, that sent me right over the edge without so much as unzipping my jeans.

I could even hear her voice, as if she were right there next to me, whispering seductively, "Brendan. DeLapp is my married name."

Chapter Six

THE NEXT DAY WENT ALONG with something approaching normalcy until mid-afternoon, when I got a phone call from the mayor's office. His assistant was on the line, and once I picked up, she said, "Hold, please," and I held, and then Mayor Accardi hopped on the line, and he got right to the point. "My sources tell me that Karl is out indefinitely. So, I need to know, what's the backup plan?"

"Sir?"

"Kid, I'm pretty sure I didn't stutter."

"No, sir."

For what it's worth, I wasn't a kid who called a lot of adults "sir" or "ma'am," but with the mayor, it really felt like the only possible option.

Mayor Accardi certainly wasn't going to return the favor (not that I blamed him). "Kid," he said, "I want to be very clear. I've been in before. I'm on the list, you get me?"

I agreed with all of that because agreement seemed like the safest choice going.

"Two things keep this city running," the mayor went on. "Taxes, and me."

"Yes, sir."

"Oh, for—. Do you have the key, or don't you?"

There it was, the elephant in the room. Now I had to decide, did I flat out lie to the mayor? Or did I buckle under and tell the truth?

Curiosity, see, it's one hell of a motivator. Curiosity killed the cat, or so we're told, but which cat? Maybe that particular cat wasn't being sufficiently cautious. Maybe a different cat would have been just fine.

Let's face it: I'd had the better part of a day to sit at my post and stare at the Elvis door and to feel that key in my pocket, rubbing a small dent in my thigh. No cat in the history of the world was as curious as I was right then. Besides, I was the kid who liked pouring gasoline on any given fire, or dropping a squirming, squeaking guinea pig into a fifty-gallon tank with a live snapping turtle just to see what would happen—and I'd done that, no kidding—so I told the mayor the truth, or at least the part he wanted to hear.

"Sure, I've got the key," I said. "Is there a particular time you want to drop by?"

For a moment, the only answer I got was distrustful silence. Then he said, "And is the deal the same as before?"

I had no way to know, but I could tell which answer would play best. "The deal," I said, "has not changed."

"One hour. Anyone tries to cut in line, tell 'em to get lost."

Was my city lucky or unlucky to have a mayor who told the competition to "get lost"? I honestly wasn't sure.

Vinyl Wonderland was empty during that call, and I was just getting off my rear to add some new stock to the Soundtracks section when the front door opened, and a woman with Irish freckles and curly red hair tip-toed inside. She was fortyish and well-dressed, round-faced and round-bodied, and being in my shop apparently made her so nervous that she wouldn't let go of the door.

"Hello?" she said, looking at me and my armload of albums. "I think I'm supposed to say, 'Katie sent me.'"

"Katie."

"That's right. She said you'd know what to do."

"Okay. So, you're not here for records."

The woman's laugh was high and nervous and faltering, like a trickle of water echoing its way down a drain. "Not for records, no. It's just, you know how it is. I have a problem."

I was sorely tempted to say, "Don't we all," but the angel on my right shoulder muzzled the devil on my left, leaving me with a question. "Did Katie say anything about a door?"

The woman nodded vigorously, and her hair bounced around on her head.

"Well," I said, "I can let you in, I guess. But I'm not responsible, right?"

With an emphatic shake of her head (and more bouncing curly hair), the woman said, "Definitely not. Whatever happens, it's on me."

I set the records on the counter and headed for the back of the store. The red-haired woman hurried to follow. When I got to Elvis, I took out my keys and said, "Who should I say is coming?"

This, see, was a crucial question. I'd spent a good chunk of my supposedly hard-working day mulling over what the woman in the coveralls had given away, which wasn't much, but I thought I understood a little more about the whole Elvis-door process now. If Karl let someone in, he was supposed to alert the woman at the desk; he was supposed to call ahead. Presumably, that meant using the phone.

In response to my question, the woman clasped her mitten-covered hands and said, "Do I have to say?"

I shrugged. "Yeah, you kinda do. But I don't keep records if that's any comfort."

"Is that a joke?"

Baffled, because I hadn't been joking, I looked to her for clarification, and she swept out an arm, indicating the shop as a whole.

"Ah," I said. "No, not that kind of record. Obviously, I keep records."

And still she wouldn't say her name, which I found more intriguing by the moment. Celine had come alone. The furtive shopper who'd glanced at the door hadn't so much as spoken to me. The mayor, who generally traveled with an entourage, had come by himself, and the man with the missing tooth hadn't been nearly as brave about his mission from "Roger" as he liked to pretend. I didn't know much, not at that stage of life, but because I knew shame so intimately, I could spot it in others a mile away. The people who wanted to pass through the Elvis door were people with secrets, people who desperately valued their privacy—and that discovery was, frankly, thrilling.

The woman hesitated yet again. "You are Karl, right?"

Apparently, "Katie" hadn't bothered to describe Karl. No doubt she'd simply said he was the guy behind the counter, since once upon a time, that had always been true. How many years had Vinyl Wonderland been open, anyway? I realized that I had no idea.

To the woman, I said, without batting an eye, "Sure. I'm Karl."

"All right. I'm Judy Treviso."

She began spelling the last part, and I held up a hand to cut her off. Then I pulled out my keys. "One thing you won't want," I said, as I worked my way through the endless albums to reach the door, "is all that winter gear."

"Oh! Is it warm in there?"

"Hot."

She nodded. "Good. I spend every New Years in Florida. Is it like that?"

"No," I said, even though I'd never been to Florida. Wherever it was that the tunnel led, it didn't match up to any description, photograph, or movie of Florida that I'd ever seen. As I spoke, I got the key in the lock and turned it. For a moment, the mechanism stuck, as if it didn't want to let Judy Treviso pass through, but then it gave way. I opened the door.

Wide-eyed, Judy peered in, then looked at me. "I just…go?"

"Yeah."

"It's kind of dark."

"It gets brighter pretty fast."

"You don't understand."

I couldn't argue with that, since I had no idea what she was getting at.

"Women learn," she said, very patiently, as if I were an inattentive, wriggling four-year-old. "They learn early. Mothers teach their daughters. Don't go anywhere alone. Especially don't go anywhere dark."

That made sense, and I started to offer up a rote series of protests, but she just gave me a pat on the arm and said, "It's okay. Katie said it would be…disconcerting. And dark. But, I have to go, right? I have to."

And with that, she went.

I closed the door behind her, and I wasn't sure if I was supposed to lock it, but I decided against, and then I hurried to the counter and grabbed the phone. How to dial? If zero dialed the operator, and 9-1-1 would get the police, then what about just plain old number one, by itself?

I tried it.

It worked.

"Karl?" said a woman's voice—the woman, presumably, from the desk in the junkyard.

"No, it's me. Brendan. We met yesterday. You've got a guest, incoming."

After a microsecond's pause, the woman said, "How'd you get this number?"

"Hey, you're the one told me to call."

"But I didn't say how. Never mind. Who exactly is headed my way?"

"A woman named Judy Treviso."

"She's not on the list."

There it was, another small nugget of information. There was a list, and first timers weren't on it.

"She said someone sent her. Katie."

"Katie Blaine?"

"I don't know. She didn't say."

"Okay, well, so far so good, but Brendan, next time? Get the full name of the reference."

"Sure thing."

Again, the woman paused, and I could hear that dry wind passing over the receiver like a papery, whispering ghost.

"Gotta go," the woman said. "She's almost here."

"Okay."

"But that was nice work, Brendan. You don't belong where you're sitting, and you're not Karl, but you're quick on the draw. Maybe you'll do."

"Wait!" I said, before she could hang up. "The mayor is coming, too. Tony Accardi. He said he'll be here in an hour, less."

"And?"

"Well, I don't know, can I let more than one in at a time?"

Her laugh was unpleasant, laden with outright contempt—though not, I was pretty sure, for me. "Honey," she said, "if need be, we've got room for the whole city. Sad but true."

In the background, I could still hear the wind, but I also heard a sort of high-pitched squawk of alarm, which I presumed had to be Judy Treviso arriving, dumb founded.

"Toodles," said the woman in the coveralls. "We've got company."

47

of high-pitched squawk of alarm, which I presumed had to be Judy Treviso arriving, dumb founded.

"Toodles," said the woman in the coveralls. "We've got company."

Chapter Seven

THE MAYOR WENT THROUGH THE Elvis door not long after Judy Treviso, but he arrived back first, with his fancy coat over his arm and a sheen of sweat standing out on his ski-slope forehead. With his free hand, he closed the Elvis door behind him, and even once it was closed, he gave it a firm push, as if hoping to ensure it would never open again.

For a moment, he said nothing—not until he'd walked past the L-bend in the shop, to make sure that he and I were the only people present, which we were, other than Jefferson Airplane on the stereo. Grace Slick, singing lead, was explaining (as she likes to do still) that one pill makes you larger, and one pill makes you small.

The mayor, still sweating, said, "If I had a lick of sense, I'd have this place bulldozed."

I could not for the life of me think up a response, so I pretended I was busy jotting notes on a pad of scratch paper. When I glanced up, the mayor was unfurling his coat, preparing to do battle with the December weather outside, and I caught a glimpse of something clutched in his hand, a coral-colored sheet of cardstock, smaller than a regular sheet of paper, and perhaps twice as long as it was wide. Possibly he'd had it in a pocket on his way in through the Elvis door, but I doubted it. This seemed like something he'd brought back, a token of some sort. A trophy.

Eager to know what he'd found and why it mattered, I said, just to keep him talking, "Sorry about the temperature changes. Nothing I can do about that."

The mayor adjusted his coat over his shoulders and gave me a hard, unfriendly look. "Don't act like October," he said, and when I looked blank as a wall at that, he clarified by saying, "Don't act like one of *them*. You're not, I'm sure of it. You're just…I don't know what you are. You've got acne."

This was, regrettably, true. Most days, my brushes with pimples weren't bad, especially compared to so many of my (former) classmates, but for whatever reason, that morning had begun with a flare-up. One thing for sure, my skin was definitely not something I wanted to discuss with the city mayor, of all people, so I nodded at the card in his hand, changed the subject, and said, "Did you get what you went for?"

His eyes narrowed. I'd just asked for specifics from a man whose job it was, like all politicians, to avoid clear, specific answers. Or, looked at another way, I'd just demanded information from a man who was used to demanding information from others.

Nevertheless, he held up the card, and now I realized what it was. I'd seen one in Mrs. Felsen's English class the year before, when she'd taken a day that was supposed to be reserved for Hemingway's *The Old Man and the Sea* and spent it on civics and citizenship, instead. "Voting," she insisted, "will change what needs changing." Whether this was true, I still wasn't too sure, but it was thanks to her that I knew that Mayor Accardi was holding up a voting card, the kind that people used on election day to cast their ballots.

"Four votes," said the mayor. "All I need is four."

Sure enough, the card had been punched through exactly four times. The card showed plenty of other little numbered boxes available, but the rest were intact. This struck me as bizarre. Was Celine DeLapp so worked up about the Elvis door because she wanted to cast some sort of vote?

"See you 'round," said the mayor. "And do me a favor. Keep your trap shut."

For a guy who was supposed to be beyond salvaging in the "ethnic" department, he sure talked a lot like my dad.

Anyway, after he'd gone, I turned off the stereo so I could bear down and think with a clear head, which of course meant another swig from my nearly empty bottle of bourbon. Then I took a second toke because, what the hell, who was there to stop me? But then I really did get down to brass tacks. Mayor Accardi had mentioned votes, but we weren't in an election cycle, and besides that, he'd said he only needed a grand total of four votes. Therefore…

I turned this over for a minute, trying to link these ideas into a useful sort of mental Mobius strip, and then I grabbed my coat and headed out, locking the shop's front door behind me.

Down the block, I found what I was looking for, a pair of curbside newspaper boxes, one for the *Dispatch* and one for the *Citizen-Journal*. I chose the *Citizen-Journal,* fumbled in my pocket for change, inserted the coins into the slot, and retrieved a copy of the paper. It was cold out, so I hustled back to Vinyl Wonderland, re-opened the shop, and spread the newspaper on the counter, smoothing it down with my palms.

Sure enough, there it was, front page, bottom right: a headline piece describing an ongoing tussle down at city hall. According to the article, only three of the city council's members were prepared to pass the mayor's latest budget. To get that budget approved, the mayor needed one more vote, for a simple majority of—that's right—four.

The thoughts in my head did a series of ungainly cartwheels. If I was putting all this together correctly, then the Elvis door, it was like a genie. It granted wishes. And I was the one with the key!

But this giddy interpretation didn't hold water for more than ten seconds, see, because before I'd entered the picture, Karl had presumably had the key for years and years, and his life was several country miles from perfect. If the Elvis door was a gateway to a genie and nothing more, then surely he would have milked that cow for all it was worth, and done it a long time ago, too.

Best, then, to take it slow. That was a phrase my mother had lived by while teaching me to drive on the city's icy roads one winter prior to this. *Best to take it slow, and keep your eyes peeled.* Those had been her exact words, and I hadn't heard her so clearly for months. It was like she was right there with me in the shop, breathing in that mildewed record-cover scent and extending a gentle hand to caress my hair.

But that line of reality popped like a bubble the very next second, when

Judy Treviso opened the Elvis door and stepped through. She looked as if she'd just received terrible news from some long-distance relative but hadn't yet digested what she'd learned. Using both arms, she clutched (of all things) a bulky, taupe-colored ottoman.

"Okay," she said, more to the room than to me. She seemed to get her bearings, took a few steps into the shop, and tried to push the door closed with one foot. "Would you mind...?" she said. "This isn't heavy, but it's—well, it's big."

I jumped up and hurried to assist, after which I locked the door and replaced Elvis. The King looked pleased. He looked ready to say, "Thank you very much."

Unlike the mayor, Judy still had her winter clothes on—or maybe she'd put them back on before trudging through the tunnel. I was pretty sure she knew how to find the front door without my help, but I was beginning to wonder if she needed a physical push, or some sort of cattle prod. She was just standing there, arms wrapped around that ottoman like she was pregnant and was about to give birth to a piece of furniture.

"That," she said at last, "was not what I expected."

I badly wanted to ask what she *had* expected. What, exactly, had her friend Katie told her? But that wasn't the part I'd been assigned to play.

Judy cleared her throat. "I mean, I don't know what I thought would happen, not really, but that? I can't even..." She blinked, and her eyes welled. "I mean, what kind of a choice is that? Who sets that up? Who would dream up forcing anyone to make *that* decision?"

Confused, wanting to be helpful, I pursed my lips and started to say, "Um..." but Judy cut me off.

"You," she said, shooting an accusatory glare my way, "will never see me again."

And with that, she finally got a move-on, hoofing it at high speed toward the front door. She banked off the door frame on her way out, ottoman first, and yelped when the rebound sent her smacking into the door, but at last she made it through, and away she went, tottering down the street with her precious ottoman leading the way.

I stared after her, slack-jawed, for as long as she was in view. It was just too bizarre. The mayor needed votes, sure, so he got a paper ballot. But how could Judy Treviso have some sort of desperate need for a glorified cloth-bound footstool? That didn't track, not in a million years.

I figured I had three people I could hit up for answers. The first was Karl, but Karl was out of reach, at least for now. The second was the woman in the coveralls, but I had a bad feeling that if this whole scenario were reduced to a soccer match, that she'd be playing for the other team. The third option felt more attractive, and that third option wore military surplus boots and a fabulous leather jacket and went by the name of Celine DeLapp.

Now, it was true that I didn't have her number, but back in those days, see, one of the most vital objects in any home or business was the phone book, a fat paper doorstop that was divided into the *Yellow Pages* for area businesses, and the *White Pages* listing residential contacts. Almost everyone in the city and its many surrounding towns chose to be included.

With that in mind, I rummaged behind the counter, pulled out the Vinyl Wonderland copy of the *White Pages*, and flipped through it until I found the surname DeLapp. The print was tiny, and my eyesight wasn't maybe as perfect as I liked to pretend. My personal mythology said I had twenty-twenty (and so, of course, I did), but was I glad that Karl kept an excellent magnifying glass behind the counter. Did I put it to use with that phone book? Oh, my, yes.

As a name, DeLapp wasn't common as dirt, like Smith or Jones or Brown, but even so, the *White Pages* listed eight possible DeLapp households. Two were women, and not named Celine. Three were men, with no female name co-listed. (The *White Pages* always listed men first.) But the other three showed the names as Mr. and Mrs., including, teasingly, an entry for "DeLapp, Stan and Seely."

Close enough. I read off the attendant phone number under my breath, and I was all set to dial, when I was struck by a new thought, and I rifled the *White Pages* again, searching for my last name, Purcell.

The newsprint pages dried my fingertips, and I had to lick them to get them to separate where I wanted, but I got the right one at last, and I used my index finger to scan down to the Purcell header. In the entire region, the *White Pages* listed only three. Sure enough, there was my father, Frank, and lurking there in his wake, surviving in the phone book even after death, was my mother, Lauren.

I stared at her name for a long time, then I slapped the book closed. I checked the date on the cover: Fall/Winter, 1984. That was depressing. My mother had been dead and buried for months before this edition even went to print, but in its pages, she lived on. Society could hold a memorial service and stick a body in the ground, but it wasn't organized enough to delete a name from the phone book. People could still look her up, decide to give her a call. My father would likely be the one to answer.

Hello, may I speak to Lauren Purcell?

I imagined my father hearing that request and sagging, knees buckling, his hand reaching in vain for the nearest handy chair to provide support, to prevent him from collapsing to the floor.

Well. I re-opened the directory, located the Purcell listing for a second time, and ripped out the page. A futile gesture—I could just imagine myself, hustling through the city, ripping that same page out of every resident's *White Pages*. It would take years, and more would be delivered, so I'd never catch up—but for a moment, I lived that choice in all its glorious impossibility.

A few minutes later, I was recovered enough to get on the phone and dial the number for Stan and "Seeley" DeLapp, but after the first ring, I hung up. The odds were good, given that this was the middle of the day, that Stan DeLapp was at work. Somewhere. Doing whatever a guy named Stan DeLapp did for money. His absence, however, was not a guarantee, and I needed a plan in case he answered—him, or really anyone other than Celine.

When I dialed again, I got a message machine after the eighth ring. The voice that clicked on was male, deep, and imposing. It said, with dull predictability, "You have reached the DeLapps. We're not in. Leave a message after the beep."

The recording ended, and the beep beeped. Showtime.

"Hello," I said, and tried to sound responsible, older, like some of my better teachers. "This is Brendan from Vinyl Wonderland, and I'm calling to you let you know that the special order you requested has come in, and we're open tonight until eight."

I almost made a crack about the special order being an album by the

Doors, but that, I knew, would have ruined the effect, and possibly forced Celine into a lie, so I restrained myself. Barely.

Celine didn't call back—no surprise there—but she showed up that evening, just after I'd started in on my supper, a deli sandwich I'd ordered from across the street. Timing is everything. There I was, wanting nothing more than to impress a pretty girl—woman—and the pretty girl managed to walk in the door at the exact moment that I had a too-big bite of salami and bread in my mouth, not to mention grilled onions dribbling down my chin.

"Lord above," she said, as she took in the food on my face. "You had damn well better not be my special order."

Chapter Eight

BRINKSMANSHIP WAS SOMETHING I'D BECOME expert at in my time as a teen troublemaker. I had long ago learned that the answer to the question of "Who blinks first?" determines winners and losers in all sorts of contests. Reckless behavior, see, especially in groups, typically involves drawing a line in the sand and seeing who dares to cross, and back in those days, most of my peers didn't want to cross the lines I drew, not unless they had to. They'd learned not to even try; they'd learned because I'd taught them.

I guess you could say I was an educator.

Dealing with Celine, however, required an entirely separate order of negotiation. I had something she wanted: access. She had something I wanted: information.

After I'd dealt with my sandwich and found a napkin for my face, I told her as much, and to her credit, she took the high road and tried to save me from myself. She said, "You don't get it. That door back there, it really is a case of the less you know, the better."

"Sure," I said. "Poor little Brendan's not tough enough, or smart enough, or old enough, to handle whatever's on the other side of that door. Oh, well. Poor little Brendan can't seem to find the key."

She objected, or she tried to, but mostly, she fidgeted. Now that she was so close, now that the key was available, she could not wait to get through the Elvis door, and it showed. Every moment's delay had her shuffling her feet, rearranging her fingers, cocking her head, shifting her gaze. At one point, she crossed her legs and squirmed as if she needed a bathroom.

"Fine," she said at last. "What is it you're so desperate to know?"

I hopped up on the countertop, a thing Karl would never have done, and once there, I leaned on my hands and swung my legs and basked in my little victory. "First off," I said, "what's the name of the woman in the coveralls, the one with the desk?"

Celine closed her eyes as if I'd disappointed her, and now it was time to ask a higher power for patience. When she opened them again, she looked sad.

"What?" I said. I had never appreciated pity, especially after Mom's death, and most of the time, that's what sad eyes seemed to mean.

With no change to her expression, Celine said, "You weren't supposed to go through."

"How do you know?"

"You weren't sent. Nobody told you."

"Oh, so this only works by referral? Please."

"As far as I know, yes."

"Well, I didn't leave the tunnel, if that's any comfort."

She chewed on this, considering. "That's probably good. And the woman's name is October. October Roberta."

I assumed I'd misheard, although I remembered now that Tony Accardi had made a reference to "October" earlier in the day. I said, "Don't you mean Roberta October?"

Celine shook her head, and her bangs wandered low over her eyes, like half-drawn curtains. "No. Her first name's October. Or at least, that's what she told me."

"Okay. So, this place is an invitation-only party, and the bouncer's name is October Roberta."

"It's not a party, and I don't think she's a bouncer."

Frustrated, I rolled my eyes. "I was employing a figure of speech."

Celine crossed her arms and stopped wriggling in place long enough to plant her feet. She said, with a total lack of sincerity, "I apologize for underestimating you and I promise with sugar on top not to do it again, but can we hurry this along? Do you even have another question?"

"How about the rules of the game? You go in, you get what you want, you come back out, end of story?"

Celine actually laughed at that, but it was the kind of laugh that makes others feel like total chumps. She said, "You go in, yes. October checks your name on a clipboard. She says, pick a road, pick a path—or, if you're lucky, she'll give you some direction. Then she'll say something like, 'Take as much time as you want, and when you're out there, wandering alone through all of that junk, you get to select one thing and bring it back.'"

"One thing, and one thing only?"

"If you need a Q-tip, there's a drug store on the corner."

I gave her a screw-you look, but I didn't disbelieve her. Her answers were consistent with what I'd gleaned already, but even so, I had the distinct sense that Celine was leaving out something crucial. Judy Treviso had said there'd been a choice, one she was aghast at having had to make, but Celine was implying that the choice of what to bring home was no more difficult or meaningful than picking the frosting color on a sheet cake.

"Are we done?" Celine said. "Can I go in now?"

By way of answer, I jumped down from the counter and pulled out my key ring. Celine's eyes got big when I held up the skeleton key. If I'd shined it up and dangled it from a chain, I'm pretty sure I could have hypnotized her on the spot, sent her to sleep, then advised her to cough up her best, most precious and tawdry secrets, one after another, until she had no more secrets left.

"I'll open up," I said, "but I'm still confused. How do you know what to take? That stuff looked like it went on for miles."

"Oh, it does. And it took me a long time, that first trip, to find what I needed."

She moved the Elvis standee for me as she was speaking. Next to her, I fitted the key in the lock and gave it a hard turn. As it clicked over, as I opened the door and held it for her, I said, "I don't get it. If you already found what you need, why are so gung-ho to go back?"

"Why am I—?" She stifled a rueful laugh, then tried to cover that with a smile, but it looked like the grin on a death's head. Refusing to meet my eye, she stared into the depths of the corridor, toward the point where it bent to the right and led away, elsewhere. She said, "Brendan, I'm going to give you an answer to that question, and the answer is, 'None of your damn business.'"

"Hey," I said, one hand firmly on the door, "I thought we had a deal."

Quick as a wink, she dodged into the doorway so that I couldn't shut the stupid thing without closing it on her. She said, "I gave you information, and that's what you asked for. But my personal life? That is not your concern, and if you pry any harder into what I'm doing here, I will kill you, do you understand me? I will kill you dead."

Now, I didn't believe for a minute that Celine could actually murder me, or even do me any serious harm, at least not if I was awake. She stood maybe five-foot-three, and like I said, I'm over six foot, and I was never a beanpole. Opponents who wanted to knock me off the ball in a soccer game, or who thought they could win in some shoulder-charge shoving match, well, they lost. I had meat and muscle to spare, and even my steady diet of all things alcoholic hadn't wrecked my build. My parents had given me a set of weights for Christmas three years prior, and I used them, on a regular basis. In fact, in the wake of my mom's death, I'd been hitting the weights harder than ever, sometimes right after breakfast, sometimes late at night, sometimes both, so having Celine DeLapp claim she was going to cook my goose seemed about as likely as a meteor strike. Still, her threat reminded me that at least for her, this was serious business, and she had turf to defend. Fair enough. The last thing I wanted was to fight with this girl.

Woman. Whatever.

"Okay," I said, which was my version of surrender. A new line had been drawn, and I had just agreed not to cross. "You go do your thing. I'll make sure October knows you're coming."

Celine nodded, slapped the door with her palm once, hard, as if that would somehow buck up her courage, and then she disappeared into the corridor. I closed the door behind her, got Elvis back in position, but with enough room for the door to swing open once Celine returned, and then I hurried to the counter to dial the phone.

October (what a name) picked up on the second ring. "Incoming?" she said.

"Incoming. Repeat customer. Celine DeLapp."

It's amazing what a telephone can give away. I could just about see

October frowning and shaking her head.

"That woman," said October. "Flirting with disaster."

"Why? Is she not supposed to be there? Should I have said no?"

"Not your decision to make."

I thought about this, then said, "If she's making a mistake, can't you just, I don't know, ban her?"

That drew a snort from October. "Sounds to me like my new custodian has a crush."

"I don't have a crush, I just think it's okay to look out for other people, you know?"

October said, "You're a sweetheart, and maybe that gets you laid on Valentine's Day, but if a person finds their way here in the first place, from there on, we've got an open-door policy. Pun intended. For life."

Good to know, I thought. And useful, also, to discover that Celine DeLapp came and went more than most, that she was the equivalent of a dedicated barfly, the regular whose attendance is so ingrained that she has her own stool. As for the notion that I was a sweetheart, all I could think was that October Roberta clearly didn't know me very well. I found that last part especially encouraging.

"Hey, Brendan."

"Yeah?"

"Are you locking these people in, from your side? Because you do need to keep that door locked at all times, you hear me?"

"So, they knock when they're ready to come out? Or do you call ahead?"

October let out a low chuckle. "You call *me*, Brendan, but I do not ever call *you*. Are we clear on that?"

"Sure. Clear as a bell."

"Good. And yes, they can knock when they want out."

"What if I've got other people in the store?"

"Just don't make it a big production. Most people only see and hear what they're ready for—and people as a group, the general public, they are nowhere close to prepared for what we have to offer. You might say, they're lucky that way. Anyhoo, your lady love's here, so. Gotta run."

The line went dead, and I replaced the handset in its cradle. As soon as I'd done so, I realized I had another question, and that was how long was I supposed to wait for Celine to come back? Officially, I was scheduled to close in thirty minutes. Was I now under some sort of unspoken obligation to stick around longer, to wait for Celine to resurface?

I considered dialing October's number again, but I was pretty sure that wouldn't go over well, so instead, I put on a big band LP, Woody Herman and his Thundering Herd, and then I walked to the back corner and locked the Elvis door up tight. Following orders at school had never been my strong suit—in fact, I was pretty much dead set against the whole concept—but when it came to Vinyl Wonderland, both the basic job and the demands of the Elvis door had felt like systems that were worth upholding. It even occurred to me, as I once again pocketed the key, that my newfound willingness to play by the rules was a sign that I was growing up. I kind of hoped that wasn't the case. I didn't know a lot of happy adults, and the one I'd known best, well. She died.

Maybe it was unavoidable, my mother's death. Only the good die young, right? Man, but I hated statements like that. I still do. I suppose they're meant as a comfort, but they come off as pious, unfeeling. Maybe it's true, though. Given the inordinate number of mediocre or just plain appalling people traipsing around this world, it's not an idea, even now, that I've been quick to brush off.

For the sake of getting the facts squared away, my mother didn't commit suicide, and she wasn't killed in a highway crash. She didn't capsize in a sailboat in a storm, and she didn't get herself engulfed in some raging mountain avalanche. No, all my mother did wrong was to visit her favorite cousin on their farm out in rural Guernsey County, and a ragged line of thunderstorms came along, nothing so unusual for April, but the cloud formations were so dark and spectacular that my mother and her cousin stepped outside once the storm had passed and the rain had lessened, in order to get a better look. They were just standing there, hoping for a rainbow, and shading their eyes against the glare of a sudden sunbeam when a section of corrugated sheet metal swooped out of the sky and clipped my mother in the back of the head.

It hit her hard, and it hit her clean. Doris Arnold, my mother's cousin, wasn't even one yard distant, and she got off without a scratch.

Later, Doris swore up and down that there was nothing gory about the event, that it was almost immaculate. The sheet metal hit my mother, and both dropped to the ground. End of story. Doris's husband, Fitch, came to the same conclusion, and so did the coroner. "Not a lot of blood loss," the coroner remarked to my dad, at a moment when I was supposed to be out of earshot. "Probably because she had such a thick head of hair. Just blunt force trauma. I'm so sorry."

Sheet metal doesn't often take to the sky, but given the right conditions, well. Earlier that day, see, one of the many storm cells sliding across Ohio had spawned a funnel cloud, and that baby twister touched down just long enough to chew its way across another farmstead, a few miles to the southwest. Among the souvenirs it stole were the corrugated metal sheets the property owner there had used to roof a pair of outlying sheds, and after lofting those sheets who knows how high in the air, the storm lost power, and its various airborne treasures scattered back to earth.

Wrong place, wrong time. Death by storm-tossed roofing.

Because she was the only witness, Doris was, for a while, a suspect, but she had several points in her favor. First, the supposed murder weapon was impossibly unwieldy. Second, other scraps of storm debris had landed around the farm, all of which could be traced back to the same source. Third, my mother and Doris had always been close. There wasn't a motive.

"I would have traded places with her," my father said, sometime during the endless night that followed the accident. He meant my mother, not Doris, and mostly, he couldn't speak at all, not for a day or so. Whenever he tried, he'd start to shudder, then sob, as if to refer to my mother out loud were somehow sacrilegious, inadmissible.

Later, in the last week of April, with the whole northern hemisphere in bloom and the birds erupting into song every morning starting at four, my father came into my bedroom. It was early, long before sunup. He shook me by the shoulder to wake me, then sat heavily on the edge of the mattress. The springs creaked like a graveyard gate as I sat up, rubbed sleep from my eye, and did my best to stretch without coming out from under the bedclothes.

"Brendan," he said, "I want to die."

It's true that I have never wasted an iota of my time reading up on how to raise kids right, but I'm pretty sure that young people aren't supposed to hear thoughts like that from their parents. And I'm pretty sure that if they do, there's supposed to be help, of some sort, the kind that's easy to find, available in plain sight. Somebody is supposed to step in and set up regular appointments with a therapist. A distant, unlooked for relative is supposed to appear on the scene, as if by magic, like Mary Poppins, and take firm charge of the situation. At the very least, a school counselor should step in. Something. Anything.

Well, my dad was in no condition to coordinate any sort of rescue, not for himself and not for me, and we didn't have a network of close family, and as it turned out, all of my parents' friends were really my mother's friends, so once the funeral was over, they dropped away like beetles scurrying for shelter. At school, the only counselors I had access to were "guidance counselors" plus a school nurse, certainly nobody with psychiatric training, not back then. I kept expecting that I would at least be called into the principal's office, where I would be asked avuncular questions like, "How are you doing, son?" In return, I would dutifully follow the script and respond that I was fine, and the principal, because it was the easiest thing to do, would accept my answer as if my word was my bond—which at Whetstone, let's face it, it never had been before.

But the principal never did call me in, and neither did anyone else. I got the impression that they were doing their level best to ignore my entire situation.

Not surprisingly, my behavior at school, which had been dicey to start with, went downhill fast from there.

At home, my dad stopped going to work, and within two weeks, he'd been fired. He made no secret of this, and he even apologized on a daily basis, announcing himself, usually through bouts of tears, as an unfit parent and a terrible example. He spent a lot of time in my mother's studio, sitting on one of her cushioned benches and staring at, I suppose, a fast-receding past. Sometimes he'd flip through the various books of clarinet sheet music as if hoping to find a helpful clue, a viable explanation for how and why the universe had betrayed him. Once in a while, he'd pick up one of my mother's three clarinets, and then he'd place the instrument on his lap, crosswise, and he'd rest his hands on the barrel and stare down at the keys as if at any moment, they'd start to talk, or divulge some sort of secret.

His drinking ramped up to the point where he no longer had any idea how much of his stash I was consuming. Prior to my mother's death, I'd been sampling here and there, a clear case of experimentation, but by the end of May, that nascent trickle had become a flood, and once summer hit, without the structure of school to contain and shape the day, I was drunk at least as often as my father, maybe more so.

The odds are huge that I would have died that summer, one way or another, if it hadn't been for that one chance meeting with Jonesy Davis. Just picturing his face—his kindly eyes, his permanently sleepy expression—was enough to keep me from getting behind the wheel except maybe mid-morning, when I was sober enough to take care of household staples like groceries and toilet paper. And back then, since I was still on the team and still enrolled in school, I had a network of friends—"friends"—to catch rides with. Most were trustworthy, although one time, a kid named Alan Geryk was the driver, and he ran us off the road, through a guard rail, and into a ditch. If there'd been a tree in the path of his sky-blue Malibu sedan, we all would have died. Amazingly, no one was seriously hurt —and the Malibu was packed that night, with two up front and three more boys in back—and once we'd extracted Alan from the driver's seat, I stood him up and punched him as hard as I could, a vicious uppercut to the solar plexus, and then I walked home, disgusted with Alan, with people in general, and, of course, myself.

The bottom line, see, was that despite everything, I didn't have a death wish. Even Jonesy Davis wouldn't have been proof against that, if that had been where my mind was headed, and really, my fury with Alan proved the point. I could be miserable, cantankerous, half-drowned in a vat of my own self-loathing, but I still had an instinctual spark that insisted I keep going—or, as my long-haired social studies teacher liked to put it, "Keep on truckin'."

Even so, summer almost did me in. What I needed was a job, but I couldn't quite bring myself to stagger to McDonald's or Arthur Treacher's Fish & Chips and fill out an application. Was this some kind of twisted passive-aggressive contest of wills with my father, who had an even greater responsibility to be out there, beating the bushes for meaningful, well-paid work? Let's just say that I wouldn't argue the point.

The one thing that got me out of the house consistently was my newfound love of used records. My first few had come from a neighbor's garage sale, three for a buck, and I enjoyed those random discs so much that it took no time at all for me to gravitate (or graduate) to used record shops. Vinyl Wonderland was the closest, and, luckily for me, one of the city's best. Eventually, that led to Karl and I bonding, and that, as I hope I've clearly set down, led to my present predicament: counting down the minutes and waiting on Celine DeLapp, who for all I knew was lost forever in endless vistas of garbage and junk.

By the time the Vinyl Wonderland clock ticked over to nine-thirty p.m., I had a serious case of ants in the pants, and I set myself a hard deadline: if Celine didn't knock on the Elvis door by ten o'clock sharp, I was locking up and going home. It was her own damn fault for being in there, and if she had to spend the night in the tunnel, well, that was on her.

But at nine fifty-four, I heard three sharp knocks, followed by more as I dug around for the key and shifted Mr. Presley. As usual, the lock stuck, so that took an extra minute to sort out, and that meant more knocking, followed by a plaintive cry.

"Brendan? Is that you?"

At last I got the door open, and there she was, looking like she'd walked through a sandstorm. In her hands, she held what I thought at first was a picnic basket, but then I spotted a mass of soft blankets at the bottom and realized that what she'd actually brought back was a wicker bassinet.

Before I could do more than stare, she stepped through the door and pressed the bassinet into my arms.

"Take it back," she said. "Brendan, for the love of God, don't let me keep this. You have to take it back."

Chapter Nine

WHEN OCTOBER ROBERTA SPOTTED ME emerging from the tunnel, she threw down her newspaper and headed my way at a fast clip. She looked as if were intending to snowplow me right back inside, so rather than give her the opportunity, I got a better grip on Celine's bassinet and dodged around until I had all those roads at my back instead of the tunnel I'd just come from.

"Brendan, what do you think you're doing?"

October had stopped. She had her hands on her hips. Twin flares of sunlight banked of her sunglasses, which reminded me, as the actual overhead sunshine somehow hadn't, that when I'd left Celine and Vinyl Wonderland, it was the middle of the night. In December. Here, against all odds, it was high noon, and hot. Again.

"Well," I said, "I'm not sure. I think I'm doing a friend a favor."

"Celine DeLapp is not your friend."

"You don't know that."

Halfway to firing off a retort, October apparently thought better of it. She took off her glasses and fitted the arms into the vee of her coveralls. With the glasses off, it was easier to read her frustration, her sense that I'd just stuck a wrench in her particular protocols, and that she didn't appreciate it.

Attempting to make peace, I said, "I'm sorry to just barge in. I know I'm supposed to call."

"Honey, you can't be here."

So much for peace. I said, "Too late. Here I am."

The bassinet was good-sized, baby-sized, so it was challenging to swing one arm in the sort of encompassing gesture that was meant to say, *Here we both are, wherever this is,* but I got my point across. Nothing had changed since I'd come last, except that now I could see the enormous horn of rock that rose from the ground near the desk, and from which the Vinyl Wonderland tunnel emerged. It looked a bit like the prow of a mountainous ship, or maybe a massive, irregular molar. There was nothing else like it in view, just the chalky, white-gray gravel-bed roadways leading off to every possible horizon and the mounds of scrap in between. No mountains, no clouds, no trees.

October, clearly trying a different tactic, was doing her level best to smile. I got the impression that she hadn't had a lot of practice.

"Look," she said, "I know you think you know the score. I get it that you're trying to help. But believe me when I tell you, it's too late. She took the bassinet. She signed for it. She walked out of here, and all the way to you, so the deal is done, right? Change of heart doesn't matter. She took what she wanted, and now she has to live with that."

Me, I was backing toward the nearest road. "I made a promise to take this back, so what I'd like to do is just hand it to you, or maybe set it on your desk, there. Either way, we call it Even Steven."

"It doesn't work that way."

"Then tell me which road to take, and I'll put it back myself."

"Come on. Have you never been in a store where the sign says, 'No returns'? That's this place, except more so."

All her obstructions were sending me right up a wall. "Last chance," I said. "Either you help me, or I go do this myself."

"Brendan, do not, I repeat, do *not* go down any of these roads."

"Why not?"

"Because you're not supposed to be here!"

"Okay, then maybe that's a good thing. Maybe all these rules you've got don't apply to me."

To my surprise, that brought her up short. I hadn't expected to make a winning point; I was basically just yelling, picking up the pieces of my side of an argument and tossing them back to see what stuck. Had I hit on something useful? Did the rules here, whatever they were, not in fact apply to me?

October Roberta drew a long sigh, scratched at one ear, and stared into the grit and gravel halfway between her feet and mine. At last she said, "You being here, you being anywhere near here, really, it's an accident. Bad luck. You've got no actual business…" She trailed away for a moment, like a minister who's lost the thread of a sermon, and then she sighed again, and regrouped. "There is nothing here for you. Not yet, anyway. On that front, I am one hundred percent certain."

This struck me as irrelevant. "But I'm not here for me. I'm here for Celine—who looked pretty messed up, by the way. She could barely talk, she'd been crying for I don't even know how long, and her clothes, her hair—I mean, what'd you do, roll her around on the ground? Get into a wrestling match?"

I already knew this last part couldn't be true. October's dull blue coveralls weren't exactly clean as a whistle, but while the cuffs at her ankles were covered in a chalk-white film of grit from the gravel underfoot, she clearly hadn't been down on the ground, using Celine as a rolling pin.

"Good to know," said October, with a thin smile, "that chivalry lives."

"What's that supposed to mean?"

"It means I still think you should get your ass back to Vinyl Wonderland as fast as your little feet can carry you, but. You might be right. Maybe you're an outlier. Maybe you can survive this place."

Survive? That wasn't an issue I'd been expecting. Hell, the mayor had visited here who knew how many times, and Celine was a regular, too. The last thing I'd been worried about, when I agreed to return Celine's bassinet, was my survival.

"So," I said, "which road? And how far?"

"Oh, you can go as far as you want."

"You know that's not what I meant."

That smile of hers just refused to widen. "Try over there," she said, pointing to a path that began between a pile of rusted-out wheelbarrows on one side and a mound of Dixie cups on the other. "Bassinets and cradles should be on the left, about two miles down."

"Two miles?"

"Honey, these roads go a lot farther than that. Be grateful it's not more."

By that point, the first trickle of sweat was making its way down my lower back. I'd intentionally left my winter gear in Vinyl Wonderland and stripped myself down to just a t-shirt and jeans, but even so, that summer sun, positioned directly overhead, was a scorcher. I did not understand how October could survive this in coveralls and not look as wilted as the flowers in a week-old bouquet.

"I don't suppose," I said, "that you've got any water?"

She didn't even bother to smirk. "If you can't stand the heat," she began, but I finished the phrase for her: "Get out of the kitchen."

"That's right," she said. "Good luck, now. Don't get lost."

That much, I figured I could manage, so I set off along the pathway she'd indicated, with the bassinet clutched awkwardly in front of me. If I'd had a red hoodie and maybe something baked, I'd have looked a lot like Little Red Riding Hood.

The road ran straight, rising and falling over gentle swells and dales, but there weren't any forks or intersections. Water was a consideration, and one I was kicking myself for not taking more seriously back at the shop. Alcohol, I knew, was a diuretic, and while I hadn't had all that much to drink over the course of the day, I definitely hadn't spent those hours prepping for a desert hike. On the soccer team, one of our favorite topics of conversation, especially on the bus for away games, was how to stay hydrated. Some kids swore by Gatorade and others proselytized with equal fervor about just plain water. One thing we all agreed on: when it came to exercise, liquor was bad news. True, not everyone on that squad had passed biology (or not without cheating, anyway), so for some, concepts like homeostasis were totally alien. Me, I fell someplace in the middle. With or without the Latin and the exact mechanics, I understood that cells functioned best when they had plenty of available liquid to draw on. On this trip, that wasn't going to be the case.

Looking on the bright side, I figured I wouldn't have to bother with a workout once I got home. Assuming, of course, that I ever did get home.

The other silver lining was that I had plenty to look at. No matter how far my gravel-covered pathway led, there were heaps of junk and refuse to either side, some of it in low piles, some of it stacked to incredible heights, and it continued on and on, for as far as I could see. Sometimes the clutter hemmed the avenue, walling it in, but then it would open up into bays and coves, each one weirdly specific: recliners here, buckets there. Over that direction, rigid blue insulation. Beyond that, a landslide of comics: *Casper the Friendly Ghost* from top to bottom.

It was as if every landfill, trash pile, and estate sale in the world had come to rest in this one place. As to who or what had done all the sorting, I didn't want to think. Wherever it was I'd wound up by walking through the Vinyl Wonderland tunnel, it clearly didn't obey the same laws as the world I lived in day-to-day. Gravity still applied, so that was some comfort, but the sun never shifted. It just stayed right overhead. The spooky part, although it took me a while to notice, is that there wasn't anything living except me. No grass, no weeds, no shrubs. In a wasteland like this, I'd have expected crabgrass, at least, not to mention rats, crows, seagulls. No such luck. Nothing moved except me, along with occasional bits of loose flotsam, set in motion by the breeze.

The walking itself was easy. The hills were gradual, and the road was clear. Water, though; I was getting thirstier by the minute. Two miles was starting to feel more like three. It occurred to me (a paranoid flash) that October might be hoping to get rid of me. Maybe she'd sent me down the wrong road, and if I walked far enough, in this heat, with this steady wind, I'd dehydrate. One minute, I'd be marching along just fine, and the next I'd be flushed, feverish, clammy. I'd sit down, not because I wanted to, but because I couldn't stand up. I'd look for shade, but with no luck. Not long after, I'd pass out, and that would be that.

But then, just as I was thinking that I'd better turn back, I came to a cove on my left that was all wicker, three encompassing walls of wicker this and wicker that, baskets and mats, coasters and flowerpots and—bingo— bassinets. Some were painted, mostly in muted reds, blues, and greens, while a bunch of the bassinets were white, and here and there, some of the baskets had been done in black. All told, the pile-up stood considerably taller than my head, and I didn't even want to think about how deep it might be. If I started to burrow in, would I ever get out?

I didn't see any obvious spot that Celine's bassinet had come from, so in the end, I walked it as far into the cove as I could go without actually climbing the sides of that wicker mountain, and I leaned it up against a mess of others, several of which were obviously broken. Celine's was in good repair, and, so far as I could see, it was the only one that came fully equipped with receiving blankets and a pad. No wonder she'd chosen that one.

No wonder, said an unwelcome voice in my head, that it had chosen her.

"Okay," I said, to the bassinet, and to anyone (or anything) that might be listening. "There you go. Back where you belong."

Having allowed myself the juvenile luxury of a sentimental moment, I turned and scuffed my way out of that wicker dead-end, with every intention of setting a steady pace for October's desk, the tunnel, and home, followed, I hoped, by a Big Gulp the size of my head, but when I got to the road, I stopped so fast I practically skidded.

Instead of one road, with a simple choice of left or right, I'd arrived at a five-way intersection.

Chapter Ten

FIVE ROADS WHERE THERE HAD been one. I knew in a heartbeat that I was in major league trouble.

I don't know if I deserve any credit for this, but I didn't waste any time questioning what I was seeing. This wasn't a dream, and I wasn't going to start in on bad movie dialogue like "This can't be happening!" The reality of what I faced was simply not open to debate. Where before there had been a single path, with a maximum of two choices for how to proceed, I now faced five.

I blew out a sharp breath and swung my gaze from right to left, searching for landmarks. Did I find any? Absolutely not. I realized that on my trek here, aside from keeping an eye out for wicker bassinets, I hadn't been paying much attention to what I passed. Sure, each mound of cast-offs was distinctly different from those around it, but after two miles' worth, even objects as disparate as rusted bedsprings and moldering leather wallets had begun blending together like so much white noise on a badly tuned radio.

With no landmarks to work from, I looked down, hoping to spot footprints, tracks from my sneakers, but the gravel didn't reveal a single tread mark, or at least not one I could read.

Having exhausted that option, I checked over my shoulder, thinking I'd anchor myself to the one point of reference I still had, the mountain of thrown-away wicker. Luckily, it was still there, creaking a bit as the wind moved through it, but otherwise stoic, unchanged.

I licked my dry lips and tried not to think about water. Then I closed my eyes, steadied myself against the wind (which seemed to be picking up, as if it could sense the acceleration of my pulse), and did my level best to cast my mind back to the moment just before I'd arrived at the heap of old wicker. Had it been on my left, or on my right? Either option felt possible, but for whatever reason, I was sure that in veering into that cul-de-sac, I had turned left.

Okay, then. Assuming I could trust my short-term memory, that ruled out at least a couple of my choices—provided, of course, that these pathways didn't simply move around at will, or at random. Which, here, I had to figure was a serious and very ugly possibility.

Eyes closed, breathing as calmly as I could manage, I worked my way back to the moment where I'd first spotted the wicker. What had I seen? What had I walked past, just prior to finding what I wanted? What had I been rejecting as the wrong sort of garbage?

I'd been thirsty, that I remembered. I'd been musing about how far I could reasonably walk in these conditions before I sweated out all the salt I needed to keep my various organs in synch. And—Hallelujah!—I recalled finding it more than a little ironic that I'd just passed by a mountain of Minute Maid frozen orange juice tubes, the kind with spiraled, tear-away cardboard and aluminum lids.

My eyes snapped open. I looked to my right, searching for the orange and black Minute Maid logo. Hot damn, there they were, lurking a short distance down the second pathway over, and on the exact side I'd expected to see them.

"Gotcha," I muttered, and I set off double-quick, before I either lost sight of that lifeline or they somehow moved off on their own.

Two miles later (it felt like ten), I caught a glimpse of the tunnel rock jutting out of the ground, and after another dip into a valley and a climb back out, I arrived once more at the desk of October Roberta. She was busy trying to put up a large red sunshade, the kind that restaurants use when they want to look European, but the mechanism for the umbrella was broken, and it kept collapsing down over her head. She was so busy fighting with the shade that she wouldn't have noticed me at all if I hadn't called her name, and when

I did, she jumped. Her upper hand immediately lost its grip, and the shade dropped and tried to close over her head. To get away, she gave the support pole a shove, and the whole thing pitched to the ground like felled timber.

"Brendan," she said. "What a surprise."

Now, October's fight with the sunshade might have been hilarious in slightly altered circumstances, but I'd had two miles at least to chew on my rising anger, which is to say two miles of hoofing it in that miserable, unrelenting heat, and I was primed and ready to tear into that woman with a heatstroke hurricane of well-rehearsed fury. Lucky for the both of us, I didn't have a lot of gas left in the tank. Also, and I have to be honest here, not only was I running on fumes, but I was more than a little frightened. Chewing out October as part of a therapeutic daydream was one thing, but I had a nasty feeling that in this scrap-yard wasteland, she held all the cards. So, while a good screaming match might have been cathartic, it also felt like a serious risk, and in the end, what I wanted more than anything else was to get back inside the tunnel and to follow it as fast as possible to the familiar, comforting normalcy of Vinyl Wonderland.

So, instead of ripping October a new one, I just stood there, and then I stood there some more, panting like an old mutt.

"Anger," said October, not unkindly, "can be useful."

"Go to hell."

"It got you back here. Powered your steps. Kept you focused."

I was starting to feel dizzy, and I lurched away from her, headed toward the tunnel entrance, but my feet wouldn't behave. I felt like a small boat fighting a series of choppy, crisscrossing waves, and the more I tried to go straight, the more I veered off course.

Behind me, October was coming closer, talking as she came. "You've got reserves. More than most, maybe. And you didn't spend your time looking for anything for yourself. That's impressive. Unusual."

I reeled closer to what I was pretty sure was the tunnel entrance. If nothing else, it would have shade. I tried to tell October she could kiss my grits, but my tongue was thick as a ham and dry besides; I don't think anything coherent made it past my lips.

"I'm going to send you home," October said, and I felt her hand at the top of my back, her palm and fingers sliding across my sweat-soaked shirt, soothing and settling. "I'm also going to repeat the advice I gave you before. Quit your job. Walk away from Vinyl Wonderland, and don't ever, ever come back. In fact, it would be best if you forgot this place ever existed. Move, if you have to. Another city, another state. Do whatever it takes so that this place does not define the arc of your life."

Again, she rubbed my back, and I have to admit, it felt good. It felt the way my mother's hand did when I was younger, when I was sick or stressed, and she'd sit with me and place her hand on my back in that impossibly steadying way that good mothers have, and I'd feel better, not in a literal sense—when you're sick, you're sick—but I knew through her presence, those simple ministrations, that I wasn't alone, that somebody cared.

"Last thing, Brendan. Stay away from Celine DeLapp."

I reached out a hand, groping toward the rock at the tunnel entrance, hoping for a solid purchase, and I made it just before I fell on my face. Thanks to the sun, the stone was warm to the touch, almost hot, like a brick at the edge of a campfire ring, but even as my vision went double, I knew I was in the right place. Shade and cool air beckoned, and in another moment, I'd staggered inside the entrance to the tunnel. The sun wasn't slamming my head, the breeze wasn't sucking all the moisture out of my mouth. Perhaps most importantly, October Roberta wasn't whispering in my ear.

I can't say with any certainty when I passed out, or how exactly I navigated the tunnel home, but I woke up on the floor of Vinyl Wonderland, with Elvis Presley looming over me and the hum and rumble of early commuter traffic purring along outside the front window. The bins of albums huddled around me in rows, keeping their own counsel. Maybe they were judging me, maybe they weren't. It kind of felt like they were.

I pushed myself onto all fours, tasted the dry-rot stink of my own morning breath, and checked the wall clock: eight-twenty. Daylight, but barely.

As I got to my feet, I heard October Roberta's voice sounding in my memory, low and insistent, *Quit your job. Walk away.*

I had to admit, that was starting to sound like the smartest idea I'd ever heard.

Chapter Eleven

IF ALAN GERYK HADN'T CALLED, who knows how long I would have slept. My body, after that trip though Vinyl Wonderland's desert, felt like I'd played an entire tournament's worth of soccer. And, if I'm being honest, I hadn't exactly collapsed into bed the second I'd made it home. No, in a stress-induced departure from my usual slow-sipping style, I put back three shots of Jack Daniels pretty much as soon as I got my hands wrapped around the countertop bottle.

If I'd made it to my bedroom, I would have slept right through Alan's noon-time wake-up call, but I'd passed out on the living room couch, and the phone was just around the corner, wall-mounted in the kitchen. Getting my carcass close enough to answer was a Herculean task; my hangover, in combination with being dehydrated, was the worst I'd had in memory. I felt like a sack of kittens, tossed in a river and left to drown.

Actually, I'm not sure that anyone ever feels quite like that. In fact, I'm pretty convinced that it's not humanly possible to feel like a sack of half-drowned, river-dropped kittens. Let's just say that I felt awful, so awful that there isn't a metaphor on the planet that will cover it. Maybe if I'd put more of an effort into those high school English classes, I'd have the right approximation at my fingertips, but that was a ship that even then had long since sailed.

Discovering Alan on other end of the phone line was frankly hard to believe. Our status as soccer teammates had thrown us together for years, starting long before high school, but we hadn't been social except in packs. If someone had told me to call him, I'd have had to ask for the number. I was pretty sure he was in the same situation.

His reason for calling turned out to be purely mercenary. He and a group of other Whetstone Braves had formed an indoor soccer team to tide them over and keep them sharp through winter, and they'd been playing matches at a run-down facility off Morse Road called Kicks. I knew the place. The year before, I'd played at Kicks myself, though on a different team from Alan. No surprise there: with indoor soccer, the pitch is small, so the teams have to be smaller, too, with just six at a time taking the field, goalkeeper included.

Alan's problem was a team-load of injuries. They'd started with a roster of eleven, but indoor can be a brutal game, what with the side walls and the Astroturf underfoot, and they were down to just six healthy, available players for the next match. Playing an entire game without a single substitute was a recipe to lose and lose big. The remaining players had agreed it was time to call in reinforcements. Was I first on their list? I doubted it. More likely, I was last.

"Game's at two," said Alan. "Can you make it?"

I squinted at the clock and grimaced. Vinyl Wonderland was supposed to open its doors at eleven, and here I was, almost an hour late already.

"Gotta work," I said, to Alan, and then, in almost the same breath, I corrected myself. "No, wait. Never mind about work. Any chance I can bum a ride?"

Without missing a beat, Alan said, "Brendan, the only way you ever ride with me again is if you are chained in manacles and locked in the trunk."

I was so surprised that I forgot to be angry. Or maybe I couldn't summon up the moxie. The odds were good that my splitting head and curdling stomach wouldn't have allowed me to boil over no matter what Alan said, but I sure was confused. Why did Alan think the best place for me was in the trunk of his car?

"Warm-up starts at one-thirty," Alan said, "and just so you know, I voted against including you."

"Okay," I said, as a fresh wave of body aches washed through me. "Thanks."

He hung up. I hung up. I made it to the toilet just in time.

Now, the thing about my drinking, see, even before meeting Jonesy, is that I'd always taken a certain amount of pride in being what later got to be called a "high functioning alcoholic." Most days, I drank slowly and steadily, and I thought of it as surfing. I nudged myself to the crest of a wave, and I spent the rest of my waking hours skimming along, self-medicating with additional sips as needed to maintain the high. I got really, really good at that, with the result that any seriously out-of-control drunken behavior just about never happened.

Plus, I hated hangovers. That's really the only thing they're good for: motivation.

As for the conflict between Vinyl Wonderland and indoor soccer, well, I managed to rationalize that right out of existence. My line of defense went like this: I was now the chief of staff at Vinyl Wonderland, and if I chose to take an hour off, or even a day, that was my choice. Karl didn't need the money (or so I told myself, without evidence) because he had insurance, and he and his mother didn't need the money because they had a house, and she had social security.

The fact that all of these arguments detonated logic on every possible front did not stop me from deploying them. Nor did I have the grace or insight to see how I was avoiding any comparisons to my own situation, where we did in fact need the money, and desperately, too. In fact, my father and I had money problems precisely because we had a house. Houses don't come cheap, as my father used to say, in happier, more easeful times. My mother preferred comparing a house to a small child, one that's always hungry, always asking for the next helping of money, love, and repairs.

It all came down to one thing: I was late for work already, so why not arrive later still? If I felt guilty enough at the end of the day, I could always dock myself a few hours' pay.

The next step was to kick my hangover. I knew how, but I really didn't want to do what was required. That said, maybe October Roberta had a point. Maybe I had some reserves, because even though I would much rather have gone back to sleep, preferably with an icepack on my forehead and all the blinds pulled low, I did the exact opposite: I pulled on sweatpants and a nylon jacket and headed out for a twenty-minute jog.

For the first five minutes, I felt as bad as I ever had in my life. My stomach wanted to jump up through my esophagus and hurl itself headlong at the road, half of which was still covered in packed snow and ice, with a pair of tire tracks down the middle that had mostly worn themselves to blacktop. My head felt thick, bloated, and my lungs weren't giving me the air I was asking for. But I kept going, in part because I knew this was temporary, and in part because I tried imagining that my route was actually the pathway through all the garbage on the way back from the wicker dump, and I knew that if I could push through that, I could bull my way through this.

Sure enough, by the time I was done, I felt ninety percent better, and I was ready for a coffee-and-eggs breakfast. I would have spiked the coffee—I *wanted* to spike that coffee—but my promise not to drive while jacked had teeth, and I had a game to get to.

Perhaps more importantly, guest-starring with Alan's team meant that I had a chance to prove myself, maybe even take some baby steps toward rehabilitating my image. No wonder, then, that I set off for Kicks with a spring in my step. Indoor soccer was about to provide my golden ticket back to the fold of social acceptance.

That's not how it worked out. At all.

Warm-ups went fine. Most of the other guys even managed to say, grudgingly, "Hello." But the game itself? I got off to a good start, enforcing the middle of the field the way I always did, using my body to muscle my opponents off the ball, and generally causing mayhem. But my shoes were trouble. I'd outgrown the pair I'd bought specially for indoor a year ago, which left me wearing basic sneakers—too wide at the front, like cross-trainers are now. I couldn't wrap my foot around the ball, which meant I had no touch, no control. My ability to complete passes after I won the ball was seriously compromised.

And then, well, I got a first-hand lesson in why conditioning and game prep matters. Sure, I'd been working out at home with weights, but that's no substitute for running, wind-sprints, and scrimmages. Two months back, stocking shelves at Big Bear had provided at least some basic exercise, but since starting full-time at Vinyl Wonderland, I'd been sitting on my ass for hours at a time. I'd lost muscle tone, and more importantly, I'd lost lung capacity.

Ten minutes after the balding pipsqueak of a referee blew his whistle to start the match, I was sucking wind, barely able to hold my ground much less cover the field. My every move became about playing the angles so I didn't have to run more than absolutely necessary. I'm sure my excursion into the land of garbage the day before hadn't helped; I still felt dog-tired, and my calf muscles were stiff, slow to react. Why, I thought, why in hell had I agreed to this? Why had I thought this was a winning hand?

I subbed out, but I couldn't stay on the bench for long, not with just one available substitute player for our whole team, and once I was back on, I picked up a yellow card, which was a personal embarrassment for me, since my usual m.o. was to knock people around *without* ever getting carded. That day, given how out of shape I was, my challenges weren't just reckless, they were clumsy. Sure, I still argued the point with the referee, but a card is a card—and then, in the final period, when I didn't think the game-ending whistle would ever come, I tried an even clumsier tackle and drew a second yellow.

Two yellows equal red, and so, with five minutes to go, I was sent off, and as per the rules of the game, I couldn't be replaced. My team fought through the waning moments of that match one man down and they surrendered a goal in the process. We lost, 5-4.

I'd like to report that I had the grace to apologize at the end. I'd like to say, with a clear conscience, that I told my teammates that I was sorry, and that it wouldn't happen again. Instead, I did what people now call "doubling down," and I spent my newly rested lungs on a sour-grapes diatribe about how the other team cheated, the torn-up Astroturf surface was to blame for my violent challenges, and the referee wasn't fit to officiate a toddler's game of pin-the-tail-on-the-donkey.

Well, Alan finally snapped. He stomped over, got right in my face, and told me I should have been sent off long before I actually was, that my tackles were dangerous, that I'd played like a slug, and that I wasn't invited back—ever. He was standing and I was sitting, but I just let him lay into me, and then I said, loudly enough for the whole team to hear, "That's right. Like I need advice from the guy that can't keep his car on the road."

Alan's face turned red-purple, and he clenched his fists so hard that his knuckles went white. I thought for sure he was going to hit me, and I figured that might feel good. We'd get into a proper fist-fight, where I could work off my humiliation by pummeling Alan until the other guys pulled me clear. But instead, Alan took a very deliberate step back and said, in a voice that quavered like a struck bell, "Either you're the worst person in the world, or you really don't remember."

"Yeah? Remember what?"

"The night I crashed."

"Sure, I remember. You were drunk as a skunk."

Alan shook his head, and his eyes lost that bloodshot, flinty look. "I was fine until you grabbed the wheel."

"That's ridiculous."

"Brendan, you were wasted, totally wasted, laughing your head off, and we'd agreed to drive you home, and next thing I know, you'd lunged for the wheel. We almost died. And you still think it was my fault."

Somewhere in there, his fists had unclenched. He took a further step away, then reached for his gym bag. Without another look in my direction, he headed for the exit. The rest of the group melted away in his wake, leaving me on my own. All around me, the next two teams of combatants warmed up, stretched, and tried not to be caught staring my direction.

Twenty minutes later, I was home and oh-so-ready for a drink, but the sight of my father spread eagled on the floor in the living room, one arm crooked tenderly around the nearest leg of the glass-topped coffee table, put the brakes on that. He had on a beige dress shirt, a black leather belt, and Navy slacks; I was pretty sure that if I flipped him over, I'd discover he was wearing a tie.

Now, to put this in context, my dad had passed out in pretty much every corner of the house over the past nine months, but never on the floor. It occurred to me that he might not be sleeping, that this might be a serious emergency.

"Dad?" I said, and I licked my lips, tasting a hint of residual salt from the sweat I'd worked up at Kicks. The sharpness on my tongue reminded me, despite my best attempts to stay focused on the situation at hand, of that first contact with the salted glass of a well-made margarita.

For a long moment, my father didn't respond, but then he raised the arm he'd curled around the coffee table and gave a feeble, exhausted salute.

"Hi," he said.

I wasn't sure whether to be relieved or angry. Maybe both. "Dad," I said, "what are you doing?"

After a long pause, he said, "Nothing."

"Right, I get that. I mean, big picture. What are you doing?"

"Every individual," my father said, as if reciting from a textbook, "has both the capacity and the right to mourn in their own particular way."

"Where'd you get that, Phil Donohue?"

"Who?"

On another day—a better day, the kind we didn't have any more— my father would have recognized Phil Donohue's name and been able to reference him quickly as a daytime talk-show host on TV, but a lot of things had slipped lately, like which day the trash went out, and how to pay the credit card bill, and where he'd stored the paperwork for our auto insurance.

"Gotta go," I said. "I need a shower."

"Where were you?"

"Soccer. Indoor."

He still hadn't lifted his head from the floor, but he said, with a trace of actual curiosity, "How'd it go?"

"We lost. I lost. Everybody lost."

"Oh."

I kicked off my shoes and let them clatter, one at a time, against the hall closet door, and I was just moving off to the kitchen, in search of something strong, when my father called my name.

"Yeah, what?" I said.

"I need to know what you want for Christmas."

That caught me off guard. Christmas was just around the corner, but I hadn't really applied that knowledge to my own life, my own house. At Kicks, the management had put up long strands of twinkling lights in the lobby, the new kind with the tiny little bulbs, and the grocery stores had been playing Muzak-styled Christmas hits since the week before Thanksgiving, but whatever holiday spirit was drifting through the city at large, it hadn't reached me. Karl and Vinyl Wonderland hadn't been any help. I knew there was a single box labeled "Xmas Décor" in the storage closet, but Karl hadn't dragged it out before I took over, and I hadn't given it any thought since. Day to day, sure, the weather was cold, and sometimes snowy, but that didn't mean it was Christmas. To discover that my dad was one step ahead when it came to jingle bells and mistletoe was a major shock.

Maybe if we'd been attending church, singing "Away in a Manger" come Sunday mornings, I would have been more on the ball, but church had been my mother's purview, and when we went, it was at her urging. With her gone, I'd graced a church pew for her memorial but hardly ever after that. Maybe just twice, on late spring days when my father had insisted we attend in my mother's memory. "In her honor," as he put it—but we sat in the back, out of sight, unengaged and certainly not honored. By late summer, Dad had stopped even mentioning church as something we might do. Like school, like soccer, church became just one more piece of connective tissue that we'd cut away and left behind.

"Christmas," I repeated, as if the word were new to me, foreign, and I needed to give it a road test. "I don't know. Maybe I don't want anything."

My father rolled to one side, as if my answer had pained him and now he was trying to find a more comfortable position. Then he gave up and went right back to where he'd been sprawled originally.

"I remember," he said, "when you were little. We gave you slot cars. A track. You raced those cars all day, every day, for hours. I'd hear your mother, practicing or giving lessons, from that direction"—he indicated the studio—"and from this direction, I'd hear *whirr, whirr, whirr*."

I'd heard this story before, and I remembered it, more or less—or at least, I remembered it through the filter of my father's vivid and frequently repeated memory. For him, see, that had been the best Christmas of his adult life, because it had been *my* best Christmas, the one where I'd opened every package as if the universe itself were waiting inside, shiny and fresh, newly created, and all just for me.

I still had the slot cars. They were in a bin under my bed, but I had long since moved past the point where two fake cars speeding around an endless figure-eight held any attraction at all.

My father spoke again, and this time it seemed as if he might actually sit up. "When *is* Christmas, anyway? What day of the week?"

"Hang on," I said, and I went into the kitchen to check the wall calendar that my mother put up every year on the side of the refrigerator. I didn't like looking at it. I didn't like considering how, on December 31ˢᵗ of this year, the calendar would become useless, and my mother wouldn't be on hand to put up the new one, for 1985.

After I'd figured out the date, I called to my dad. "Today's Sunday the sixteenth. Christmas is ten, nine days away. Tuesday."

When he replied, his voice sounded so tired, it barely made it out of the living room. "Just tell me what you want," he said, "and I'll get it for you."

I returned to the hall, so I could hear him better. I thought about kneeling down and putting a hand on his back, the way October had done for me. The way my mother would have done, for either of us. "Dad," I said, "it's okay."

This time, he managed to roll onto his side, so he could catch my eye. He said, slurring gently, "No, I'm serious. You name it. Books. Toys. Gift certificates. Or, I know, how about a car? You want your own car? I'll get you a car."

"We can't afford the car we've got."

"You must want something."

Did I, though? Was there anything I actually wanted? Right at that moment, I wanted a shower, a meal, a drink, and a chance to convince myself that Alan Geryk was deluded. Those weren't things I would ever find under a Christmas tree (except maybe the drink, in bottled form). What did other people want? Alan wanted to win. Karl wanted his mother to heal up. Karl's mother wanted Karl to heal up. Judy Treviso, for some reason, wanted an ottoman. Mayor Tony Accardi wanted votes. Celine DeLapp wanted…well, I wasn't sure what she wanted, but it was important, whatever it was, and it made her upset enough to cry in front of me, some teenager she barely knew.

So, what did I want?

"Okay," I said, "are you being serious? You really want to know what I want?"

My father struggled up on to his elbows. No question, he was hung over. He looked like he'd been the victim of a hit-and-run, and I knew for a fact that he felt right now the way I felt when I'd first woken up. Even so, he rallied. He squeezed his eyes shut, then forced them open and said, "Just tell me. Tell me what you want."

So, I told him. No sugar coating, no beating around the bush. I said, "Dad, I don't know what I want, but I know what I need, and that's you. Functional."

Man, the look on his face. It was like I'd just shot Bambi's mother, right in front of him, and he was Bambi.

For a moment, he looked as if he might try to wince his way past that pounding hangover headache and say something coherent, but then it was all too much. He lay back on the floor, wrapped himself up against the coffee table, and started to cry.

That was enough for me. I marched back to the kitchen, swiped a half-full bottle of vodka, and headed for the bathroom and the hottest possible shower.

Maybe there'd been worse Sundays in the history of the world, but right then, I sure as hell couldn't think of one.

Chapter Twelve

ON MONDAY, VINYL WONDERLAND WAS always closed, which gave
me an unfortunate excuse to keep right on wallowing in a deep, cavernous
lake of self-recrimination. That catastrophe of an indoor soccer game kept
replaying in my head. Not just the game, moment-to-moment, pass-to-pass,
but the aftermath. I took some pride, then and now, in telling the truth—in
being brutally honest, if not to the world, then at least to myself. Alan Geryk's
version of his car accident suggested that I wasn't doing a very good job.

The Elvis door and what lay beyond it probably should have been
uppermost in my mind, but incredible though that was, it felt impersonal,
not really about me. Sorting out the truth, the truth about myself, that felt
far more pressing than figuring out an alternate reality that I probably didn't
have the right tools to explain no matter what.

So, I called Derek Glasscock.

To hear my folks tell it, I'd known Derek since I was born. We were
delivered on the same floor of the same hospital, thirty-six hours apart,
and because we'd wound up at the same schools starting in kindergarten,
our families had been tracking a nearly identical social orbit for well over
a decade. I had the better life, because it's hard to make fun of the name
Purcell, whereas Glasscock is just about the worst surname a boy can be born
with, at least in English. I know for a fact that Derek had plans to change it
just as soon as he turned eighteen. "No kid of mine," he'd say, darkly, "will

ever have to suffer with this stupid name."

He wasn't a bad guy, Derek. He'd developed into a passable outfielder come springtime, and in the fall, he was a half-decent right fullback for my former Whetstone soccer squad. In fact, he was one of the few I actually kind of missed. He was a little down-in-the-mouth, like a human Eeyore—a partly cloudy day, for him, always signaled incoming rain—but he could be funny, too, and because he'd grown up on the receiving end of so many jokes, he was never funny at anyone else's expense.

Most importantly, Derek had been in the back of Alan Geryk's Malibu on the night of the crash. In the middle spot, no less. Not as bad as front passenger, the so-called "death seat," but bad enough. If anyone besides me had had a near-death experience that night, it had been Derek.

Oh, and did I mention? Derek Glasscock was militant about telling the truth, and unlike me, he told the truth to the world at large.

Calling him was tricky, since it was a school day, and I wasn't awake until what for Derek was second period. Let's remember, see, that this was decades before cell phones, so I couldn't exactly send him a text. Instead, I twiddled my thumbs, took the occasional nip of peach schnapps, and waited for the school day to be over.

When I finally dialed, I got his mother first, and she pretended she was glad to hear from me, and she asked all the right questions, and claimed more than once that she missed my mom. The odds are good that she was sincere; Melinda Glasscock had always struck me as a fine example of what happens to generally decent, good-natured people when they grow up.

But Derek, on the phone, was hard to read. We hadn't talked in a long time, and for whatever reason, he hadn't been part of the indoor soccer group at Kicks. So, he sounded friendly, but friendly didn't cost a dime. Mostly, he was mystified about why I'd called.

I didn't leave him twisting in the wind for long. "Listen," I said, "the night Alan's car crashed. Did I have a hand in that? And if so, what did I do?"

Derek swallowed so hard that I could hear him gulp over the phone line.

"Good idea," he said, as if I'd just suggested we go play a friendly game of tennis. "I could meet you in, I don't know, how about half an hour?"

Lucky for the both of us, I was quick on the uptake. Alan's crash clearly wasn't a subject Derek wanted to cover on the phone—like us, his house had only one telephone, and it was in a very public location—so a burger and fries sounded like just the excuse we needed.

"How about G.D. Ritzy's?" I said. "The one on High, near Jerry's."

There was a pause. "Ritzy's," he said, at last. "You sure?"

I shrugged as if he could see me do it, and said, "It's a halfway point and they make decent burgers. What's not to like?"

"Okay, but you're buying."

That sounded ominous. Here I was with my first date in months, not counting Lani Bell at Big Bear, and not only was it with a guy, but it was also a guy who didn't want to go Dutch.

Still, beggars can't be choosers, a phrase that sounded doubly apt when I had to resort to rifling my dad's wallet for cash, and he only had fourteen bucks, total. I wondered, as I pocketed those wrinkled bills, if this was the last money he had, period. If so, all the more reason for me to get back to Vinyl Wonderland, first to get myself paid, and second to keep making more.

Derek and I arrived at the same time, made nice, and got our orders placed. Once I'd paid for our grub, we picked the most out-of-the-way table possible, and we ate in silence for longer than I would have liked. I don't mind keeping my own counsel, but not when the people around me are working with information I don't have.

Well, Derek finally let go of his cheeseburger and got down to business. He had curly hair and freckles, and even his Ohio State Buckeyes coat kind of screamed out, "I'm harmless!" Which, at least with regard to me, he most certainly wasn't.

"You do understand," he said, "that this is a really weird place for you to want to meet."

I sucked so hard on my Coke that I clamped the straw completely shut. Once I'd let go, I said, "Why? What are you talking about?"

Derek gave me a look like he had fifty things to say, and none of them sounded right. "Maybe if you tell me what you remember about Alan and the crash. Then I'll know what ballpark we're playing in."

What did I remember? I ate some shoestring fries and gave that some thought. A Saturday night in May. A party someplace, unsupervised, friends of friends from another high school. Alcohol? Presumably. Weed? Not for me, but maybe others. We'd left the party, we'd headed nowhere in particular, just driving, with the goal of eventually dropping everybody at home. What else could there possibly be?

I fed that history to Derek, and he pulled in his lips, looking one part thoughtful and two parts disappointed. He said, "You don't remember picking a fight?"

"With who?"

"Dunno. Some guy at the party. That's why we left. First, we pulled you off of him, and then we got you out of there."

Elbows on the table, I spread out my hands, fingers splayed. If I'd been a magician, doves would have exploded up toward the ceiling. I said, "Derek. I have no memory of that."

"Do you know why we put you in the front seat?"

"Sure. I'm bigger than you guys."

Derek shook his head. "The rest of us didn't want you throwing up on us."

"Give me a break. I can hold my liquor."

And there it was, that look I hated more than anything: pure pity. Derek Glasscock, sitting in easy range of a good right hook, was feeling sorry for me. I frankly couldn't believe it.

"Brendan," he said, "I don't know how to put this delicately, but I am one of the many people you've thrown up on. With me, it was mostly just shoes, but it wasn't like just a little spatter. You totally unloaded. I'm actually trying to think of anyone on the team that you haven't been sick on, or cussed out, or spat on, or tried to fight."

"Man, you are out of your mind."

This time, his head shake was emphatic. "We get what happened. We all do. And we tried, we really did. But you pushed it. You pushed it past the point where we had any reason to care."

"Pushed what? I don't even know what we're talking about!"

Heads were turning around the restaurant. Lucky for us, it wasn't the dinner hour, so we mostly had the place to ourselves, but even so. G.D. Ritzy's isn't where diners expect to have ring-side seats for a serious argument.

Derek ignored the stares and said, "I'm talking about you. You went from being a fun guy to a violent, black-out drunk, and the night of the crash, you were actively trying to get yourself killed, and us along with you."

"Get out."

"You had your hand on the wheel *constantly*. Like, Alan would swat you away, push your arm, and you'd be right back, seat belt off, trying to crawl into the driver's seat so you could get your foot on the gas. We're in the back seat, like, trying to tackle you from behind, trying to pin you, and by the time we got on Cook Road, Alan was just trying to pull over so we could get you out, sit on you or something until we could get you calm or halfway sober, and next thing we know, you'd got hold of the wheel and yanked it hard to the right, and we're all flying into that ditch. And then! As if that isn't enough, as if you hadn't damn near killed every one of us, made us all a part of your death wish—and Alan with a concussion and bleeding from where he hit the steering wheel—but then you've got the nerve to haul out and hit him! I mean, what is that? It was crazy, Brendan, crazy."

From the corner of my eye, I watched as a family of four, sitting three tables down, made a hasty getaway, gathering up their food and turning what had been a festive dine-in meal into take-out.

Me, I sat back in my chair and took a long moment to assess. This wasn't just anyone telling me this crap. This was Derek Glasscock, who was not exactly a teen kingpin or conniving alpha male, and I couldn't see that he had anything to gain by making this up. At least from his perspective, he was telling the truth.

"All right," I said. "And something happened here, too, didn't it?"

Derek nodded. "You really don't remember?"

"It's a G.D. Ritzy's. I've eaten food here. It's not the kind of thing that needs remembering."

"It was mid-summer. Late June, maybe? Friday night, and a bunch of the guys decided to come here after a movie, and somehow you found out about it, and you drove over here, and you were so wasted. Like, I'm talking smashed. And you breeze in, and you go on this insane monologue about how you, you personally, had invented the G.D. Ritzy's wild mountain blackberry ice cream, and next thing we know, you're behind the counter, actually scooping ice cream, and there's this girl working the late shift, and her manager's out taking a smoke break, and it's you and her, and you decide she's cute and you, you start—I don't really want to talk about it."

I looked toward the Ritzy's cash registers, and I had a sudden memory of a black-haired girl in a Ritzy's uniform, a girl who was panicking as she tried to fend me off while I kept begging her for a kiss. Holy hell, that was not a memory I wanted to own, so I slammed the door on that entire chapter, but not before Derek and Alan and the rest vaulted over the counter and wrestled me to the floor.

"Okay," I said, and my voice was so soft, it was like I was speaking through a mute. "You can stop."

To Derek's credit, he did. He picked at his food, and he waited. It wasn't much, that waiting, that picking, but it was the finest single act of friendship that I'd seen in months.

Especially since it wasn't deserved.

After a while, I realized I was shivering, and I didn't know when that had started, and I couldn't make it stop.

I wanted to be home.

I wanted to break one of Ritzy's plate glass windows.

I wanted a drink.

Slowly, squeezing my words out like cold, stubborn toothpaste, I said, "I take it there's more?"

"More I could tell you? Oh, yeah. Lots."

I tried to say, "I guess I owe Alan an apology," but I couldn't get my tongue organized enough to get past "I guess."

Derek scooted back in his chair. "Thanks for the burger," he said, as he stood. "And if this helped, well. Then I guess I'm glad I came."

I stayed at Ritzy's for a long time after Derek had gone, mulling directionless thoughts and taking occasional sips from the dregs of my soda. What was left of my fries smelled like lard and salt, and the remains of my burger, the little wormlike curls of meat, looked revolting. I could almost hear the slaughterhouse. In the end, I dumped the lot of it in the trash, a serious rarity for me, because I always finished my food.

Or did I? My tête-à-tête with Derek suggested that I knew myself about as well as a hamster understands calculus.

I drove home on newly snow-free streets (nothing like a warm front to kill off snow), hoping against hope that I wouldn't find my dad still prone on the living room carpet. He wasn't, thank goodness. Instead, he'd found his way to the sofa, where he'd passed out all over again with Tom Brokaw and *The Nightly News* on the television for company. He had a bottle of scotch in his hand, which I pried free. He protested only once, feeble as a newborn, and then I took that and every other bottle of booze, wine, and beer I could put my hands on, and one by splashing one, I poured them down the drain.

Next morning, when I woke up and got ready for work, Dad was in bed, asleep, but sometime in the night, he'd gone out and re-supplied. He'd set five new bottles of the hard stuff in the liquor cabinet, and a twelve-pack of Genny Cream Ale in the fridge.

That was bad enough, and a budgetary disaster, but then, not five minutes after I'd opened the doors to Vinyl Wonderland, along came Celine DeLapp, and my Tuesday went downhill fast from there.

Chapter Thirteen

IN CASE I WASN'T CLEAR at the outset, even when the Vinyl Wonderland foot traffic was light, I had plenty to do. Aside from general cleaning, which (after hours) included mopping the floor, I had a backlog of well over five thousand albums that Karl had purchased but not priced. Back before Karl had his stroke, I'd been told to clean the discs and the covers if needed (and where possible), but I'd been on strict orders to leave the pricing to him. Now that Karl was gone indefinitely, and now that some of the store's official stock was starting to thin out, I'd begun adding price stickers to the discs I was sure of, which turned out to be a pretty fair number. Browse enough used record bins, and you start to see a bunch of repeats, patterns, the vinyl equivalent of the usual suspects. I was less than a year into my used-record addiction, and I found that I could price at least half of Karl's horde with a high degree of confidence, and without checking any outside resources.

As for actual customers, the in-store shoppers didn't take much time at all—the Vinyl Wonderland clientele mostly liked to be left alone—but phone calls came in, too, and those folks tended to have very specific requests. Did we have Aaron Copland's *Appalachian Spring,* but conducted by Leonard Bernstein? Did we have a British-issued picture-sleeve forty-five of Dire Straits's "Skateway"? Did we have a mono edition of *Days of Future Passed,* or a stereo edition of Otis Redding, performing live?

Not that I was scrambling. I can't honestly claim that working at Vinyl

Wonderland was busy, or hectic. It wasn't. It was pleasantly steady, and the opposite of frantic.

Or at least, that would have been the case if it weren't for the Elvis door and the people connected to it.

As for myself, I mostly came and went through the back alley, but Vinyl Wonderland's front door was glass set in a metal frame, and it was surprisingly heavy, slow to respond. It wasn't the sort of door that human beings could interact with in an emotional way. Slamming it, for example, wasn't possible; it had a pressurizer. Even just getting through it took an extra moment. It was as if our customers, in order to enter the shop, had to push through chest-deep water.

All that said, when Celine arrived that morning, she careened through that door. She entered so fast, it was like a magic trick.

"You didn't return it!" she cried, looking at me. "You said you would, you promised, and you didn't! Why?"

I was over by the Country bins, filing an armload of George Jones LPs, and I had Pink Floyd's *Atom Heart Mother* on the turntable (very strange stuff, the rock-orchestra equivalent of cows lowing in a field), and my main concern, up until that moment, was how I was going to work up the courage to dump the last of my under-the-counter bourbon down the sink. "Self-absorbed" might have been a good way to describe my mind-set. "Distracted" and "stressed out" would have worked, too.

And suddenly here was Celine—again—Celine, whom I thought I'd helped. Last I'd seen of her, she was waving good-bye through the shop's front window, looking abashed and tearful as she made her way, under the dim orange glow of the streetlights, to her car.

That mood had apparently gone missing. This latest version of Celine was pissed off, and she didn't appreciate the fact that I hadn't come up with a rapid-fire reply. Sneering, she stepped closer and said, "You can't even apologize? Really? Are you that pathetic?"

The problem of her exact accusation was a stumper. I had to assume she was talking about the wicker bassinet, but I'd returned that, exactly as ordered—hadn't I? In the wake of my chat with Derek Glasscock, I had to consider the terrible possibility that pretty much all my memories were open to question, or even flat-out incorrect.

Celine gave me a look like I'd just flunked the easiest test ever. "Look at you," she said. "You're just a kid."

Now that hurt. It hurt in part because it was true, at least in the legal sense, but worse, I really had done exactly what she asked, and it hadn't been easy. In fact, if my memory was even ball-park trustworthy, I'd very nearly collapsed from heatstroke, and all for her sake.

Well, I'd like to report that my very grown-up self reacted to Hurricane Celine with appropriate calm and maturity. I really would like to say that. But I can't. What I did instead was to drop my armload of George Jones to the floor—on landing, they made a satisfyingly loud crunching, thumping noise—and then I flung out my arms and yelled, "What do you want from me? I took your stupid bassinet, and I brought it back! Why are you yelling at me?"

I'm not proud of that moment, although I guess it was honest enough. Hollering back at someone who's distraught, not to mention confused about the facts, is a pretty terrible choice. But I wasn't exactly lacking in emotional issues at that particular moment, and sometimes if you poke a blister, it pops.

As for Celine, well, that tough-girl leather jacket didn't work as emotional armor, not by a long shot. After a valiant effort to hold back a spurt of red-rimmed tears, she said, "I don't understand."

"That makes two of us."

She sniffled, hugged herself, and shot a suspicious glare toward Elvis. "If you took it back…"

"I told you, I did."

"To where all that other wicker stuff was piled up?"

"Yeah."

"But if you did all that, then how come she's worse, not better?"

Wouldn't you know it, another customer waltzed in at that exact moment, some random guy I'd never seen before, and I managed to say, "Hey, come on in," because Karl was big on greeting every customer—"It cuts down on the shoplifting"—before getting my full attention back on Celine.

"Who," I demanded, "isn't better?"

Some people, in my experience, are incapable of delivering a straight answer. Is it about temperament? Is it about gender? Is it about emotional distress? I've come up with many theories over the years, but in Celine's case, I have to say that I think it was baked in, like genetics. So, instead of explaining who she was talking about, she asked if I drank coffee, and I said, "Sure do," because I absolutely needed something strong to take my mind off of the bourbon.

Next thing I knew, Celine was out the door, promising to be back in "two ticks," with coffee for the both of us. I just shook my head. I'd been open for less than ten minutes, and already my day felt like a whirlwind.

Now, this was a world before Starbucks and our nationwide obsession with neighborhood coffee shops, so what Celine brought back a half hour later was McDonald's finest roast, in white paperboard cups with bright yellow arches decorating the sides. As for quality, let's just say that the coffee tasted like—well, it tasted like McDonald's. I guess it could have been worse.

By then, that first customer had come and gone, and so had another, and I'd made a modest $22.50. Vinyl Wonderland, except for me and Celine, was empty.

"I've got an extra stool," I said, indicating behind the counter, "if you want to sit."

She accepted this offer without any fuss, and pretty soon we were sitting side by side behind the counter, about two feet apart, with our hands wrapped around our coffees. We looked like twin shopkeepers, presiding over our wares together.

"I have a sister," she said, after the silence between us had stretched on far too long. "She's older, nine years older. So, in a lot of ways we aren't very close. I mean, we are. It's just we're pretty far apart, you know?"

The sister, I assumed, was sick. The question on the table—on the counter—was, how sick?

Celine went on, eyes down. "She got sick last year. AML. It's a kind of leukemia, and the prognosis isn't good. Her white blood cells, they multiply too fast, and they crowd out the red blood cells so the whole immune system breaks down. Her body is wide open to pretty much anything else that comes along, so. After that first diagnosis, she went downhill really fast."

She was nodding her head, as if to reassure herself that this was all true, or maybe to keep herself calm, and I was pretty sure she was seeing pictures in her head of her sister's decline.

"There was this one nurse at the hospital," said Celine. "She was kind of—well, she wasn't your average nurse. Like, she had tattoos and these crazy bright red glasses with chains on the sides, like an old-fashioned librarian. Plus, she had these bizarre earrings—different every day. Eyeballs, one time. Bats."

"She sounds…fun."

"No, she was not in any way fun. And this one time, she kind of caught me by the shoulders, and she got way closer than anyone is supposed to get, you know? Or at least, anyone you're not, you know, getting naked with. And she said, 'Hon, I'm gonna level with you. We're doing everything that modern medicine can do, but your sister? Her body is putting up a fight, and that's good, but she's fighting the treatments, too. The cancer is winning.' And by that point, this woman basically had me pinned against the wall, and I'm starting to feel like this it's time to maybe shout for help, but then she says, 'Your parents were not ready to hear any of this. They're good people, but they think prayer will be enough, prayer and chemotherapy. Radiation targeted at your sister's bone marrow. But there is another way.' And then she took my hand and pressed this scrap of paper into my palm, and she said, and this is a quote, 'Not that going where I'm sending you worked out so well for me, but maybe, maybe for you. So, you just tell Karl that Moira Phillips sent you, and he'll know what to do.'"

Celine paused to take a slurping sip of her coffee, then set it carefully down again, as if the cup were old bone China, highly breakable. "You can guess, right?" she said. "The paper had an address on it." She nodded toward the front door, where the street number had been added in gold with a black border. "This address. Vinyl Wonderland."

I said, "So you first showed up here…when?"

Celine let out a little puff of air and said, "Over a year ago. And Karl was waiting, as promised, and when I told him that Moira Phillips sent me, he unlocked the door back there, and I went in, and….yeah."

But all this history wasn't what really had me interested. "I don't get it. What's your sister got to do with that wicker bassinet?"

She looked faintly annoyed, as if I already had all the puzzle pieces and was just playing dumb for no good reason. "But you've been in there," she said. "You know."

"Except I'm not supposed to be a part of this. Karl only wanted me full-time for a few days, and then he was going to be back at least part-time, to run the shop and deal with the Elvis door."

"Is that really what you call it?"

Shrugging, I toasted the Elvis standee with my still-steaming coffee. "We give the King his due. My point is, if there are rules to that place beyond 'keep the door locked,' nobody told me."

Celine thought this over, and finally said, "I think there's only one hard-and-fast rule. You can take one thing, and one thing only."

"And the basket isn't what you wanted."

"No, it's exactly—!"

She cut herself off, and hunched lower on her stool, as if trying to make herself as inconsequential as possible. When she spoke next, she began with her eyes closed. "What happened was, I went in, and I was totally freaked out, right? Because of the place, and October Roberta, and all that junk, and the complete impossibility of it all, and October said, 'We have what you need, and we have what you want, but remember: you take one thing, and one thing only,' and she pointed me down this one particular road, and I walked down it for I don't even want to think how long—it felt like forever—and then I found this little corner table, like for curios or a vase, or maybe a telephone, and it was all by itself in front of this mountain of old sponges and scrub brushes, so it was almost like I was supposed to see it, and on top of it was a pair of hiking boots. Women's hiking boots. And I stopped, and I stared really hard at those boots, because my sister loves to hike, and suddenly she couldn't, because she was too sick, and then I looked closer, because there was this little white paper tag on a string, attached to one of the eyelets. It was basically an old-fashioned price tag, but instead of a price, it had my name on it."

Another pause, another unhappy sip of coffee. I waited. I knew there was more coming.

Celine said, "So, I picked up the boots—and I know, October said 'You take one thing and one thing only,' but these were clearly a pair, the laces were even tied together—and I turned around and I headed back, because this was clearly what I was supposed to find, and I wasn't sure why, but I could see the connection, kind of, sort of, except that as I headed back, just when I was starting to feel relieved, sort of halfway hopeful, like maybe this would all work out, I heard—well, I heard a baby. I heard a baby cry. And I'm talking about that very first cry, the one in the delivery room, the one where the baby's lungs are pulling in oxygen for the first time, and I turn around, trying to figure out where it's coming from, because, well, you've been there, right? That wind can be tricky, but there's nothing living out there. Not even bugs. And I turn around and I realize I'm facing this sort of wall of everything people can possibly make out of wicker, and right at the front, eye level, is that bassinet. The one I gave you. And almost everything in that pile was broken, damaged, chipped, but not the bassinet. And when I got closer, I could see it had receiving blankets, clean, spotless, like the whole thing was absolutely ready for use, and way in the distance I could still hear that baby crying, and I looked at the hiking boots, and I looked at the bassinet, and it was like October was right there next to me, whispering into my ear, 'You can take one thing, and one thing only.'"

Celine looked so small perched up there on that very high stool. I thought about reaching over, or maybe even getting up and wrapping her in some kind of awkward hug, but it was like she could sense what I was thinking, and she caught my eye and gave her head a little shake, and then she ran a hand back through her bangs.

As gently as I could, I asked, "Did the bassinet have a tag, with your name on it?"

She said, "It sure did. But I did the right thing. I left it where I'd found it. Turned my back, walked away. Walked all the way to October Roberta, and I plunked those boots on her desk, and she said, 'Good for you. You found what you need,' and I said, 'I guess,' and then she got out a clipboard with a sort of ledger on it, and she wrote down my name and the date and the word 'boots.' She took the tag off and put it in one of the drawers. 'Here you go,' she said. 'Tell your sister we're wishing her the best.' Which maybe shouldn't have surprised me, given where I was standing, but I hadn't mentioned my sister. Not a word. But October knew anyway."

It didn't take any advanced mental math on my part to understand that so far, none of this took us up to the present tense—to the last time I'd crossed paths with Celine. I said, "So, you took the hiking boots. And your sister…"

"…got better. She did. She had a bone marrow transplant. It helped. She was home, recovering. Not cured exactly, but by the end of summer, she was getting out on her own. Walks in the woods."

"Not with the actual boots."

Celine shook her head. "No. I never actually gave them to her. That felt…no. They're more like a talisman. If I physically handed them over, I don't know. Maybe they'd melt."

"So, where are they?"

"Back of my closet. In a box. In the dark."

Part of me felt like I was back at G.D. Ritzy's, sitting with Derek. I had the distinct impression that I had only half the story.

As I was thinking up ways to gently tug the rest of this crazy tale out of Celine, a customer came in, a big cheery guy I'd seen a bunch of times. He was one of those people who had a weekly budget reserved just for used records, so I knew that he'd be spending some quality time selecting his prizes. In order to give Celine some cover, I slid down from my chair and restarted the Pink Floyd disc on the turntable. Then I turned up the volume.

As the music got going, Celine's nose crinkled as if she'd just smelled rancid meat. "What," she said, "are we listening to?"

I grinned. "Pink Floyd. Before they were famous."

She shot an exasperated look at the stereo system. "I can see why."

Back on top of my chair, I said, "So, I'm still kind of lost. You got what you wanted. And as for that crying baby…I mean, you're married. You want a baby, make a baby."

Man, was that ever the wrong thing to say. Celine let out a sort of gasp and put her head in her arms, flat out on the counter. The gasp was so loud that the big guy in the corner looked up and asked if she was all right. I assured him that we were okay, just having a moment, and he rolled his eyes and went back to thumbing through Rock, letters X-Y-Z, a pile-up of Yes and Warren Zevon.

Thanks to me being a tactless idiot, it took a good long while to pry the rest out of Celine, but it came down to this: she'd been married three years already, and she and her husband had been trying to have a baby since pretty much day one. For all her tough-girl posture, what she wanted most was family, kids, and it hadn't worked. They'd been to see doctors, but there wasn't anything conclusive to point to. Her eggs checked out, and he had a perfectly normal sperm count. Which wasn't the sort of thing I had any desire to know, but I'd wanted the story, and now I was getting it.

Celine didn't have to connect the rest of the dots. She'd gone into that trash-heap wasteland and come away with what she needed, a miracle for her sister, but she'd left behind what she most wanted.

"I went back for the first time in September," Celine explained, somewhat recovered. I'd handed her a box of Kleenex, and she'd taken a long time-out to blow her nose. "I just wanted to go and, you know, look. Or that's what I told myself. I wanted to prove that I was strong enough to say no. And I was. I found the bassinet again. I picked it up. I rocked it, just like there was a real live baby in it. I even sang it a lullaby, 'Angels Watching Over Me.' And then I put it down and walked home, and you know what October said to me, on the way out? She said, 'See you soon.'"

"Not very nice."

"No."

I was trying to reconcile Karl with this whole scheme. I could picture October Roberta gloating, no problem. I was pretty sure she had a mean streak two feet wide. But Karl? When I asked Celine about what Karl had said, if anything, she was quick to defend him. Karl, she said, had tried really hard to convince her to turn around and go home. He'd all but begged her not to take a second trip through the Elvis door.

"But," said Celine, "I think he has rules, too. Or maybe, more like orders. Orders he has to follow. The first one is that he has to let people in if they've been sent. And the second one is that if you've gone in once and you want to come back, he can try to talk you out of it, but if you insist, he has to open up."

That made intuitive sense to me. It fit.

I said, "You've come back a bunch of times now."

After blowing her nose again, she said, "Yeah. Too many. That stupid bassinet, it's like—it's the closest thing I've got to an actual baby. And I know that if I take it, if I bring it home, then all these tests and all the fertility treatments, they won't be necessary. I'll get pregnant."

For my teenage ears, the word "pregnant" always came off like an alarm bell, and no wonder. I spent a good deal of mental energy making sure that I didn't get a girl pregnant. Now, here was Celine, barely older than me, and pregnancy was her primary goal.

If she noticed me looking uncomfortable, she didn't show it. She said, "This last time in, it was too much. My husband and me, we'd just had a fight. He's ready to move on, maybe adopt. He says he married *me*, not a baby we can't make, and he said something about how it's totally dominating his life— that's what he said, *his* life—and of course I can't tell him, I can't explain what I've been going through, much less that I've got some kind of witchcraft solution, so I came here, and you let me in, and this time, I didn't plan it, but I grabbed that bassinet and ran. I ran all the way back to October Roberta, and she gave me this smirk and practically ripped the bassinet out of my hands, and she took off the tag and wrote it down on the ledger, and then she crossed off 'Boots,' and that's when it hit me, when I finally realized what I was about to do. It didn't matter that I hadn't returned the hiking boots. It wasn't like a physical exchange. Just the fact of my choosing something else, that was all that needed to happen in order for my first choice to stop working."

"So, between the desk and my end of the tunnel…"

"…I changed my mind. And you know the rest."

"Look," I said, "I swear I took it back. All the way. I don't know if I got it down to the square inch of where it was supposed to be, but is it in the right pile? Absolutely."

Over in the corner, Cheery Guy was eyeballing a record. He had it out of its sleeve, and he was sighting along it, checking for warps. A careful shopper, this dude. Unlike, for example, Celine. But as soon as I made that comparison, I sensed how unfair it was. For Celine, the stakes were infinitely higher.

"I can guess the rest," I said. "Your sister had a relapse."

Instead of nodding, Celine tore the plastic lid from her coffee cup and drained the remainder of her drink with one short slurp. That done, she said,

"My sister is back in the hospital. She was having seizures, which means..." She hesitated long enough to make sure she could speak without losing it all over again, then said, "It means the leukemia attacked her nervous system. And that's…that could be fatal."

"So, what do we do? I mean, do we go looking for another pair of boots?"

This, at last, was a direct question Celine was ready to tackle. She said, "I will try anything. I will do anything. And first thing this morning, I would have said no to getting your help. But standing in line for this coffee, I had a—well, call it a revelation. Kind of simple, and maybe even kind of stupid, but I realized that even just to get a cup of coffee, I needed help. Help from somebody else. And that maybe it would be okay to ask for help for something bigger, too."

The Pink Floyd record had reached the point where the cows, at least according to the band's musical imagination, get milked, and there was a lot of groaning and syncopated pulsing, which I guess was intended to make everyone in earshot think about industrial farming, milk, and very large udders.

Celine stared daggers at the turntable, then looked back at me, really for the first time since she'd sat down.

"Brendan," she said, "I think you're the wild card in all this. The joker in the deck. So, if you can help, then yes, I'm all in. But I'm not a damsel in distress, and you don't get to solve my problems or save my sister for me. Whatever we do, we do it together."

Why do fools fall in love? Damned if I know. But I do know the exact moment that I fell head over heels for Celine DeLapp.

Whatever we do, we do it together.

"I'm in," I said. "All in."

Chapter Fourteen

THE PLAN WAS SIMPLE, AT least in terms of timing. I'd close Vinyl Wonderland early, and then Celine and I would open up the Elvis door and gang up on October, two against one, until she put those magic hiking boots back into play.

Honestly, I would have gone sooner, but Celine said she had to put in a few hours at work first, and that played out nicely for me, too, since I really wanted to get back and check on my dad. The dinner hour seemed like the right time to do that, so me and Celine, we agreed we'd rendezvous at Vinyl Wonderland at seven p.m.

Sorry: as my mother would have told me, that's "Celine and I."

Mothers. When they're not around, you wind up missing them for the oddest reasons.

Now, most days, even after my mother's death, going home had been a comforting choice. Home meant familiarity, food, support, my very own room, and my very own bed. Even broken into pieces, home was a refuge. But in recent weeks, with my dad getting worse instead of better, that kind of assumed safety was starting to feel like a very distant memory. I'd taken to steeling myself before turning the corner onto our street, never quite sure what I'd find once I stepped through the front door.

Well, this time I didn't even have to be inside before spotting trouble. As I rounded the corner and got a look down the block, there was my dad wrestling a queen-sized mattress down the driveway, headed for the street. It was well past dark, so I only had a couple of widely spaced streetlights to see by, but there was no question about what was going on. My father was throwing out his bed.

Since I didn't want to risk hitting him, I parked along the curb, and I jumped out. "Dad!" I said, as I vaulted over a fast-melting snowbank. "What are you doing?"

It's funny how people ask that kind of obvious question, when what they really mean is, "Why are you making this clearly insane choice?"

My dad's response was to dump the mattress at the curb, in the same spot where the trash cans normally get set for their weekly pick-up. The effort of dragging the queen all by himself had him gasping for air, and he bent low, put his hands on his knees, and said, "Not your concern, Brendan."

I spun around, checking to see which neighbors were watching our performance. Maybe I was grown-up in a couple of superficial ways, but I was still a teen when it came to caring viscerally about what others thought. The last thing I wanted was for the people in the houses around us to be turning me into their next serving of extra-juicy gossip.

"Dad," I said, "let's get you inside."

"Sure," he said. "You can help with the box spring."

"No! Where are you going to sleep?"

"I'm starting over. I can sleep in a chair."

I threw another wild look up and down the street, as if the news cameras from Channel 4 were already seconds away. "Dad," I said, "can we at least talk about this inside?"

That wasn't a hard sell, but stopping him from going after the box spring turned into an actual wrestling match, very clumsy, in the hallway. He was sloppy drunk, see, something I hadn't spotted outside, so it was like grappling with a life-sized doll, heavy but pliable. He never tried to hit me; I never tried to hit him. He just kept working his way toward his bedroom, mumbling about how the box spring had to go, and I kept dragging him back the other way until at last, he was on the ground, with me splayed over top like a blanket, and next thing I knew, he was snoring.

All right, that's not strictly true. First, he told me to go to hell. Then he said he wished I'd never been born.

That hurt more than I cared to admit, and it made me think of Jonesy Davis and his dictum that for some people, drinking was a good thing: it brought out their best. *I'm a happy drunk*, wasn't that what he'd said? But for others, alcohol gave their demons free rein.

I left my dad prostrate in the hallway like a human bearskin rug, and I stepped over and past him and headed outside to recover his mattress. I didn't know the specifics, but I knew that beds were expensive. We couldn't afford a new one, and the sidewalks were slick and damp with snow melt. Leaving the poor thing outside for even another hour would probably wreck it for good.

As a general life lesson, I'd offer the following: never move a queen mattress by yourself. You can't lift it; it's not possible. You have to drag it, and when you do that on a concrete driveway, whichever side is on the bottom gets pretty chewed up.

Anyway, I got it inside eventually, mostly by telling myself that if my dad could haul this thing around, then I could, too. (I guess stubborn runs in the family.) After that, I got hold of the big fan that we mostly used in summer, and I aimed it at the mattress, which I'd left propped against the wall by the living room, hoping that the extra air flow would help the mattress dry out. Only then did I think to check the time.

Crap. It was already six forty. In twenty short minutes, I was supposed to be meeting Celine back at Vinyl Wonderland. The drive would take ten minutes easy, and I had a lot to get ready.

Well, I had planned to enjoy a leisurely bite to eat, even if it was nothing but a frozen TV dinner, but instead, thanks to the mattress debacle, I went racing around the house like the proverbial chicken with its head cut off, gathering supplies. The most important thing was a decent backpack because I sure as hell wasn't going into October Roberta's junkyard without a ton of water, and I needed something to carry it. That meant dumping everything out of my school pack, which I hadn't so much as glanced at since the day I dropped out, and then it was on to the kitchen, where I loaded up with soda and Gatorade. That done, I dug like a woodchuck through the cabinets, looking for pretty much any kind of thermos or sealable bottle. This was years before bottled water hit the big time, so this wasn't as easy a job as it might sound. Even so, by the time I was done, I figured I had almost two gallons worth of drinks in the pack—man, was that thing heavy—and then I dug out the Coleman camping jug that I usually brought to soccer practices and filled that up, too.

Sun hats, check. Sun block? Nope. First, because back then it was called "suntan lotion," and second, we didn't have any. Then I added a flashlight, a package of Oreos, and a couple of apples, one of which I was already biting into as I raced out the door.

The other thing I'd hoped to do at home was sneak a drink or two. Sure, that would have violated my don't-drink-and-drive rule, but I knew my limits, and I knew I could handle a couple of shots, no problem, so long as I put a full meal in my belly. Plus, I'd been such an angel at work. Post Celine, I'd finally found the mid-afternoon courage to dump out my bourbon, although I admit that I allowed myself a regretful taste at the very end by running my finger around the inside of the bottle's neck and then popping my finger into my mouth. That didn't count as drinking, did it?

Anyway, I got back to Vinyl Wonderland ten minutes late. The apple core went flying into the dumpster, my backpack went on my back, and my key went into the rear door's lock. I hurried through the rear hall and into the shop, leaving the lights off so that any potential evening customers wouldn't get excited and try to come in.

Celine was on the sidewalk out front, pacing back and forth and smoking. I had the crazy idea that I wished I was that cigarette, held first in her fingers, then sucked into her mouth. The strangeness of that idea did not make it in any way less erotic, and I would have been happy to simply stand there and watch her, to appreciate at a distance what I knew I couldn't have, but I got hold of myself and walked to the door, unlocked it, and let her in.

"Thought you'd stood me up," she said, as she sidled past me, inside. "Thought you'd left me at the altar."

"Never," I said, and I meant it. The image of me and Celine standing together at a fancy church altar, exchanging vows, exchanging rings, it all but froze me in place. It was a good thing I had the concrete realities of keys and doors to deal with, or who knows what I might have said next. Something soppy, for sure. Something equal parts romantic and heroically hopeless.

Like me, Celine had a backpack, but hers was leather and classy, like some weird hybrid of a chic handbag and a sturdy piece of airport luggage. I was beginning to think that either she or her husband made a pretty good salary. Had she ever volunteered what she actually did? If she ever had, my memory had once again betrayed me.

As I finished locking the front door behind her, I asked, "Did you bring water?"

Her pack was slung over one shoulder, and she gave it a pat by way of an answer. "You," she said, "brought too much. You can't even stand up straight."

I had no intention of admitting that she might be correct. Be prepared, right?

"Come on," I said. "Let's get this show on the road."

"Brendan. You're a big guy, but you're not exactly Hulk Hogan."

This was getting old fast, and I admit I kind of snapped at her, told her to mind her own business, but she snapped right back, reminding me, all too accurately, that the whole reason we were here was her business. So, we had ourselves a little impasse, with Elvis keeping watch, and wouldn't you know it, I was the one to back down. I shrugged off my pack and dug out the four glass-bottled sodas (Frostie's root beer, my mother's favorite), and set them aside.

"Happy?" I said.

She wasn't. "Give me at least one of those Gatorades. I've got room."

I put one bottle into her outstretched hand, and she squirreled it into her pack without letting me see what else was in there. That done, she gave me a long look, like I was a car, and she was considering a test drive.

"You need to know," she said, "that I'm used to being in charge."

"Okay."

"I wear the pants at my house. Laugh all you want, but it works for us."

"Okay."

"Stop saying 'okay.'"

It was all I could do not to say exactly that.

"My point," she said, "is that going in there as a partnership—doing anything, really, on equal footing—that's hard for me. I like to be in control."

My dad had once explained, in confidential tones, that giving up control was the great burden of men in the world, because men desired, always and forever, to be in charge, but more and more, as the 20th century wandered toward the 21st, men had been forced to surrender that position. This was trouble, my father said. Big trouble.

Oddly enough, Jonesy Davis had tackled the same topic, in his usual sideways manner. It was late summer, and I'd joined him for a morning of weeding and maintenance at the Park of Roses.

"Speaking for myself," said Jonesy, his expression rapt and his gloved hands patting down mulch, "I'm a boat on the river of life. And these days, that sits pretty well. Drifting and boats, that's a good combination. I'm ex-Navy, did I mention? That's right: you're looking at an actual honest-to-God World War II vet. I know, I don't look it, do I? Old and short and soused. But I was there. Pacific theater. Saw my share of action, too. And then, because I'm nine ways a fool and twice on Sundays, I stayed in. Korea came along, and there I was, still sailing the seven seas. I was at Inchon, and then a few months later, we hit a mine, and I got to take a long swim in the drink. The U.S.S. *Partridge*, that was. February 2nd, 1951. Lost a couple of buddies that day, and my God, was that water ever cold. Anyway, my point is—what were we talking about?"

I reminded him: boats and drifting.

"That's right. And Brendan, when it comes to drifting, take it from me: that won't ever work for you. Not for long, anyway. You're a fellow who likes to steer the ship. Hands on the tiller. And once you come to terms with losing your mom, I'll bet my bottom dollar that you'll be a pretty good pilot."

That conversation had taken place long months ago, and was I any closer (as Jonesy put it) to "coming to terms" with my mother's death? No. Definitely not. Not by a mile.

To Celine, I said, "I don't know what we're going to solve by discussing a problem we haven't even had yet."

I could tell that she didn't agree, but she nodded as if she did. "Then let me at least say that I apologize for saying, before, that you're just a kid."

Part of me wanted her to say more, to state out loud her belief that she saw me as a full-grown man, but that wasn't forthcoming.

"No problem," I said. "Now let's go fix your sister."

Elvis gave way; the door swung wide. The cobblestone corridor beckoned, and so did the tunnel beyond. I could already feel the breath of that desert breeze as it ghosted its way through the darkness.

The first time I'd gone in, I was too surprised to be properly afraid. On my second trip, I'd had a clear goal, and something to carry, plus Celine's frantic tears at my back. This time, even though I finally had company, I realized I was frightened. That wasn't an emotion I was used to, and I guess everyone responds to that kind of stress differently. Under pressure, some folks turn into chatterboxes. Me, I clam up, and that's exactly what I did that day. I marched into the tunnel, leaving Celine to follow, and I didn't offer a word of encouragement, not even as we emerged, on schedule, as expected, into October Roberta's world of jettisoned scrap.

Working on the assumption that we needed every advantage we could get, I hadn't called ahead on purpose, so we caught October napping—literally. She was sitting tipped back in a ripped-up leather office chair with her feet on the desk and her hands folded over her midriff, and while I couldn't be sure-fire positive thanks to her inscrutable sunglasses, it looked to me like she was fast asleep.

Celine nudged me with her elbow. "Maybe we just go on by?"

I nodded toward the various paths and roads, twelve at least, with more (I presumed) on the opposite side of the tunnel rock. I said, "How would we know where to go?"

Her response was equally dubious. "She might point us the wrong way no matter what."

"Feels like a chance we have to take."

She didn't push back, so I headed toward October, and when I got close enough, I rapped on the top of the desk like I was knocking on a door. "Wakey-wakey!"

Well, October's response was downright gratifying. She shot backward in her chair, then completely over-balanced and wound up rolling over in a somersault that left both her and her chair in a heap on the ground.

"Sorry," I said. "Did we scare you?"

October got herself into a sort of crouch, as if she thought we might be two attack dogs, ready to spring at her. Her coveralls were smudged in chalk-white smears from the lime-dusky gravel, but her sunglasses, miraculously, hadn't shifted so much as a millimeter.

"Nice," she said. "The both of you together, it's like the ultimate unholy alliance."

"I go to church," said Celine, which frankly surprised me. "I'll bet my next paycheck you can't say the same."

Smirking, October got to her feet and began brushing herself off. She said, "I'll allow that church and I have a complicated relationship. Now. What can I do for you?"

I had my mouth open to explain, but sure enough, Celine stepped up and cut me off. "Brendan returned the bassinet," she said, "but you're acting like I still have it."

October smiled. It was not a pretty picture. "So, your sister relapsed?"

"Don't act like you don't already know that."

"Actually, I don't. The information I get is…spotty. But it doesn't take a genius to guess. And I did warn you. You take one thing, and one thing only."

Like an angry parrot, Celine said the last part with October, in tandem. "…and one thing only, we know. But I gave the damn thing back."

October's jaw jutted toward Celine like a battering ram. "You gave it to Brendan. Not the same thing."

"And Brendan put it back!"

"That's true," I said, "and you know it."

October cocked her head and grinned at me. "Poor little Brendan. So self-righteous. And so in love."

I should have seen that one coming. I should have had my guard up. Instead, I do what the guilty always do once accused, I turned bright red, then blustered my way through a series of sputtering denials.

Did I fool anyone, most especially Celine? Nope.

"Great," she said. "Just great."

October shook her head at Celine as if she were gravely disappointed. "I'm surprised you didn't notice."

Celine looked away, toward the horizon. She was facing into the wind, leaving her bangs to flutter across her forehead.

"Fine," I said, "so I've got a crush. Big deal. What we want to know is, how do we get you to accept the idea that the bassinet is back? That all Celine wants is the boots, the boots she's already got."

October cast a skeptical eye on Celine's army surplus boots, which frankly ticked me off. "Not those boots," I said. "The ones she took for her sister."

For a long moment, October said nothing. The sun beat down, every bit as hot as I remembered it, and I was just about ready to dig in my pack to pull out the two sun hats when she said, in a playful voice, "Brendan. Is that really what you're here for? To help Celine's sister? I bet you've never even met her."

"That's right, I haven't. But I did a job, and I didn't get credit for it. Neither did she. So, I'm asking again. Nicely. How do we fix that? How do we make it right?"

Again, October gave herself a lingering moment to think things over before she steepled her fingers and said, "The thing is that normally, in here, you explore alone. Bringing a friend

is—well, it misses the point. But I tell you what, just this once, I'll make an exception, and here's how we'll do it. I'll give you the tag back. The one that came with the bassinet. You two go out there, and if you find the bassinet and reattach the tag, we'll call it quits. Deal?"

Celine said exactly what was on my mind. "No tricks?"

Digging into the top left-hand drawer of the desk, October said, "Tricks are beneath me." After rummaging for a moment, she found the paper tag she wanted and held it up, dangling it by its string from a pinched finger and thumb. "Here you go."

Celine reached out and took the tag. "I return this to the bassinet, and we're square? The hiking boots…?"

"They'll be just as effective as before. Which isn't perfect, by the way. The human condition is, after all, a downhill race to the grave."

Celine's eyes narrowed dangerously, but she slipped the tag into one of her jacket pockets. "Let's go," she said to me. "Let's get this over with."

"Which road?" I asked, and October pointed to one that I was one hundred percent certain I hadn't taken before. It was flanked by ruined lawn chairs on one side and a truly revolting pile-up of food refuse on the other, mostly Jell-O salads.

"You sure?" I said. I was looking around for the path I'd used before, the one that started off between wheelbarrows and Dixie cups.

"Oh, I'm never wrong," said October. "But Brendan. A word of warning. You think you're here for Celine, but out there? You never know what you might find."

"Doesn't matter," I said. "I've got my marching orders."

"Very sweet. But don't forget: if you want to give God a laugh, tell her your plans."

Well, I didn't like the sound of that, not one bit, but Celine was tugging at my elbow, urging me to get a move on, so I nodded a good-bye to October, and off we went, Celine and me, into that wilderness of garbage. I remember feeling loose, confident. We'd worked out a deal, and counting the big Coleman jug in my hand, I had enough water to last for days. What, I thought, could go wrong?

The one-word answer to that question turned out to be, "Everything."

Chapter Fifteen

FOR THE FIRST MILE OR so, we took turns pointing out the oddest or most spectacular piles of refuse. A whole mountain range of silvery metal shopping carts, for example. A hundred-yard stretch of teddy bears, most of them missing an arm or an eye. Wooden rowboats, most with massive holes, washed up for as far as the eye could see. Farther along, tubes of skin cream. Typewriters. Empty cans of wood stain, the cans themselves dripped on and mottled by their former contents. I can't speak for Celine, but I felt like we were tourists visiting a really screwed-up national park. The lake of melted ice cream cones was especially impressive.

"How deep," said Celine pausing at the lake's steep banks, "do you think that is?"

"Don't fall in, and we'll never have to find out."

For a while, we made a guessing game of everything we saw. As we passed a hill of old Pez dispensers, we tried to guess how many there were. Or, a little farther along, how many tractors in the tractor mound? We toyed with methods that might make our estimations more or less accurate, but in the end, we gave up completely, because we never had the answers. Maybe October could have told us, but I doubted that.

After a while, the novelty of having a companion to talk to wore off, although I would have talked to Celine about anything if I'd thought for a moment she was actually interested. The longer we held our tongues, the more the strangeness of the place settled over us like a shroud, until it reached the point where it seemed downright rude to break the silence, and all that was left was the wind, the junk, and our steady footsteps on the crunching gravel underfoot.

The longer that silence stretched, the more awkward it became, at least for me, because now that my initial bout of fear had settled down, I really did want to talk. I had this heady urge to share every last detail of my life. Every thought in my head felt crucial, worthy, simply because I wanted Celine to know me better, to get a long, slow look at the mixed-up food processor that called itself my brain. And, of course, the longer I kept silent, the stronger the urge became to just give in and babble about pretty much anything in hopes that something would stick—that Celine would crack a tiny, shy smile, or maybe even laugh.

That's one of the great parts of a crush that people forget, later on, that sheer giddy joy that comes from unburdening yourself. It's as if people are canisters of propane, with everything held in check until the right connection comes along, and then all that pressure gets released in a torrent of words and feelings and unrelated nonsense.

It's a fact that I thought up that analogy as I hiked along with Celine beside me, and for about thirty seconds, it struck me as sheer brilliance, a genius-level insight. It had to be shared, spoken out loud, presented like a delicate gift at Celine's feet!

But then, after we'd walked a little farther and passed by a heap of broken mouse traps and the world's largest dump of old guttering, I started wondering about what the propane canister was like when it was empty, all hollow and cold, and I decided that maybe this was an idea I'd better just keep to myself.

It was a very good thing that I'd brought water. Even with our sun hats, we stopped frequently to drink. At the same time, I was happy that Celine had made me leave some behind. I was sweating hard thanks to the extra weight I was humping, and the back of my t-shirt was soaked through from top to bottom.

After close to what must have been an hour of steading tramping, Celine said, "I don't remember it being this far, before."

"Neither do I."

But we didn't make any move to stop, and a few minutes later, she said, "Do you trust her?"

"Who, October? No."

"But I do think there are rules. Rules for her, rules for us. We may not know them all, but it's like driving—or, I don't know, music. The rules exist, and maybe she can lie or cheat in certain ways, but in others, like with a key signature, sharps and flats, I think her hands are tied."

Since I didn't see any reason to disagree, I said, "Makes sense," and then, because I couldn't stand to have her so close and still know so little about her, I said, "What do you do, for work? Like, where did you go this afternoon?"

She tucked her bangs up under her hat and kept walking. She said, "Those are two different questions."

That was Celine in a nutshell, and I kicked myself for having forgotten so quickly that direct questions—personal ones, anyway—were essentially inadmissible.

"Okay," I said, "but you do work."

"Sure."

"And you don't want to tell me what you do."

"How about you guess."

I gave it a half second's pause, like a stand-up comic, then said, "You deal high-grade coke."

That was a slam-dunk victory: she laughed.

"Wrong," she said. "But nice try."

"Can we do hot and cold?"

"What are we, ten? Playing 'I Spy'?"

"Hey, you're the one that turned this into a guessing game."

We paused for a water break, and I doled out the Oreos, which she refused, and then I assured her that yes, we were indeed ten years old, and guessing at her work life was exactly like 'I Spy.' My next guess was that she worked in a doctor's office, and she made a buzzer noise, like I'd struck out, but she allowed that this was maybe closer than running illegal drugs.

The only thing I knew for sure was that she didn't work full-time—or that, if she did, her hours were her own to set. That ruled out a bunch of prospects like teacher or day-care worker, not to mention the other stand-by for women, secretary. Back then, the term "office assistant" might have existed, but it sure wasn't the default.

"How about…stewardess?"

Celine said, "Not warm, not cold, just…wrong."

"Bus driver."

"Nope."

I was starting to realize that the world contains an awful lot of possible professions, and I'd barely scratched the surface. Wracking my brain for clues, I thought of Karl, and then I remembered Celine's comment about key signatures. I said, "You play in a band. No, the orchestra."

At this, she gave me an approving, questioning look, like a tutor whose stumble-bum student has just made a surprising cognitive leap. "Warmer," she said. "Hot, even."

"But you don't actually play in a band."

"I could."

Music, then. But indirectly. "Okay," I said, "you tune pianos."

"Scorching hot."

I liked those words, especially coming from her. I wanted her to say them again. "You work at Coyle Music," I said. "You're one of the salespeople."

"Yes and no," she said. "I don't work *at* Coyle, but I freelance. My specialty is instrument repair."

"Ever work on any clarinets?"

"Woodwinds and brass are ninety-nine percent of what I do."

This was beginning to sound downright creepy. Were the Gods of Coincidence about to inform me that Celine DeLapp had known my mother?

Celine, picking up on my hesitation, asked, "Why? Do you play?"

"No. But my mother did." Before Celine could zero in on why I'd put that in the past tense, I said, "Did you ever do any work for a Lauren Purcell?"

Celine brightened immediately. It's funny how name recognition can do that. Humans: we like knowing who's who.

To me, she said, "Sure, I remember Lauren. Nice woman. Wait, she's your mother?"

That would have been the time, the moment to explain, but all I said was, "Yeah. That's my mom."

"Funny," said Celine. "Small world. I actually haven't seen her for a long time, but usually with me, that's good news. It means nothing's broken. The clients I don't see are right where they're supposed to be, making music."

As she spoke, we crested a low hill and found ourselves surrounded, on both sides, by a tumble-down slag heap of abandoned clarinets. Some were plastic, some wood; most were in pieces. The keys were tarnished, the cork eaten away. One of the ones lying nearest to me was so crushed, it looked as if it had been run over by a tank.

Celine swore under her breath, and we both stopped. "This," she said, "was definitely not here before."

I licked my lips, wishing I'd thought to bring Chapstick. Plus, I'd been craving a drink of something stronger than just plain water for a long while now, and all these ruined clarinets weren't helping.

"Come on," I said. "This is October, trying to get under our skin."

But Celine wasn't so easily dislodged. She'd knelt down at the edge of the pile-up, close enough to run a finger over the cracked bell of the nearest instrument. "I could fix this," she murmured. "Brendan, I could fix *all* of these."

"Ah, no, Celine. Think about what you just said."

"They're *instruments*, Brendan! People should be playing these!"

"Yeah, that would be amazing. But look around you. We're looking at what, five thousand clarinets? And that's just the ones in easy reach of the road. Come on, stand up—no, I'm serious. Stand up and stretch as tall as you can and look at what you'd be dealing with."

Reluctantly, slowly, she stood. Clarinets, in horrible disrepair, stretched for as far as the eye could see. Presumably, they'd eventually bump into another road, or a separate landfill of something different, but until then? The pile was effectively infinite.

"You cannot," I said, "fix this."

"I could try."

"No, walk away. And if you can't, I'm gonna pick you up and carry you."

"You wouldn't dare."

"Try me."

Indignant, she looked away from the endless array of keys, mouthpieces, and barrels, and glared at me like I was the lowest form of garbage on earth—which, in that moment, was exactly what I wanted her to do.

"Now," I said, "don't look back. Walk."

"But…"

"No buts. Come on."

I guided her gently, one hand on her elbow, but she didn't need help past the first few steps. Whatever charm the clarinets exerted, it had precious little pull once she'd turned her back. Better still, she seemed newly aware of what had just happened.

"Wow," she said. "I could have spent some serious time there."

"Pretty sure that was the idea."

She gave me a very different look this time, one that felt to me like a wholesale reassessment. "You're all right. You really are."

Now, I'll admit that I loved hearing that, no two ways about it, but at the same time, I was wondering who would disagree, and the list was long. Alan Geryk, for example, or the ice cream girl at G.D. Ritzy's.

After the clarinet dump ended, the next half-mile of junked leftovers didn't feel so personal. First came rebar and concrete, then newspapers, all the same one, endless back issues of the *Manchester Guardian*. But then, just as I was starting to think that we were on safer ground, we ran into a horde of miniature liquor bottles, the kind they serve on airplanes, and wouldn't you know it, every last one was full.

"Whoa," said Celine, and she took a small step closer. "This is like a lifetime supply."

There were more brands in that dump than I could count, with every possible type of hard liquor represented. The sheer variety of glass—shapes, labels, colors—it was jaw-dropping. Bottle after bottle, the contents catching the light and winking in the sun—winking, it seemed, directly at me.

Celine stepped closer, as if she were halfway hypnotized. "Want one?" she said, and she looked back at me for confirmation.

"Don't," I said, shaking my head. "One thing, and one thing only remember? No free lunch out here."

"Right," she said. "Sorry. Don't know what I was thinking."

She moved off, headed down the path, disappointed but not really challenged. No surprise; this roadblock, for her, was a minor distraction. For me, however, well. As I ordered myself to keep walking, to follow Celine, my whole body went into open rebellion. All that alcohol, so near at hand, so available. Those bottles, in combination, were like one vast electromagnet and I wanted nothing more than to let them pull me closer.

"Brendan? Are you all right?"

She'd stopped several yards ahead of me, and she was looking back, a quizzical look fighting to peek out from behind her bangs, which had once again slipped down from beneath the brim of her hat. I realized that I'd stopped, too—that instead of following her, I'd taken a step closer to the mound of bottles.

In the face of my total failure to respond, Celine came back and mounted a rescue. She put one arm around my waist and got a good grip on my arm with the other. "It's okay," she said. "October's going after you this time. Clarinets for me, booze for you. You need to rise above. Come on, now."

Slowly but surely, she steered me away from those glinting, tempting bottles and edged me a few steps down the path. When I twisted my head to look back, she said, sharply, "No, no. Look at me. Brendan. Look me in the eye."

If anyone had told me, even five minutes before, that I'd be reluctant to look Celine DeLapp in the eye—and at close range, too—I'd have said they were thirty-one flavors of nuts, but right then, the competition was stiff, and it took a serious effort to bring my head around. But, once I met her gaze, the shock of having her so close flipped a switch. I forgot about the liquor bottles and blinked hard, as if I'd just been woken up.

"Better," she said. "Now, remember, I'm the one you've got a crush on, so keep your eyes on me and keep walking."

"Sorry," I said, as I did my best to staunch a wave of profound embarrassment. I'd seen her cry plenty of times, but I sure as hell didn't want to change places.

"No apologies necessary," she said. "We've both got our fair share of weaknesses. This place knows how to exploit them."

After another ten yards, I tried to pull away, but Celine kept tight hold—so tight, that I could feel the side of her breast slide against my upper arm as we moved.

She said, "I'll let you loose when we're out of sight," by which she meant the liquor bottles.

I gave in and allowed myself to notice again as my arm rubbed companionably against her. It wasn't exactly skin-to-skin—she was wearing a blouse and a bra—but even so. The need for a drink eased, and my interest in all things Celine grew by the step. Was this a weakness, too? If so, then I had to assume that this reckless mix of desire and head-over-heels puppy love was just one more thing for October to manipulate.

Next thing I knew, without warning, and with no sign of the Minute Maid orange juice dump as a landmark, we'd arrived at the mountain of all things wicker. Sure enough, there was Celine's bassinet, lying exactly where I'd placed it.

"Okay," I said. "Let's do what we came to do."

She licked her dry lips, bobbed her head yes, and remained exactly where she was.

I figured that meant it was my turn to steer her, so I got hold of her hand and started forward. She followed, but I could feel her trepidation right through her fingers.

"Celine," I said. "You've got a sister, remember?"

That got her moving, and we worked our way into the cove, with the wicker junk-pile rising up higher and higher on three sides. When we'd gone as far as we could without climbing, Celine fished the price tag from her pocket. I could see her name written on it, the lettering done with slender calligraphic swirls.

"Tie it on," I said. "You can do it."

"Can't," she said.

"You can."

"But I don't want to."

Now, I don't know where inspiration comes from. Never have, never will. Probably nobody does, so believe me, I surprised myself big-time when I heard myself say, "Celine. Tell me about your sister."

"What? Why?"

"Just tell me."

"Like what?"

"You could start with her name."

Celine gulped as if she were trying to dry-swallow a pill. "Joanne. Her name is Joanne."

"What's her last name?"

"Varney. She's not married, so that's my maiden name."

"Keep going."

Very slowly, with fingers clumsy with nerves, Celine reached out to thread the price tag's highly uncooperative, almost weightless string through a handy loop of wicker on the bassinet. As she did, she began narrating very deliberately, like one of those formal, colorless voices from the film strips we'd get shown at school.

"My sister's name is Joanne Varney. She is thirty-two years old. She has brown hair, shoulder-length. She stands five-foot-four, so she is one inch taller than me. She has a mole on her right cheek. She calls it a 'beauty mark.' She works as a bookkeeper for a restaurant supply company in Westerville. She has leukemia. She's had a bone marrow transplant. She was in remission until this past week, but even so, her odds of surviving past five years from her date of diagnosis is less than twenty percent. She has always treated me like an idiot. Meaning, she works hard to make me feel second-best. And I know it's a sin, and I try every day, I try my hardest, but I do not love my sister. Brendan, God help me, I've tried, I swear I've tried, but I don't even like her."

As she said this, her fingers finished with the tiny strands of string, and the price tag was once again firmly attached to the bassinet.

"Okay," I said. "Good job."

As if the bassinet were a much-loved pet, Celine let one hand rest lightly on its edge and said, "I don't understand why I'm doing this."

"Look, we got what we came for, right? Time to go."

"But if I'm being honest—and isn't that what we're supposed to be, honest?"

"Celine…"

"This is crazy. I would trade my sister for a baby in a heartbeat."

In a way, she meant what she said. But she'd reaffixed the price tag.

She'd come all this way. And her hand, still draped over the stiff, unyielding lip of the bassinet, hadn't tightened to grip and claim it.

I took a chance and put my hand over hers. "This isn't the place, and it's probably not the time."

Then I curled my hand under hers and lifted it off the bassinet. Touching her like that sent shivery little surges all through my body, but I did my best to concentrate on helping her turn away.

"Come on," I said. "One foot in front of the other."

She walked with me, step by step, until we reached the path and turned right. The road looked normal enough. The way home seemed as if it would be long, sure, but also simple and straight-forward.

Then Celine nudged me. "Do you hear that?"

I looked around, head cocked. "Hear what?"

"There's a baby."

My stomach fluttered nervously, but even trying my best, I couldn't hear what she was hearing. I said, "Celine, there's no baby."

"But I hear it! It's crying!"

As she tried to pull away from me—I still had hold of her hand—I became aware that the quality of the light was changing. The world was dimming. Mystified, I looked up to gauge the sun. It was still there, of course, straight overhead, but a layer of cloud was strafing across it, moving fast and rapidly thickening.

It turned out that it wasn't clouds, or not exactly. It was fog, see, a proper fogbank, and it was rushing in so quickly that in another instant, everything around us had gone gray. The temperature plummeted; I could feel cool droplets peppering my sweat-soaked skin. The trash heap to my right vanished into a wall of soft gray mist, and a moment later, so did the one on my left.

Then Celine pulled free from my hand, and before I could make a grab for her, she was gone.

Chapter Sixteen

I CALLED FOR CELINE REPEATEDLY but got no response whatsoever. It was like she was a radio signal, and I'd just driven into a tunnel. All around me, the fog slid past, skidding along, impossibly dense, propelled by the still-steady breeze. Even Celine's footsteps, which should have been clearly audible on that crunching gravel, had been stolen away.

"Celine! Come back! Follow my voice!"

But she didn't, or couldn't.

I spun around, searching for some slight gap in the shapeless gray, something solid to orient myself, but there was nothing but colorless, featureless fog. Worse, I realized that between reaching for Celine and then turning around, I no longer had any idea which way I was facing. I was still on the path (I could just make out the gravel at my feet), but beyond that? No idea.

Calm down, I told myself. Be cool. It's weather. It'll pass.

Resigned to wait, I took what I hoped would be a steadying breath and planted my feet. Moving in any direction felt dangerous, and the idea of sitting down for the sake of a rest felt doubly so. I knew I wasn't anywhere near a busy street, but I couldn't shake the notion that if I sat, some incautious driver would come careening along, headlights useless, and I'd be smashed flat. Ridiculous, of course. The nearest functioning cars were somewhere on the far side of Vinyl Wonderland.

Five minutes passed, and I tried calling a few more times for Celine, but the way my voice simply melted into the fog creeped me out, and I finally gave it up.

Ten minutes. Fifteen. I began to seriously consider the notion that I would have to find my way back in this stuff. It was a damn good thing the road was straight—assuming, of course, that it hadn't changed and become as curvy and kinked as my dad's old green garden hose.

After what must have been at least twenty minutes, I was beginning to feel like I'd stumbled into a giant isolation tank. For better or for worse, it was time to make some tracks.

Step one was to turn in the direction I thought I should be going, and I shuffled forward, not so much lifting my feet as scuffing them, moving like a cross-country skier, but with much smaller strides. I held my arms in front of me, feeling for any impediment, but the Coleman jug was still full of water, and with my arm outstretched, it was too heavy, so I gave that up and kept going with just one arm out in front.

My feet ran into the bottom edge of a junk pile before my hand gave me any warning, which made sense: mounds, hills, and mountains all start at the bottom. Curious, I bent down to see if I'd recognize what I'd found: bottle caps, all from Tab soda, that horrible diet stuff my mom used to put away on a daily basis. Coincidence? Or was this a sign that October was laughing at me?

Using the toes of my shoes as prods, I worked my way along the edge of the pile until I had a sense of how it lay in relation to the path, and then I stepped away from the bottle caps and into what I hoped was the center of my road home. I advanced like a sleepwalker, slowly, with one arm out, feeling my way forward as the fog slid around me, damp and clammy.

Had high school readied me for this situation, and I'd somehow failed to pay attention? Had either of my parents provided useful advice? Had anyone, ever? Maybe Jonesy Davis?

No, and no again.

For the second time, I bumped into a junk heap feet-first. I frowned, wondering if this meant I'd veered too far to the right. One thing for sure, I wished that I'd veered almost anywhere else. The mess at my feet was a truly disgusting mound of half-eaten lasagna. Some of it had been thrown out still in the pan, and the rest lay in a horrible, slimy mountain of limp noodles, rotting ground beef, and putrid red sauce. The smell reminded me of stewed tomatoes blended with raw sewage, and I backed away, trying not to breathe.

How all that pasta hadn't been baked solid by the wasteland's usual constant sunshine, I had no idea. Not that it was sunny anymore. The way this fog was acting, I was starting to think that sunshine, as a concept, had been outlawed.

And I'd lost Celine.

I tried calling for her again, but it was so disheartening, the way my voice sank into the air without leaving any sort of trace, that I gave up. Again.

One step at a time, I moved farther away from the lasagna until I decided (for right or for wrong) that I was back on the path. It was a pretty arbitrary decision, but once I was "there," I kept going, inching along, terrified that the next thing I'd find would be a cliff or a gorge. If that's what October chose to provide next, I figured I'd be over the edge before I could so much as scream.

But then, just when I was starting to get genuinely chilly, just as I was starting to consider the possibility of dealing with actual hypothermia, the fog thinned. It broke into tatters, sections I could get a fix on, and when I looked up, the sun appeared as a whitish, watery disc. It was still straight overhead, and it was clearly doing its level best to burn off the churning mist. I stopped, hardly daring to hope, and held my breath as the fog continued to scatter and dissipate. In another thirty seconds, I could see the path, hemmed in by walls of trash on either side, broken reading glasses to my left, hordes of file cabinets to my right. Things I didn't need. Things nobody needed, but maybe thought they did. All junk, the unloved crumbs of everything that most people thought of as civilization.

But one thing, at least, was different. Directly ahead, in the middle of the road, stood a polished wooden nightstand, on top of which lay a cream-colored piece of paper, held in place by a round glass paperweight.

Now, I didn't like the look of that at all. Not one bit. The table and everything on it positively radiated the word "trap."

Before I approached any closer, I turned in a full circle, scanning for Celine. There was no sign of her, of course, and I didn't see that huge pile-up of wicker, anywhere. Had I really come so far? I doubted it. The lasagna was still there, looking even more disgusting now that the sun was out. If anything, it looked alive, like the whole massive glop of it could rise up like some huge amphibian and lumber into the road.

The very last of the fog flew away, following the breeze, and I got used to the idea that in a few seconds, I'd be sweating again.

Well, I knew I could walk around the nightstand. It wasn't exactly a roadblock. But I also knew that I couldn't avoid it so easily. This thing was here for a reason. This thing was here for me. Would I be able to deal with whatever I found there? I wasn't sure. But I took some comfort from October Roberta, who'd said that I had reserves. Reserves of strength, I hoped. Or character. I sure hadn't shown much of either one in the real world, but maybe here, I had what it took.

I walked up to the nightstand, put a finger on the lower edge of the paper to stop it from flipping up in the breeze, and read it over. It was a diploma, more or less. A diploma from Alcoholics Anonymous, proclaiming that Frank D. Purcell had remained sober for one entire year. It was signed by an instructor whose name was illegible and countersigned by my father. His signature was unmistakable. The date was December 1985, exactly one year in the future.

Did AA give out diplomas? I had no idea. But if they did, this was what it would have looked like, complete with a gilt border and AA's unmistakable triangle logo, the three sides carefully labeled "Unity," "Service," and "Recovery."

Slowly, reluctantly, knowing in advance what I'd find, I shifted the paperweight out of the way and lifted the diploma. Sure enough, a small paper price tag had been affixed to the back, and in lieu of an actual dollar figure, there was my name.

From behind me, a telephone rang.

Did I jump? Sure, I did. That garbage-world had a pretty limited range of sounds, and for a telephone to suddenly ring like that, loud and jangling—well, I don't mind confessing that my nerves did a serious backflip.

Turning around, I discovered there was a second nightstand, identical to the first, maybe twenty yards back the way I'd come. Had it been there a moment ago, and I'd somehow missed it? No. Not possible.

The telephone, which wasn't connected to anything, and looked just like the one on October's desk, rang again.

In my sophomore year of high school, Mrs. Felsen (the same English teacher who loved Bluebeard and adored unreliable narrators) had spent the entire year chirping her favorite phrase, "In for a penny, in for a pound." This whole situation fit that to a tee, so I gave up on the diploma, re-set it under its paperweight, and marched off to answer the ringing telephone.

I shouldn't have done that.

What I should have done is run fast in the other direction, with or without the diploma.

I set down the Coleman water jug and reached for the receiver. I lifted the phone to my ear and said, because this is what everyone used to say to telephones, "Hello?"

"Hello, dear," said a woman's voice, in a smooth, polished soprano. "Are you all right?"

The handset slipped down against my chest, and I pressed it there, breathing hard, eyes closed. I had just taken a call from my mother.

"Brendan?" she said, her voice muffled against my ribs. "Are you still there?"

I brought the handset back to my ear and said, in a whisper—it was the best I could manage—"I'm here."

"Good. I thought for a second—I didn't want you to hang up. Because it's been a long time, and I have really missed you."

"I miss you, too." What other response was there?

My mother said, "I know. And I'm sorry. This wasn't part of the plan, was it? I'm supposed to be with you. I'm supposed to be there when you graduate. I'm supposed to be there when you get your first salaried job. I'm supposed to be there when you find the right girl and get married. And instead…I can't be. Or not exactly. But Brendan, I don't know if this is too much, but if you like, if you really want to, we could still talk."

With my free hand, I was wriggling my fingers in and out of the coils of the handset cord, and I tried not to think about what she was proposing.

"Mom," I said, "where are you?"

"Oh, you know. But what matters is that we can talk. We can be part of each other's lives."

"But Mom, you're, you're—"

"Don't say it."

"We can't be having this conversation!"

"You sound angry."

"I'm not angry, I'm—! Mom, why won't you tell me where you are?"

There was a pause. The wind picked up, then died back. The sun glared as if it was a hammer and I was a nail, and it wanted to drive me straight into the ground.

Carefully, my mother said, "I know it's been hard for you. Hard for your father, too. I know he's not coping, and he needs to. He needs to pull himself together. But you could help him with that. We could help him together. Anytime you need advice, I could be there for you. Just a phone call away."

"Mom," I said, "this isn't real."

"No, you're wrong about that. A lot of things are real that we would prefer weren't. Your drinking, for example. What's been happening with your friends. The way you got kicked out of school."

"I didn't get kicked out. I dropped out, to work. Dad's not working, we needed money."

"Brendan."

I spun in place, wild-eyed, looking at every possible horizon point, expecting to somehow see her, to see my mother clutching a matching telephone somewhere in the distance. No such luck.

"Brendan? Are you still with me?"

I looked down, frightened to discover what my fingers had already found, tied by string to the curlicue telephone cord. Sure enough, there it was, the tell-tale paper tag with my name on it.

"I love you," said my mother. "I love you more than I can say. So, you know what to do, right? You *know.*"

I slammed the phone down so hard that a shockwave traveled up my arm; I felt it all the way to my jaw.

You take one thing, and one thing only.

And there it was, in plain sight at last. I could take what I wanted, or I

128

could take what I needed. October's brilliantly simple, soul-destroying trap, laid bare.

But no. Surely, there was a third option. I could take nothing at all.

Three choices, then, each one uglier and more beautiful than the next. Maybe I did need that diploma (or possibly my father did), but then again, maybe I didn't. Maybe he didn't. All I knew for certain was that I'd come here for Celine, and now I'd lost her. If I had a true need, it was to find her, or, barring that, to simply get the hell out.

At rock bottom, I guess I was a soccer player above all else, and that meant letting my feet take charge. There was a decision to make, and I couldn't make it with my head, so instead, I put my feet into overdrive. That meant grabbing the Coleman jug and setting off down the path at a seriously fast clip, and pretty soon, I'd left both those wretched nightstands in my rear-view mirror. Did I know that I was going in the right direction? Nope. At best, it was a fifty-fifty shot. But then again, I was pretty sure that my ability to get back to the tunnel rock and October's desk was entirely up to October herself, or maybe to whatever higher power had placed her on guard in the first place. The only thing I really brought to the table was determination. Reserves.

Did it take more time than it should have? Damn straight it did. Was I running low on water before I finally spotted the monolithic rock jutting skyward in the distance? Yes. My best guesstimate (not a very good one, I'm sure) was that I'd covered at least ten miles, and that killer sun hadn't blinked once.

But just as I found myself on the last downhill stretch, the one that would carry me home, I passed by a tower of badly stacked wooden crates, and beyond that, to my surprise, was nothing at all. Which is to say, the trash took a break. Crates on the near side, mufflers at the back, and rusty, beat-up bird cages beyond, with my pathway serving as the final border, but in the middle of all that? Nothing but a very clean bathroom vanity set, just one, sitting all by itself in the dirt. A mirror, a sink, and a spiffy counter that might have been marble, or might have been whatever fakery humans have invented to make people feel like they're brushing their teeth in the lobby of a fancy bank.

Now, I don't mind admitting that by this point, I was feeling pretty wrung-out. The Oreos were long gone, so I was hungry, see, exhausted, reeling a bit. If I'd been thinking clearly, I would have quickly bypassed that spooky vanity set, but instead, I was so surprised that I veered closer for no better reason than idle curiosity.

Sitting on top of the vanity were two innocent-looking heaps of black fabric. One was a lacy bra, and the other a pair of very skimpy satin panties.

I looked all around, searching for the owner, who I figured might not be dressed, and while on the one hand, that was a really arousing idea, I was pretty sure this was a lousy place to be naked, and I wanted to help if I could. But there was no around except me, so I looked at the underwear again, and I even reached out to pick up the panties, so I could rub the fabric between my finger and thumb. The satin felt clean and slick and wonderful, just the way I wanted it to.

On impulse, I looked around the side of the vanity, and sure enough, there was a towel rack, and hanging from the rack were two matching, monogrammed hand towels. The towels were white with black stitching, and the stitching read, clear as day, "DeLapp."

Probably I should have dropped those panties like a hot potato, but instead I held them up, checking to be sure, to be dead certain that there wasn't a price tag.

There wasn't, and for a moment, I breathed a sigh of relief.

Then I took a better look at the bra. Sure enough, tied gently to one of the spaghetti-thin shoulder straps, was a little white tag. With my name on it.

Honestly, I was impressed. October—or somebody—knew me really well, and the idea that simply bringing these items home could win me Celine was beyond attractive. In fact, it was straight up intoxicating.

I realized I was giggling. Out loud.

You take one thing, and one thing only. But the bra and panties were clearly a set, like the hiking boots for Celine's sister.

The temptation was fierce. But. I closed my eyes, brought the panties to my face, and pressed them against my nose and mouth. I took a deep breath, inhaled what I could, and then let them drop from my fingers.

Time to go.

In another hundred yards, cursing myself all the way, I arrived back with October Roberta. She was perched on her desk with her feet on the chair, both hands wrapped around her knees and looking right at me, as if she'd been expecting me. Which I'm sure she was.

"Brendan," she said, "you are a puzzle."

Compliments weren't what I was after. I said, "Where's Celine?" and kept coming, rapidly closing the gap between us.

"Safe and sound," said October. "She got back hours ago."

"With or without the bassinet?"

October laughed, but for once she sounded more or less pleasant. "You can ask her yourself. Assuming you ever see her again. You sure there's not something you want to go back and grab?"

I wasn't sure, not at all, but I wasn't about to admit that, not to October. "I did what I promised. And now I'm going to go."

Nodding appreciatively, October said, "People who keep their word are rare birds around here."

"That was then," I said, referencing a book I'd been marched through in ninth grade. "This is now."

"Maybe. But you'll be back."

"I bet you say that to everyone."

October's smile was predatory, shark-like. "Time will tell."

As I entered the shade of the tunnel, I fought down one last urge to turn around, to retrieve at least one of the princely, priceless gifts I'd been offered—it hardly mattered which—and kept my feet moving. The tunnel felt longer than usual, and I half-twisted my ankle on an uneven patch of floor, but at last I reached the left-hand turn and found myself facing the Elvis door. I pushed it open, closed it behind me, and leaned against it as I breathed in the familiar, gently moldy scent of Vinyl Wonderland.

It took me a long time to move from that position, but eventually I got the door locked and went over to the counter, where I noticed a piece of paper, folded in half and tented so it would stand up and grab my attention. It hadn't been there when I left, and sure enough, it was a note from Celine. Outside, it was still dark, which made me reluctant to turn on the shop's overheads, so I held the paper close to the front window, where it could catch the glow of the nearest streetlight. This is what I read:

Brendan,

You did a good thing tonight. Maybe I did, too.

I did wait for you. First on the road, and then at October's desk, but she was obnoxious, and I was running out of water. You understand.

I also knew that if I didn't get out of there, I'd change my mind and go back for the bassinet.

Is it possible that admitting to weakness is the key to being strong?

Listen: you need to do us both a favor. Keep your distance. I'm married. You're in high school. We weren't meant to meet in the first place. If you can let me get on with my life, I'll let you get on with yours.

May the road rise up to meet us both.

Yours / not yours

Celine

Chapter Seventeen

THE NEXT MORNING WAS WEDNESDAY, and within five seconds of opening my eyes, I made it my life's mission to make certain that the entire purpose of this particular Wednesday would be to forget all about Tuesday.

Is there a living soul who would blame me for that?

Not that stuffing Tuesday in a box was easy. I mean, it wasn't exactly a daily occurrence that I was offered a three-pronged choice between fixing my dad, reconnecting with my dead mother, or winning the affections of a girl—woman—whatever—that I was increasingly crazy about.

So, I figured the best chance I had of keeping Tuesday at bay would be to fix my mind on a set of specific, achievable goals—and that's what I did, beginning with a nutritious breakfast that didn't involve alcohol, followed by a trip to visit Karl in the hospital.

Unfortunately, Riverside Hospital remained one seriously rule-bound institution. I wasn't family to Karl, and Karl wasn't family to me. Nor could I claim that Karl was my guardian, and I definitely wasn't his. My status as a Vinyl Wonderland employee cut no mustard either, so I finally asked if I could at least call Karl's room. The nurses explained he didn't have a telephone, and then they let it slip that he wasn't in any condition to use it, even if he had one.

"Go home," said the nurse, who reminded me of Maria from *Sesame Street*. "I'm sorry about your friend."

After being turned away, I drove to Vinyl Wonderland, ready to open up and get on with what I hoped would be a normal day, but I thought about Karl as I went, and how awful it had to be for him, assuming he was even remotely conscious, to be stuck in a hospital bed and not be able to do anything for himself, much less give me some direction. I was pretty sure his mother hadn't visited—she could barely get out of bed herself—and who else was even allowed in? My guess was that Karl would have wanted to see his various bandmates, but they weren't family any more than I was, and rules (at Riverside) were rules.

The news that Karl wasn't improving, at least not quickly, settled like a ten-ton weight on my shoulders, because it was one thing to run Vinyl Wonderland for a few days, but it was a whole different situation if I had to take over long-term. Would it even be legal? I was seventeen. At the end of the month, there'd be bills to pay, and I didn't know how to do that. I certainly didn't have access to the shop's bank account. I didn't even have the combination to the breadbox sized safe that Karl kept under the counter, tucked behind a stack of envelopes. The idea, initially, had been to just let money accumulate in the till, and then Karl would empty it out after the first few days of my tenure. But that had never happened. A few days back, when I'd run low on one-dollar bills, I'd had to close the shop and beg the bank across the street to break a hundred.

As for the carbons from the credit card imprinter, what on earth was I supposed to do with them? Were the shop's payments from Visa and MasterCard going into a bank account someplace, or did I have to do something to make that happen? I had no clue.

As I pulled into the alley and parked, an even bigger problem loomed: taxes. If Karl wasn't back by April 15th, Vinyl Wonderland would be in violation of who knew how many laws. That was months away, but as far as I could tell, so was Karl's potential recovery.

Lucky for me, no matter how untenable my situation felt, the basics were still easy, and entirely in my control. It was my set of (borrowed) keys that opened the shop doors, and my fingers that found the wall switch and turned on the lights. I was the one who washed down the windows and swept stray leaves away from the front entrance with the old corn broom. It was my smiling face that greeted the day's first customer, and not too long after, I was the one who took his money.

So, moment to moment, I could cope. I could pretend that I was a small business owner, and that I had the world at my feet. It was only when I looked past the simple stuff and started to ask questions that I got into trouble.

Normalcy was what I wanted, see, and for once, normalcy was what I got. For the entirety of Wednesday, nobody asked about the Elvis door. Did I spend the day thinking over what all had happened the day before, in the fog, even though my entire goal was to avoid that subject? Absolutely. And I was tortured by a crushing need to call Celine, but I didn't. Instead, I read over her note at least fifty times, and tried to distract myself with the albums I threw on the in-store turntable.

Did any of that work? No.

But I did have another victory to celebrate. I hadn't started the day with a drink, and I got through my entire shift clean as a whistle. The trick, I knew, would be staying on the wagon once I got back in range of my dad's liquor stash.

Closing time was painless, but I didn't go straight home. Instead, I drove to Karl's house. It was cold and dark on the porch, and the outside light wasn't on. As I approached, I felt like some minor-league criminal, or maybe a door-to-door salesman, the kind that does his best to smooth-talk old, housebound women with broken hips.

After a third round of knocking, I was ready to cut bait and go fish, but then the porch light fizzed to life, and I heard someone fussing with the door on the living room side. When it opened, I found myself facing a woman I'd never seen before, about my dad's age, and after explaining who I was, she let me in and guided me to the back bedroom, where Karl's mother sat in bed, propped on a stack of plain white pillows. She had a book of crossword puzzles open on her lap and a number two pencil clamped in her wildly crooked teeth.

"The boy from the shop wanted to see you," said the woman who'd let me in, and Karl's mother pulled the pencil out of her mouth and waved me into the room.

"Come in, come in. Is everything all right? I'm sorry Karl's gone and left you in the lurch."

I figured the best way to ask an opening question was to simply be polite, so I said, "I'm sorry to bother you, especially so late, but I wanted to ask about how Karl was doing, because the hospital really didn't want to give me any news."

She used her pencil to scratch behind her ear and said, "He's got me worried sick. He can answer yes and no questions by patting his hand, once for yes, twice for no. But it's so hard for me to get there to see him, so I haven't been, and the doctors tell me he needs to come home, that he doesn't need hospital care anymore, but I know I can't care for him. He's supposed to be the one looking after me! So, I don't know. I'm all in a dither."

"Not what the two of you had planned, I know."

She shook her head with real vigor. "Not at all," she said. "First, I wasn't supposed to get old. Break a hip. I know, nothing I could do about any of that, but even so. I object! And don't think I don't know what you see when you look at me—an old woman with blue veins and falling-out hair—but I'm still little me inside. I look in the mirror, I don't recognize myself one bit. I'm supposed to be a little girl, or a high schooler. Maybe thirty, but never a day over forty. And as for Karl, he had plans on top of plans! You know he only opened up that shop because, well, because it was supposed to be temporary. He had a deal, he said. He was going to be a star! That's what he said. And he certainly was working hard enough, what with all his music friends. I hardly ever saw him. He was always off somewhere, rehearsing. And then he'd come home, cook up a meal and give me a kiss on the forehead and tell me, 'Don't worry. My ship's coming in any day, and when it does? Easy Street.' That's what he'd always say. He'd tell me Easy Street was just around the corner."

Had Karl ever mentioned that his mother was such a talker? Not that I could recall, but clearly, she had a few thousand things on her mind. Worried that she'd gather a new head of steam, I said, "Do you know, does Karl own the shop outright?"

"Well, he doesn't own the building. He pays rent to the landlord, just like everyone else on the block."

My mind whirled through the possibilities. Was it conceivable that the landlord knew what was waiting behind the Elvis door when he'd rented out the space? Or maybe Karl had known, and the landlord hadn't? Or maybe neither one had known, and it was all just a case of, "Here are the keys, the rent is due monthly, and good luck to ya'."

Karl's mother had gone back to staring cock-eyed at her crossword puzzle. Just as I was about to ask another question, she said, "What's a six-letter word beginning with M for a 'Worker, one of many'?"

"A minion," I said, without thinking about it, surprising myself at least as much as her.

"Bullseye!" she crowed, and she scooped up her pencil and started scribbling. "Thank you, dear. You should stop by more often."

I said, "Hey, Karl didn't leave any messages for me, right? I mean, I don't know how he would, but he didn't say 'yes' or 'no' to anything related to Vinyl Wonderland, right?"

"Not that I'm aware of, no. But it's a great relief to me, knowing that you're keeping the place open and running. We need the money, you know. Now more than ever. Because I know Karl was going to make it big, and I know Easy Street was just around the corner, but he clearly hadn't gotten there yet, and now? With the stroke?" Frustrated, she swiped away a tear. "He's too young for this, much too young, So, if you want to know what I think, when it comes to my son, his future? All plans are on hold. All bets are off."

That sounded about right to me, but if all of Karl's plans were shot to hell, whatever they were, then who or what was in charge? If the answer to that fill-in-the-blank was me, then I figured I'd better come up with something better than just 'Show up for work and make a few bucks.' For my dad's sake, for Karl's sake, for my sake, what everybody connected to Vinyl Wonderland needed was a new set of plans.

Those were the thoughts that were clattering around in my head as I showed myself out—but then, at the last moment, I did a U-turn, made a garbled apology to the neighbor woman who was holding the door, and showed myself right back in again. After all, it was still only Wednesday, which meant it was just one day after Tuesday, and Tuesday had been the sort of day that just wasn't going to stay corked in the bottle.

I paused at the bedroom door, but Karl's mother had heard me coming, and as I arrived back in view, she said, "Yes?"

"I just wanted to ask," I said, as my voice caught, "do you miss your mother?"

Clearly, that wasn't what she'd expected to hear. Her shoulders drooped and she blew out a long breath, and she set her pencil carefully in the fold of her crossword book.

"Brendan," she said. "That is your name, isn't it?"

I nodded.

"Did you lose your mother just recently?"

I gave her the basics and she listened and drummed her fingers on her lap. When I was done, she said, "How old are you? Nineteen?"

Was it a lie to let her believe that? I suppose so, but I didn't contradict her, and so, in the blink of an eye, I went from seventeen to nineteen.

"Wounds," she said, "need tending. But I have Karl to worry about, not to mention myself, and these crosswords don't really help. I know, old people are supposed to offer good advice. Wisdom. I guess I'm not that sort of old person. I'm sorry."

She reached for her pencil, then blinked her deep-set eyes at me. She was clearly waiting for me to go away. Somewhere in the space between us, the ghostly voice of my mother hovered, lingering, listening.

I left in a hurry, feeling rebuffed, let down, unreasonably annoyed. I'd handed Karl's mother a piece of my heart, and she'd barely even bothered to pass it back.

Home was no better. My father was awake, which was something, and he was sitting at the dining room table, on which he'd spread the newspaper's classified ads, the "Help Wanted" section. This should have felt really promising, and he seemed excited about it, explaining at great length how he was ready to get back into the job market, but when I finished heating up a nasty frozen pizza for my supper, I realized he'd been crossing out each and every ad, one at a time, with a fat black magic marker.

"Dad," I said, "what are you doing?"

No surprise, he was one hundred percent ready to be offended. He let the marker drop, and it landed with a wooden *plunk* on the newsprint, and he said, "None of these are right, okay? I'm looking, but every one of these jobs is completely wrong for me."

I wasn't fool enough to think that the best jobs the city had to offer were necessarily listed in the classifieds, but even so, I was sure there had to be something. So, I stood over my dad's shoulder and chewed my pizza and squinted at the miniscule newsprint to get a sense of what little was left—which wasn't much. My father had done a very thorough job of inking out over a hundred possible entries.

He said, "You're making me very uncomfortable."

"I'm reading."

"I don't like it when people stand over my shoulder. Especially when they're chewing."

"Okay, just let me look at these—"

"Brendan!" Without any warning, he scooted back his chair and stood up, twisting as he did so that we were nose to nose. Red-faced, he said, "Do not read over my fucking shoulder!"

His breath was sour, fermented, horribly strong. I backed away and kept my dinner plate between us, which I intended as a gesture of complete surrender. "Fine," I said, as I scooped up the classifieds section. "I'll be in my room."

So, me and my cardboard pizza hunkered down and hid, and small-print visions of job possibilities bounced around in my head and made it just about impossible to taste what I was eating (which might not have been such a bad trade-off). As for the job postings, they did look to be less than ideal, but they were also effectively endless and included openings for fast food, filing clerks, YMCA swim instructors, loan officers, private security, and long-haul drivers with (or willing to obtain) a class C driver's license. But would my father be able to get, much less hold down, a single one of these? I wanted to think that yes, of course he could. His breath told me he'd likely forget about any interview he managed to schedule within minutes of arranging it.

I had an unopened bottle of rum in my sock drawer, and with my pizza done, I rose from my bed and pulled it out. I'd left the bottle there on the night of my purge, figuring that an emergency supply might be important.

Not that I'd specified what the emergency might be, but this whole night was beginning to feel like a solid candidate, so I took the bottle with me to the bed, and I sat on the edge, bare feet on the floor and the rum clutched to my chest, and I tried to think up a good reason not to take a long, hard pull.

In the end, I let the bottle be. I did this for five reasons: first, because I didn't want to be what my father was fast becoming; second, because I didn't think that Celine would approve; third, because I knew my mother wouldn't approve; fourth, because I was pretty sure that October Roberta would see it as a victory; and fifth, because I had decided, somewhere over the course of the day, that I wanted to go back to school. There was no chance of that happening right away, but maybe I could re-enroll for what would have been my senior year, and would now, presumably, be a second shot at being a junior. Knocking back what I could of a fifth of rum, in bed, alone, wouldn't be a banner start to making that dream come true.

From the far end of the house, I could hear my dad doing his best to sing along to something on the television. To drown him out, I turned on my stereo system, an unimpressive all-in-one set-up made by Realistic, no less, the store brand for Radio Shack. I thought about putting on a record, but I knew that would end before I nodded off, so I punched the FM button instead.

Well, the classic rock deejays must have been in a mellow mood that night, since the first song that came up was the Beatles' "With a Little Help from My Friends." And, because I was a depressed teen, of course I knew without question that John, Paul, George, and Ringo were singing the song specifically to me.

Not that I had any friends, not anymore. But I knew how to find one, and I knew how to win her. All I had to do was pay one last visit October's wasteland of trash.

"What are you here for, Brendan?"

That's what October would say, or something like it, and I'd answer that my mom was gone and my dad was lost, so I'd take what was left: Celine.

Chapter Eighteen

IDLE HANDS ARE THE DEVIL'S playground, or at least that's what the youth minister at my old church used to say. In fact, he liked that old saw so much that he said it pretty much every week, and thanks to what I'd found on the far side of the Elvis door, I now had every reason to believe him. In fact, from where I sat, idle hands struck me as just the beginning. When you work in a place with a door that grants wishes (more or less), the only way to not go barging through is to stay constantly, compulsively busy.

That's what made the next two days at Vinyl Wonderland into a relentless, unceasing battle between me and the Elvis door. Every time I looked toward the King, the door scored a point. Every time I got through an hour without glancing his way, I got to mentally scratch that point off the scoreboard. Customers came, customers went. I priced and sorted records. I even bought a small collection (cash on the barrelhead), and thanks to a couple of fifties-era Eddie Vinson LPs and a certain contact in Karl's Rolodex, I made a small profit on that investment by closing time that very same night.

I resisted calling Celine. I avoided taking a drink. I took from the till only what was absolutely owed me at my five-dollar-an-hour rate, and not a penny extra. I was, by any measure, a model citizen—until late afternoon on Friday, with the store empty at last (the previous shopper had cheerfully headed for home with three different Donnie and Marie Osmond records), I lost my staring contest not with the Elvis door, but with the telephone. I had a question for October, and I couldn't quash it any longer.

So, I let the Styx LP on the turntable come to an end, and as the stylus arm rose and lofted itself back to its resting place, I picked up the phone and dialed the number one.

October answered on the seventh ring, just enough of a delay to make me wonder if she was maybe taking a lunch break. Did she need a lunch break? Did she eat? Was she human?

"Hello to my new favorite custodian," said October. "You got someone coming through?"

"No. Tunnel's empty."

"Then why are you interrupting my beauty rest?"

That certainly prompted another question: did October Roberta sleep?

"Listen," I said, "I don't know what you think is happening out here in the real world, but the guy who is supposed to be sitting where I am, your official custodian, I'm not sure he's coming back. Maybe ever."

October replied in a tone that implied that no topic could be more boring. "My sources tell me that Karl's inability to return is a distinct possibility."

"Okay, sure, and I wasn't expecting you to be sympathetic, but I need to know, since I'm the one on the hot seat, right? I'm the one with the keys. What exactly did Karl do? Like, what's his deal? What did he work out with you?"

"Sorry. That's not a question you get to ask."

My temper flared, and to help keep a lid on it, I caught the eye of Frank Sinatra from a giant poster on the wall and pretended that he was October. That gave me something to focus on, a place to aim my anger.

"Too late," I said. "I already asked."

"But I don't have to answer."

"You do, because if I don't know the rules of the game, I'm not going to be able to play, not properly, not for your sake or mine. And I know you think you've got me over a barrel. I know you think it's a matter of hours, not days, before I go charging back in there and take something home, but you need to seriously consider the possibility that I might do the opposite. That I might walk away, take the key with me, and never come back. If I do that, and Karl's incapacitated, you're out of business."

I didn't add, although I wanted to, a crack about "whatever business you're in." If I'd learned one thing from my speech class (first semester, sophomore year), it was to drive to the end of a statement, and never tack on extra clauses, or anything else, at the end. Never.

Well, October thought about my ultimatum for a full two seconds, which is pretty close to an eternity on the telephone, and then she said, "Brendan. The world's a big place, and there are other doors. Other ways in. Desperate people, they find a way."

"Sure," I said, "maybe, but what we've got here is a door that's in good working order, and I'm pretty sure you like visitors."

Now, if I'm being scrupulously honest, I hadn't actually known that until the moment I said it, but I guess sometimes necessity really is the mother of invention. The second those words were out of my mouth I knew I'd scored a hit.

October's sigh was audible, and it washed through the receiver as a breathy, intimate whisper. She said, "The deal with Karl was very straightforward. He would act as our custodian, our gatekeeper. In return, we'd keep his business afloat, and eventually, we'd give him the break he's been craving since, well, pretty much forever."

"What do you mean, 'keep the business afloat'?"

She laughed, and as with most of her laughter, it didn't sound in any way good-humored. She said, "Come on, kid. You're smarter than that. You don't seriously think that shop you're baby-sitting pulls in enough dough to feed a household, pay somebody's mortgage? Last time I checked, you've got more inventory than a Ford dealership, but you don't sell enough in a day to even cover your pathetic little paycheck."

The last part wasn't strictly accurate, but the rest? Truth hurts, as my former youth minister (of course) liked to say.

To October, I said, "Let me get this straight. Near-sighted, overweight, funny-looking Karl was going to transform, with your help, into an honest-to-God rock star, provided he put in his time first, as your personal doorman."

"Gee whiz and gosh golly, Brendan. Do I have to start calling you Sherlock?"

"No, but you could tell me how long the poor guy was supposed to sit tight and wait. I mean, he's, like, almost fifty."

"Exact terms of service were never specified. And he wouldn't have wanted them laid out like that, believe me. No, no. Think about it. Was I supposed to flat out tell him, in advance, the day his mother is going to die?"

That brought me up short. Talk about a deal with the devil, this was worse than Celine and her sister. If I was hearing correctly, October had rigged the world so that for Karl to get what he most wanted, his mother had to die. Maybe that wouldn't have been so awful if they didn't get along, but from everything I'd gathered, Karl adored his mom. He'd do anything for her. In fact, my entire presence in this screwed up scenario was precisely because he was trying his best to do right by her.

"Brendan." October's voice had grown stern. "Can we agree that I've answered your question?"

I was still engaged in a killer staring contest with Frank Sinatra, but I managed to say, "I've got another question."

"Sure. Come pay me a visit. I'll point you down a path that'll take you to ten million old Ann Landers columns."

"Ann Landers wouldn't know the answer to this one. But you will."

October sounded like she was giggling. "Well, aren't you just the original cock-eyed optimist."

"I need to know about me. Because I made a deal with Karl, sure, but I never made a deal with you. Except about the bassinet, and that's done. Am I right?"

Silence from the telephone, except for the hiss of dry, desert wind.

"Hey. I'm not kidding, I need an answer."

"You're in the clear, Brendan. You're what I said before. An outlier."

"Until I take something. From in there."

She chuckled. "Try it and see."

As good old Frank won our staring contest for something like the fifth straight time, a new idea struck me—although in the moment, I wasn't sure how I was hoping to make use of whatever answer October gave.

"You do realize," I said, "that I'm currently sticking you full of pins."

"What?"

"I built a voodoo doll. Of you. Got it on the counter right in front of me. Here, hang on, I'll just stab another pin through your eye. You can't feel that?"

Her voice turned cold like the underside of a glacier. "No. I can't."

Gotcha, I thought. It sounded to me like she'd swallowed the lie that I was holding a voodoo doll, which meant that she couldn't see what was going on in my life, at least not moment to moment. No specifics. No detail. Her knowledge, which sometimes seemed omniscient, really was spotty at best. Not that I was yet sure how that would be useful, but it felt like crucial, critical knowledge.

"Too bad," I said. "Maybe next time. But I'm betting you have to go. I mean, you lead a pretty busy life in there."

The glacier got colder. She said, "You have no idea," and hung up.

The notion that I'd put one over on the mighty October Roberta had me so energized that I dug out the box of Christmas decorations and gave the whole shop a makeover, including a taped-on Santa hat for ol' Blue Eyes. I put Christmas forty-fives on the turntable, one after another, including the Chipmunks, the Ronettes, Brenda Lee, and Bruce Springsteen & the E Street Band. For no good reason, for a little while, life felt kind of festive.

But then, just as I was putting on "Grandma Got Run Over by a Reindeer," in walked the man with the missing tooth. I'd forgotten he even existed, but I recognized him the second he showed up. A face like that, gap-toothed, is impossible to forget, and on top of that, he still smelled like sweaty socks from the bottom of a mud-caked rugby team's gym locker.

"Hi there," I said, hoping that if I was chipper enough, he'd either ask for something simple, or maybe just turn around and leave. "Welcome to Vinyl Wonderland. Anything I can help you with?"

He said, peering at me, "You were here before."

"I was, yeah. I work here."

"But you're not Karl."

I said, "Maybe I am, maybe I'm not. Who wants to know?"

Man, was that ever the wrong answer. His eyes darted in every possible direction, and he started taking these tiny halfway breaths. He said, "I'm not giving out my name. Nobody said nothin' about giving out my name."

At this point, all I wanted to do was relax him. I mean, the poor guy hadn't even moved past the doormat, but all I could think of to say was, "It's safe," which I immediately regretted. Was Vinyl Wonderland safe? Not for this guy, not in a million years.

The man with the missing tooth stuck his thumbs in his belt loops and said, as if daring me to contradict him, "Roger sent me."

"Okay."

"I need a loan."

"Okay."

"Just to tide me over, right? I'm good for it. You know I'm good for it."

Every word out of his mouth made me think of movies, cop shows on TV. It was like he'd cribbed his dialogue from a bunch of taped-together screenplays. But what he was saying didn't feel any less true for being second-hand. He was seriously down on his luck, that was clear, and someone—probably the wrong someone—Roger—had directed him here as a last resort.

Except that I didn't want to be the last resort. Could I help? Maybe. Could I at least send him through the Elvis door, and then later, once he was back, could I go home and sleep the night through, content in the knowledge that this guy would have what he needed to stave off his emergency? Sure. But if I turned his trip into a weather forecast, I figured there was a one hundred percent chance of torrential rain. On his way out, he'd find something he wasn't expecting, and it would have his name on it, and whether he took it or left it behind, it would tear him apart, brick by brick and bone by bone.

"Listen," I said, "I'm just closing up. You should maybe come back later."

A tremor ran through him, bottom to top, as if a localized earthquake had rumbled up through the floor, into his feet, and out through his head. Then, just as he had on our first meeting, he reached into a deep coat pocket and pulled out a pack of cigarettes. As he tapped one into his palm, he said, "Can't come back. It's gotta be now."

"Okay," I said, surrendering. "But you can't smoke."

He paused, as if this might be a deal-breaker. "You sure?"

"All the way inside, maybe. But not in the shop."

"Inside," he repeated, as his fingers worried the cigarette. "Inside where?"

"Come on," I said. "Let's get this over with."

I led the man with the missing tooth to the Elvis door, and once everything was ready and the door was open, he gazed in as if I were his executioner, and the corridor I was asking him to step into was a prison cell, one with no exit.

"I told you," he said, "I need a loan. And Roger said you could help. Why do I have to go in there?"

"Look," I said, "Roger sent you, right? And you trust Roger."

He puffed out his cheeks, shuffled his feet, and pulled out a cigarette lighter, a cracked purple Bic. "Roger," he repeated. "Maybe I used to trust him. Now?"

"Walk on through," I said. "I know you've got questions. I do, too. But on the other side, if you're lucky, that's where you get the help."

"But Roger said to ask for Karl! You're not Karl!"

We argued back and forth for at least another minute, which was doubly unpleasant, not only because his body odor was so incredibly foul, but because I had to keep convincing him to trust the whole Karl-to-October system, which I frankly didn't trust myself. But how else was I supposed to get this guy out of my hair? How else was he going to reach what little assistance he might actually get?

Eventually, I didn't so much convince him as I wore him down. I herded him bodily into the corridor, and then, just as Elmo & Patsy finished explaining how others might say there's no such thing as Santa, I locked the door behind him. I got Elvis back on guard duty, and then I hustled over to the phone, so I could alert October that she had a visitor—and a nameless one, at that. But when I picked up the handset and put it to my ear, there wasn't a dial tone, and as my index finger got ready to spin the rotary, I heard my mother's voice say, "Brendan. It's been days. Why haven't you called me back?"

Well, I didn't quite fall over, but I did kind of tip sideways, so that I wound up leaning on the wall.

Through the phone, my mother sounded sharp, harried. "Brendan. I'm talking to you."

"Yeah," I said. "I know."

"It's not that I'm trying to pressure you. It's just that not all deals last forever."

I said, "Mom, maybe we don't need a deal. I mean, we're talking right now."

She snorted, as if that were the most idiotic thing I could possibly have said. "We are, yes, but that doesn't mean we can do it again. I'm not even sure—if I get caught, doing this, I don't even know…" She let that thought slide away into the telephonic depths, and then she marshaled her forces and started over. "Let's not fight. How's school?"

I fought to find an answer that wasn't an outright lie. "School is school," I said, at last. "I feel like sometimes it gets away from me."

"Oh, I remember feeling exactly that way. And I could help with that, I definitely could. I can help with homework, or getting ready for college, or even—and I don't want to intrude or make anything awkward—but I could help with girls. Help you understand what they want, how they think. It's very difficult to be a teenage girl. I should know, right?"

It didn't matter that almost every word she spoke sounded out of place, weirdly cloying. It didn't matter that my actual mother had never once offered to "help" with girls. What mattered was her voice, the simple fact of hearing it, and how it gave me a sense that she was with me, nearby, in proximity and coming closer, and that she cared. I wanted this conversation to go on forever.

Except I also wanted it to end, and fast. My mother was dead, I knew that as a visceral fact, and talking with her like this violated everything that I'd ever understood about the ground rules of life.

"Brendan," said the voice of my dead mother, "how's your dad?"

"Oh, he's…well, he's okay. Coping. You know."

"He's a good man, Brendan. I don't think he expected to be a single parent, but I know he'll be there for you."

Eyes squeezed shut from guilt more than anything, I said, "Listen, I have to go. I have to make another call."

"Oh. Are you sure? Really?"

I wanted to scream at her, don't pout! My mother doesn't call me out of the blue, from beyond the grave, and then give me a hard time for being busy! But I kept my cool, told her the call I had to make was genuinely important, and then I told her that I loved her.

"I love you, too, kiddo. And you know that we can talk like this any time. If you make the right choice."

I ended the call, breathing hard—I felt like I'd just done a set of wind sprints—and dialed the number one to reach October. She picked up in the middle of the first ring.

"A little late on the draw, aren't we? He's already here."

"Sorry."

"Brendan. Wakey-wakey. What's this guys' name?"

"I don't know. He wouldn't give it."

"Okay. Do we know anything about him?"

"He said some guy named Roger sent him."

October paused, although whether the name meant anything to her was beyond me. At last she said, "All right. I guess I'll give him my usual warm welcome." And with that, she hung up.

I put the phone down. I looked around the shop. I took in the posters, the records, the spotty but festive decorations. None of it was enough to lift my spirits. All the energy I'd felt when I dove into Karl's Christmas box had melted like so much slushy snow.

As I stood there in the empty shop, listening vaguely to the traffic sliding past the big front windows, my new mood coalesced into something at least halfway concrete. I felt like I was living what Mrs. Felsen sometimes tried to explain about essay-writing, about how rhetoric and rules were great, but that sometimes the conscious mind isn't always the best tool for solving problems, and sure enough, without my really meaning to try, the first spark of a plan began to stir at the back of my mind. Even calling it a plan was a stretch. It was more like a wriggling, awkward chick trying to peck its way out of the shell. There was a kind of an end point, sort of, but absolutely no middle, and there must have been a hundred missing connections, so I really couldn't see how it would all work out. That said, I knew one thing right away, and that was how to begin.

It was time to pay a visit to Mayor Tony Accardi.

Chapter Nineteen

I WON'T DWELL ON FRIDAY night, on my father's self-pitying rants, or his disastrous, pathetic, comical attempts to put up our artificial Christmas tree. My paltry efforts at decorating Vinyl Wonderland looked downright professional by comparison.

Instead, I'll skip on to Saturday morning, but before I do, I should mention that the whole reason that my family had a plastic-and-wire tree was because of my mother, and her fears—phobias, my dad said—about live trees and house fires. Growing up, she'd known not one, not two, but three families whose houses had caught fire thanks to hot lights and Christmas trees. One of those houses burned to the ground and took the family with it, pets and all.

On top of that, my mother had grown up with Swedish grandparents, and to hear her tell it, on Christmas, those folks wore wreaths with real candles in their hair, and the trees had candles, too—lit. My mother had a seemingly endless supply of shocking stories about hair getting singed, wax dripping in red-hot rivulets onto people's skin, and, of course, Christmas trees going up in flames.

With hazards like that as a backdrop, my mother would have been happy to have no tree at all, but my father clung to his traditions as best he could, and every year, a week or so after Thanksgiving, they'd get into a heated tiff about the possibility of purchasing a real spruce tree. My father always insisted that because nobody in the house smoked, flame from that source wasn't a problem, and besides, the long strings of holiday lights had very small bulbs now, the kind that never heated up enough to cause outright combustion.

My mother remained unmoved. Christmas trees were fire hazards, pure and simple, and so their "compromise" remained in effect, and up went our fake plastic tree. I was used to it, in part because I'd never had anything else, and the tree was, as my father claimed every year as he unboxed it, "very high quality," which I guess made him feel better about not being allowed to display the real thing.

This year, of course, the debate over whether to break down and buy a real tree hadn't happened. My mother had missed that appointment by a good eight months.

Anyway. Because time is what it is, Friday night gave way pretty fast to Saturday morning, and I shocked even myself with how early I was up. It's funny how not drinking makes it possible to rise with the sun. I'd kind of forgotten how closely linked those two things can be, and I wondered, as I hurriedly showered, what else I'd forgotten over the past several months. I had a bad feeling that if I ever arrived at a laundry list of answers, I wouldn't like a single one.

The reason for my hurry and my out-the-door, eat-in-the-car breakfast was that I didn't want to let the mayor slip through my fingers. I figured he'd have a busy schedule, even on the weekends, and I was pretty sure that if I showed up at his actual office, I'd get turned away. No one knew my name, and I had zero political clout. But I was convinced that if Tony Accardi understood that a representative of Vinyl Wonderland was paying him a home visit, no matter how unexpected, he'd be willing to hear me out.

Mayor Accardi lived in Bexley, a city within a city, surrounded on all sides even then by Columbus proper. What Bexley lacked in size it made up for in prestige and wealth. A Bexley address meant a winter-time heating bill that would rival the monthly mortgage on most normal homes.

Anyway, I wasn't one hundred percent sure of the address, and Tony Accardi wasn't listed in the phone book, but I knew what the house looked like—more or less. I'd driven to it during a soccer team joy ride almost exactly a year ago, with a know-it-all senior named Darrel at the wheel.

I'd been in the back for that trip, leaving good old Alan Geryk to enjoy the coveted front seat, and when Darrel said, "Let's go visit the mayor!" we'd all cheered like that was the best idea since sliced cheese. I don't think a single one of us believed that Darrel knew where he was going, but, after a twenty-minute trip, he coasted to a stop at the foot of a driveway decorated by a gate, walls, and two hefty stone lions. The lions were painted white, and they had their paws up on large stone balls, as if they were taking a breather between stunts at the circus.

"That," said Darrel, with enough wonderment in his voice that he might just as well have been pointing out the final resting place of Atlantis, "is where the mayor lives."

There were hardly any lights on—no surprise, since it was the middle of the night—making it close to impossible to get a proper sense of the place, but the house was clearly enormous, and was set well back from the street. It also didn't exactly come with a sign that said, "Mayor's House," so we were skeptical, and Darrel knew it. He said, "You think I'm jerking you around."

"Well," said Alan, who surely didn't want to risk his ride home. "Either way, it's a pretty incredible house."

Darrel twisted his neck around and looked each one of us in the eye. "You want proof? You got it." Then he faced front, stuck out an arm, and leaned hard on the horn.

"Darrel!" Alan yelled. "What the hell are you doing?"

"Just wait," Darrel replied, as he honked again. "Watch."

From around the nearest corner, a guy in a uniform jogged into view. Maybe he was a cop, or maybe he was private security. It was hard to tell to tell in the dark, but the guy waved at Darrel, and Darrel laid off the horn and rolled down his window.

"Hey," the officer said, as he closed in, "unless you want me to run you in for disturbing the peace, you need to move on."

"Sorry," Darrel said. "My friend in back bumped my arm."

He sounded so incredibly innocent. He had that gift, Darrel did. A cherubic face, and devils on both shoulders.

"I don't care who bumped what," said the officer. "Get lost."

"Did we wake up anybody important?"

"Yeah. Me, for starters." the officer said. "And probably the mayor. Now beat it, and don't come back."

We beat it, and we didn't go back. But, thanks to Darrel's shenanigans, I had a working idea of where I needed to head. For one thing, on our way out of that neighborhood, Darrel had driven past the Drexel movie theater. I figured all I needed to do was locate the Drexel, and then drive in ever-expanding circles, staying patient and keeping an eye out for two white stone lions.

It wasn't the sort of plan that wins the Academy Award, but it worked. Not a half hour after leaving my driveway, I'd found the mayor's house. Better yet, the gate was open. Was it an oversight? Pure luck? A sign that somebody else was expected? I didn't know, and I didn't care. I spun the wheel, nosed the Cutlass into the narrow gap between the two lions (they now had evergreen wreaths draped around their necks), and drove on through.

Ahead of me, a brown van labeled United Parcel Service was on its way out, and after we squirmed around each other, I parked by the three-car garage, underneath a basketball hoop with a net that was so ratty, it looked ready to fall off if I so much as glanced at it. When I got out, I made sure to close the Oldsmobile's door as softly as possible, with my hip. The house was stone, the gray kind that in summer makes for a strong contrast with green lawns and towering trees, but in frigid December, it mostly just looks like more of winter. Still, it was impressive: two stories high, blocky, and easily a hundred years old. It was the sort of building that made me think that maybe I should have put on something spiffier than last week's blue jeans and a Whetstone "Go Braves!" t-shirt.

The front door, white-painted, was at least a foot higher than any normal front door, but sneaking around the back to find something less grand felt vaguely criminal, so I reminded myself that I was there on important business, and that the mayor would want to see me, even if he didn't quite know that yet.

Well, somebody must have spotted me, because the door opened as I reached for the bell, and it swung inward to reveal a stocky, sour-looking guy wearing a dark blue track suit with racing stripes down both sides. I wasn't sure if he was a bodyguard or some sort of household staff, but I figured either way, I'd better announce myself before he hauled out and hit me, which he looked perfectly ready to do. But just as I was opening my mouth to give my name, he raised a finger to his lips and said, very quietly, "Ssshhh. People are sleeping."

"Oh," I said. "Okay."

He looked me up and down, then stepped through the doorway to my side, gently closing the door behind him. "Kid," he said, "I don't know what you want, and I don't really care. You need to go home."

"I'm here to see the mayor."

The man in the track suit cracked a smile brimming with fake patience. He'd clearly heard statements like mine a thousand times before. "The mayor," he said, "doesn't fix individual problems. He takes care of the city as a whole. Okay?"

This was getting me nowhere, and my temper was starting to feel like cooking oil as it spatters across a hot griddle. Plus, I had a sudden craving for a really strong drink, and it occurred to me that the mayor, once I got inside, might even offer one.

"Tell the mayor," I said, "that Karl is here to see him."

The man's eyebrows cinched up a fraction. "You don't take a hint, do you?"

I gave him my game-day stare, the one that once upon a time, I'd used on soccer field opponents to let them know that I was about to make their lives a pure misery, hell on earth. "The mayor," I said, "will want to see me."

"He might want to know your last name before he books you for trespassing, but that's about all he's gonna want from you."

"Fine," I said. "I'll head back to my car. And,"—thank you, Darrel, for the inspiration—"once I get there, I'm gonna lay on the horn until this entire neighborhood is wide awake, and then the mayor, he's gonna look out the window, and he's gonna to realize it's me, and he's going to send you out here to stop me from driving away, because he does in fact know me and he does in fact want to see me. So, at this point, it's up to you. I either see an angry mayor where everyone's awake, or I see a calm, happy mayor where everybody else gets to sleep in."

It looked for a minute like the man in the track suit was going to call my bluff, but then he let out a disbelieving chuckle and said, "Kid, you've got balls where your brain oughta be, but I tell you what. Go stand by your car, where you can see all the windows. That way, the mayor can get a look at you. If he says come in, fine. Otherwise, go home. Deal?"

"Tell him I'm from Vinyl Wonderland."

The guy gave me a sharp look, like I'd just tried to steal his wallet. "So much for Karl, huh?"

"Karl from Vinyl Wonderland. Tell him."

"Sure. 'Sir, there's a kid named Karl from a flooring company here to see you. He thinks your kitchen tile needs an update, and he wants to quote you a good price.'"

My crossed arms and my best glare earned me a smug chuckle from the man in the track suit. He reached for the door, and said, "Fine. 'Karl' from Vinyl Wonderland."

Without another word, he slipped inside, and I could hear the deadbolt clicking into place behind him. Annoyed, I trotted down the stairs and went to the car, where I leaned against the trunk, hands in my pockets, feet crossed at the ankles, and tried to look unruffled, unhurried, and infinitely cool.

It took a while, but sure enough, an upstairs curtain parted, and I caught a glimpse of a face. Was it the mayor? The light was poor, and the window glass held a sheen of slanted reflections, so I couldn't tell if the watcher at the window was man or woman, adult or child, but a minute or so later, the front door opened, and there stood Mayor Tony Accardi, in a purple and black checked robe, tightly cinched at the waist. He stuck out an arm, pointed at me, then crooked his index finger to indicate that I should make tracks his way, on the double. I did exactly that, and in another instant, I was inside, and the mayor was closing the door behind me.

"This way," he said, and he led me down a formal hallway to a back-of-the-house office, painfully formal, full of gilt portraits and glass-fronted legal bookcases. Two very skinny, very tall glass windows looked out on the back yard, where a heavy limb on a giant old oak supported an old wooden swing. It would have been idyllic, in summer, especially with a child perched on the swing, bobbing back and forth.

The mayor strode around to the far side of a grand wooden desk that was almost as big as October Roberta's, and then he turned to face me.

"Close the door," he said. "Sit down."

I closed the door. I didn't sit.

"Or stand," he said, and he stuck his hands into the pockets of his robe. The light coming through the windows was watery and pale, and even his robe, which had been vivid in the hallways, looked washed out.

"Now," said the mayor. "Explain yourself."

I'd known from the get-go that if I got this far, a face-to-face with the mayor, he wouldn't beat around the bush, so I was ready with my answer, and I said, as straightforwardly as possible, "I want you to bulldoze Vinyl Wonderland."

Whatever it was he'd thought I might say, that clearly wasn't it. He hesitated for a moment, then dropped into his chair, brown leather, studded with brass, and leaned back with his hands folded over his stomach. This looked like good news to me. He was settling in, apparently ready for a proper discussion.

"Remind me," he said, "of your name. And don't say Karl."

"Brendan Purcell."

"Thank you for that little tidbit of honesty. Brendan Purcell. You want to know one of the things that makes me good at my job, at being a politician? It's never forgetting a name. Or a face." He tapped the side of his forehead with one finger. "You were lodged in here before. Now? It's forever."

Determined to wait him out, I said nothing. Looking back, I have to say that in this regard at least, I'm impressed by my younger self. I didn't wilt in the face of authority. Probably I should have wilted, or at least have shown more respect, but the past is the past. What's done, or so I hear, is done.

The mayor said, "I remember conversations, too. I seem to recall telling you that I myself wanted Vinyl Wonderland bulldozed."

"Yes, sir. You did."

"Well, people say a lot of things on the fly that they don't entirely mean. Even the mayors of large cities have been known to make that mistake, so let me be very clear. I do not have the authority to demolish your building. Or any building. There's a metropolitan housing authority, a whole department. A whole process. The conditions under which the city takes down an existing building mostly come down to one of two things. Eminent domain, for something like a new park or a new highway, and safety. Now, I already know that there aren't any public projects in the works for the block around Vinyl Wonderland, so I think what you're telling me is that the building isn't structurally sound."

I hesitated for a split second, then told the truth. "No, sir. The building needs to come down because it's not safe."

"Exactly what I said."

"No, you said—"

"Kid. Brendan. I know what I said, and I know what you said. But I can't take a building down because of situations that don't exist. Right? So, if this were a process that I thought was important, I'd have to go the route of certifying the building as structurally unsound. Which is to say, 'not safe.'"

He paused, leaned further back, and put his feet up on the desk. "The thing of it is, Brendan—Brendan Purcell—I don't want to do any of that. Also, you're not Karl, and, as you yourself pointed out, the 'deal' hasn't changed. If it were going to change, that would be between me and Karl, or maybe October. Correct me if I'm wrong."

I was trying to work out if it would be okay to sit now, or if I'd missed my chance. I didn't want to give any sign of weakness, but interviews like this were so far out of my comfort zone that I really had no idea what body language would signal what. Feeling increasingly lost, I finally said, "Karl had a stroke. He's in the hospital. It's been days and he still can't talk."

The mayor took a moment to rub at one eye, then he frowned at his cuticles and said, "When I was your age, I learned to hate desks. Any time I ran into someone in a position of authority, they were on the far side of a desk. Now that I'm older, I've come to love my desk. It reminds me that even in this situation, which, let's admit, is not quite normal, I'm the one in charge. Are you sure you don't want to sit down?"

This game was getting complicated. Was he just being polite, or was he trying to get me to surrender whatever advantages I'd arrived with? Unable to decide, I elected to stick with the status quo, and I told him I was happy where I was.

"Suit yourself," he said. "And really, I don't know why I'm suggesting you sit, because I'm pretty sure we're done."

"No!" I blurted, before I could stop myself. "We need to close that door!"

With one eyebrow cocked, the mayor glanced at the office his. "Looks closed to me."

"That's not what I meant."

"I know. But you're assuming that I want your precious door closed. I can see that *you* want that, or maybe even that you need that."

He shifted position suddenly, swinging his legs down from the desk and bringing his chair forward so that he could lean his elbows on the desktop. I'd thought I had the man's full attention before, but this felt like a whole new ballgame. Mayor Tony Accardi was staring at me the way a drill bit stares at a plank, fully focused, absolutely devoid of mercy.

"Most people," he said, "are weak. They won't be able to handle what your shop offers. But don't for a moment make the mistake of putting me in that category. I've been through that door dozens of times, and I've gotten what I need on each visit, and I have never once strayed from my reason for going. If other people fall apart, if they can't live with their choices, that's not my problem. Understood?"

I nodded, because he seemed to expect it, but I somehow found the courage to say, "None of that matters. It needs to come down."

The mayor stood, pushing himself to his feet with the flats of his palms. "I will not be mayor forever. Eventually, term limits will kick in, even if the voters don't turn fickle first, but I promise you that on the day I am out of office, within the hour, I will be going through that door again, one more time, so if you think, for a moment, that I have any interest in demolishing that property before then? No. Not going to happen."

Having made this point, Mayor Accardi strode from his desk to the door, which he opened and held for me. "Brendan Purcell, since you seem a little out of your element. The fact that I've opened my office door means that the interview is over."

Beaten but not willing to admit it, I shrugged and slouched past him, into the hall. "You're making a mistake," I said.

"Am I?" The mayor followed me out, closed the door behind him, and passed me in the hall so that he could take the lead. "I tell you what. Let's go meet my kids."

Since he was showing me his back, he couldn't have seen the double-take I did at the mention of meeting his kids. For one thing, I hadn't realized he had children, and for another, why on earth would he want me to meet them?

We wound through the house, at one point passing the stocky man who'd first blocked my entrance, and he gave me a curt nod, as if to say, "Don't try this again." Then, just as I was getting ready to make a perfectly sincere comment about the impressive grandeur of the house, the mayor stopped in an open doorway and gestured for me to look through.

"Hello, rug rats," he said. "I want you to meet a loser named Brendan."

Inside the room, given over mostly to stuffed animals, picture books, and board games, were three kids ranging in age from five to perhaps twelve. All three were in the midst of strapping on various layers of winter gear, most of which matched, including (for the girls) the scarlet bows in their hair. All three stared my way with moon-platter eyes, and I was nodding a respectful hello before I fully processed that I'd just been introduced as a loser.

"Brendan," said the mayor, "these beautiful moppets are Vera, Michael, and Lydia. We're getting ready to go ice skating, aren't we?"

All three smiled and bobbed their heads, but Michael not so much, and only then did I realize that he was holding himself up using braces that wrapped partway around each of his arms, like specialized crutches. My first impressions quickly reorganized themselves to allow for the fact that Michael's two sisters were helping him get ready, assisting with socks and zippers and everything else that winter required.

Michael realized I was focusing on him, and he smiled weakly. "I won't be skating," he said. "I do like ice, though."

"He sits down," said Lydia, the oldest, "and then we give him a good push."

"He goes round and round!" squeaked Vera.

"That he does," said the mayor, at my shoulder. "And does anyone remember *why* we are going ice skating this morning?"

"It's an event," said Michael solemnly. "Santa's going to come and skate 'round the rink, and then our dad will give an award for outstanding service to the city."

"That's right," the mayor said, clearly pleased with Michael's recall.

"Mr. Claus, however, is not the one receiving the award. No, I will be giving the key to the city to three outstanding philanthropists who have spent their lives doing their best to help, to give back. Because that's what good people do, right, kiddos? Good people help others."

The three children giggled, clearly uncertain as to where their father's lecture was headed.

For their sake and for mine, I was relieved when the mayor clapped me on the shoulder and said, "So, we have places to be and so does Brendan."

"Nice to meet you," I said, and almost before I'd finished, the mayor had swung me away from the doorway and down the hall.

"I would like," he said, in an undertone, "to play basketball with my son, or push him on a swing, or even take a fast walk. But Michael has muscular dystrophy. He's nine, and in another year or so, he'll need a wheelchair full time. According to the best doctors this fine state has to offer, he won't live past the age of twenty-five. No, don't say anything. I simply want you, before you go, to understand that there is a day coming when I will revisit October Roberta without the responsibility of being mayor pressing on my shoulders. And when that day comes, I will take what I want, and what Michael deserves."

We reached the front door, which the mayor swung wide. Cold air drifted in, bringing with it the morning gloom of December.

"So," said the mayor, and he tightened off the belt on his robe. "Do we have an understanding?"

My face surely wasn't making that sort of promise, but I gave some vague assurance and wished that the man would stop blocking the doorway so I could escape.

"Brendan," said the mayor, "you will never come back here. My connection to your store—Karl's store—is not a matter of public record and it's not going to become one now. Your shop will remain open, and I will continue to have access to that door any time I want it, as per my particular and I think unique arrangement with—well, with Karl and his friends. Last but not least, what you do is suspect at best and certainly does not make you a model citizen, so as I head off with my two girls and my very ill son, you are going to drive back to wherever it is that you live, and you are going to contemplate your life choices thus far, and when you find them wanting, which you clearly will, you are going to make a plan for how to make a difference in the lives of those around you. Are we clear?"

"Yes, sir."

The mayor pivoted out of the doorway. I moved past him, feeling newly cowed, and hurried down the steps to my car.

It was still too early to open up Vinyl Wonderland, so I headed home, and twenty minutes after leaving the mayor's house, I walked in my own front door, fully expecting silence, or perhaps snoring.

Instead, I heard a honking, semi-musical squawk, followed by another, and another. I knew the sound, and I knew where it was coming from, but even so, I was deeply surprised. My father was not the musician in the family, but there he stood, in my mother's cramped, chilly, little studio, with one of her clarinets in his hands, trying his best to make the reed and mouthpiece work.

"Dad?" I said, when I arrived in the doorway.

He turned and lowered the clarinet from his mouth, but his fingers stayed locked on the keys in a death grip. He was holding on so hard, it was like he was free climbing a cliff, and those clarinet keys were his only remaining handholds.

"Hey," I said. "You alright?"

He said, as a plain-spoken fact, "I can't make notes."

"It's okay. You don't have to."

"I thought…I thought that in coming out here, picking this up, I thought that maybe, if I could make this work, then maybe I could hear her. Because this is how she spoke best, you know? How she expressed herself."

"I know."

He was trembling, and the clarinet was shaking in his hands. Neither of us had been in this space in so long that I could smell the dust, the stale air, the oppressive disuse.

"I thought it would be easier," my father said. "But clarinet, it's not like a piano."

"No."

"A piano, you maybe can't make music, real music, good music, but you can press a key, any key, and you get a note. This?" He looked down, shame-faced, at the floor. "I just wish there were a way I could talk to her."

I'm pretty sure that that's the moment I would have given him a hug, an urge that hadn't hit me since the day of the funeral, but he was still clutching the clarinet, and the way he was holding it, the way it was blocking my path, it might just as well have been a full-size Medieval shield. Quick as a breath, the moment passed, leaving me to muse on my father's words, his newly spoken desire to talk with my mother. That was a scary, terrifying idea, because it left me thinking of the Elvis door, and of Judy Treviso, and Celine DeLapp, and of nine-year-old Michael Accardi, and I knew that there was every chance that I held the key—quite literally—to my father's request.

I just wish there were a way I could talk to her.

I had the power to make that happen. Probably. Maybe. And maybe, if I succeeded, that experience would be enough to right my father's capsized world.

But it clearly wasn't a sure thing, and so in the end, in that poised, dangerous moment, all I said was, "Dad, how about some breakfast?"

Chapter Twenty

ON SUNDAY, KARL GOT MOVED to an outpatient facility. His mother called me at the shop to let me know. She said, "Their rules are completely different. They let me make a list of all the people I thought that Karl might want to see. Your name, dear, is right at the top."

As soon as I hung up, I flipped the front door sign from "Open" to "Closed," and took an extended lunch break. I figured Karl wouldn't mind. It was one o'clock in the afternoon, and I hadn't made a single sale since opening at eleven. What would one more penniless hour hurt?

The building where Karl had been warehoused was long and low and essentially non-descript, except that the parking lot didn't have enough spaces. I had to park on the street, then walk two blocks back, so my expectations were pretty low by the time I got to the front desk, and it's just as well that they were, because the woman who signed me in was surly to the point of being monosyllabic. When she told me where to find Karl, all she did was point and say, "There."

Let me be very clear: this was no swanky paradise for the rich and famous. This was where people wound up when they graduated from the hospital but for whatever reason couldn't be at home. This was the care facility where no one involved was in any way confident about who would be paying the bills.

I'd like to report that the rest of the staff was friendly, but they weren't.

I'd also like to say that the floors were clean, and the lights all worked, and that the windows weren't grimy. Unfortunately, if I claimed any of that, I'd be lying. Even my house was cleaner, and God knows that nobody at my address was doing the housework.

Poor Karl had been stashed in a long, narrow room with a series of seven beds all on one side, set at right angles to the wall. In movies and on TV, the beds in facilities like this always matched perfectly, as if they've been dropped in place by the batch, all fresh from the factory, but here, it was odd lots from end to end. Some of the bed frames were olive green, as if they'd come from the army. One was eggshell white. Another was wood, heavy-duty, and looked as if it might once have lived in a fancy upper-crust home. As for the sheets and bedding, they were every color of the rainbow, stripes and paisley included. The effect was so motley, it reminded me a lot of October's wasteland of trash.

The patients in this room were all men, and most were ancient, with wispy white hair or no hair at all. There were two attendants—I won't glorify them by calling them nurses, though it's possible that they were—and they were busy flipping the man on the last bed in line from his stomach onto his back. To say that they treated him like a sack of potatoes would be putting it much too kindly.

As for Karl, he was lying on a mess of pale gray sheets, and his metal bedframe, the fifth one along, was daffodil yellow. A clipboard hung from the rail, and I glanced at it long enough to see that it had more to do with rotations for diaper changes than it did with actual medical care. When I finally gave up on the clipboard and forced myself to walk to the head of the bed, I was surprised to see that not only was Karl missing his glasses—I'd never seen him without them, not even for a heartbeat—but his eyes were open.

He had very small eyes with thick, bulbous lids, and he was staring right at me, but this wasn't the blank, comatose look I'd been expecting. No, sir. Karl Wickett was wide awake and fully alert.

Unfortunately for him, he couldn't speak.

I say "for him," because I'm not sure I wanted him to speak. I was frankly kind of terrified that I wouldn't like whatever he had to say.

Not that he didn't try. His jaw worked like he was chewing his way through an impossibly thick cut of beef jerky. His arms remained at his sides, but his fingers stiffened and stretched, contorting into all kinds of uncomfortable positions.

"Karl," I said, "it's okay. Everything's okay."

I didn't want to presume or be too familiar, but I also wanted to talk without being overheard, so in the end, I sat gently on the edge of the bed. Karl was still trying his best to speak, but it wasn't working, and while I didn't want to interpret based only on his expressions, I was pretty sure he was furious. Not at me, I decided, but with himself, with his impotent inability to make coherent sounds. For a moment, Karl reminded me of my father trying to play the clarinet.

"Listen," I said, "everything's fine at Vinyl Wonderland. Okay? We're making some sales, and I'm getting the new stock priced. I know you'd do it better, and a whole lot faster, but I've got your old ledgers to check for the ones I'm not sure of, plus the price guides you showed me, so it's fine. I figured out who the landlord is, so you don't need to worry about dealing with rent at the end of the month, and I know this isn't ideal, but everything's in good shape. Full speed ahead."

Karl, with a massive effort, said, "Ellllll."

Reading lips was not a skill I had—in fact, until years later, when I met a woman who was Deaf, it wasn't even a skill I believed in—so all I could do was cock my head, lean closer, and say, encouragingly, "Try that again?"

"Elllll."

"Okay. Yeah. Got that part."

"Viss."

I sat back straight and gave Karl an emphatic shake of my head. "You said leave it alone. That's what I've done."

Unlike lip reading, lying was a skill I had down pat. If my recent soccer encounters were any guide, there were whole days where I'd done pretty much nothing but lie. What bugged me about this particular falsehood (and my regret was instant) was that I hadn't planned it. It just came out, a defensive reflex.

Karl was still trying to speak, and his eyes were bulging with the effort. Then I felt his arm press against my hip, and I shifted to give him room. As

I looked down, I realized he'd gotten his hand flipped up toward the ceiling, and he'd managed to press all his fingers together, as if he wanted me to put something in his palm.

"Eeeeee," Karl said.

Like an idiot, I repeated the sound, but as a question. "Eeeee?"

Karl blinked hard, wrenched his jaw sideways, and forced out a single, clear word. "Key!"

"Oh! You want the key? The key to the Elvis door?"

His attempt at a nod looked more like a tremor, but he also patted his near hand once on the mattress, and I got the message. Unfortunately, I wasn't prepared to honor his request, and just like that, out slid a whole waterfall of lies. I said, "Karl, I don't have that key. I've got front door, back door, that's it. Those are the only ones you gave me, remember? Are you saying you want me to get the key to the Elvis door? Where do I get it? From your mother?"

Some nerve I had, that's for sure. I had the key to the Elvis door right there in my pocket; I could feel it digging into my thigh.

As for Karl, he responded by lolling his head back on his pillow and staring at the ceiling. I was about to give his hand a supportive squeeze—which took some doing, let me tell you, because in those days, I was seriously squeamish about touching another guy, unless it involved a handshake or knocking him over—but then I became aware of footsteps behind me. One of the male nurses—orderlies—assistants—whatever—had come over to check on us.

"He doing okay?" the man said.

"He was trying to talk."

"No kidding? Well, that's good. It's hard after a stroke. Some people got to re-learn everything from scratch. Language, muscle control, the whole bit. But Karl's motivated, aren't you, buddy?"

The nurse gave Karl a slap on his leg, as if they were the oldest of friends. I might or might not have noticed Karl grimace in response.

"Physical therapy," the nurse said, sounding chipper. "That's what's on the menu here. And you know what'll be the best thing of all?"

I shook my head.

"Knitting. We are going to teach old Karl here to be a world champion knitter."

I glanced from the nurse to Karl in time to see him roll his eyes. Disdain aside, that felt like progress. I wanted to say, "Awesome! Do it again!" but then I started worrying that the eyeroll wasn't sarcasm, that Karl was having a seizure. As I leaned closer, his eyelids fluttered, then slid shut.

"Hey," I said. "Karl?"

"'S okay," the nurse—orderly—whatever—said. "Sometimes that's how it happens. They work really hard to impress a visitor, show 'em how well they're getting on, and next thing you know, they're out like a light. But I think he likes you, so don't be a stranger, okay? Knitting is great for fine motor skills, but for the folks in here, there's nothing like seeing the people they love to really get 'em back on their feet."

Looking past the nurse, I stared around at the room's other occupants, none of whom had visitors, and most of whom appeared to be at death's door. Voice low, I said, "Level with me. How many of these guys actually make it out of here?"

The nurse rubbed at his nose, a thumb-and-finger motion that couldn't have been sanitary. "If I gotta be brutally honest, it's one in ten. But that doesn't mean that your buddy, here, can't be the one who wins the jackpot."

On the way back to work, I stopped off at the drugstore for a pack of cigarettes. I hadn't smoked in a while—I preferred alcohol—but I had the urge, and maybe because I'd been so strict with myself regarding drink, well, I gave in without a fight. My dad would have had a fit if I'd smoked in the car, but once I got parked in the Vinyl Wonderland alley, I sat on the trunk and lit up, intent on trying to sort out whatever loyalties I still had left.

It was cold that day, really bitter, and I was a human ice cube inside of two minutes, but I stayed where I was, because life right then felt like I was wading through waist-deep sewer sludge, and no matter which direction I went, the sludge got deeper. A lot of things that had seemed to be pretty concrete even a week ago now felt like they were on the verge of crashing downhill in some sort of existential avalanche. What was I still sure of? The only thing that jumped to mind was that Vinyl Wonderland (the record shop part) needed to stay open, for Karl's sake, for his mother's sake, and, for that matter, for mine. I could get another job, sure, but would anyone be hiring two days before Christmas? Even a temp job as an elf or a gift-wrapper at some big department store would be tricky to land this late in the game, and the period between Christmas and New Year's wouldn't be much better.

So, those were my clear-cut reasons for towing the line on the status quo, for staying mired in my private bog of sludge. But then there was the Elvis door, and the more I thought about it, the more convinced I became that the world according to October Roberta was a flat-out danger to everyone it touched. Every solution she offered came with a briar-patch of entanglements, temptations that ate her visitors from the inside out. Was a single person who'd gone through that door happier as a result? I knew I wasn't.

But then I got to thinking that maybe I wasn't the litmus test the Elvis door required. If I'd succeeded in my (highly impulsive) visit to Mayor Accardi, then I would have condemned the whole building to the chopping block, and the results of that—well, they were confusing, at best. If the mayor had agreed to bulldoze Vinyl Wonderland, presumably that would maroon Karl. Even if he recovered from his coma, his would-be professional life would never go where he wanted it to. If Vinyl Wonderland came down, I had to assume that that would steal from Celine any hope she had of conceiving a child. And as for nine-year-old Michael Accardi, well. Given that Western science insisted that he had an incurable, fatal disease, did that mean that his only hope lay in some parallel wasteland wilderness where the normal laws of biochemistry and physics could somehow be suspended?

This was all pure speculation, since the mayor wasn't going to be any help, and I supposed it would stay that way, unless I got serious about taking this bull by its very ugly horns, all on my lonesome.

Was I truly ready to do that? Was I in any way equipped to take action all by myself?

As I stubbed out the cigarette and crushed it into the mud at the edge of the alley, I allowed myself a quick, idle daydream about stealing a bulldozer, piloting it down High Street in the middle of the night, and smashing it through Vinyl Wonderland's wide front window. The image was exciting, straight out of Hollywood, but the reality was idiotic. Even if I could find a bulldozer, I wouldn't know how to start it, or drive it.

Therefore…what? My mind seemed curiously reluctant to follow these thoughts to their logical conclusion, but as I got the back door open and set about turning on Vinyl Wonderland's lights, I forced myself to accept the fact that I, at age seventeen, was seriously contemplating the sort of homegrown action that in later years would come to be labeled "domestic terrorism."

True, I was only pursuing this idea for the best of reasons, and I certainly didn't want to get anyone injured in the process. I wasn't some upstart Timothy McVeigh (a walking reprobate who wouldn't burst on the scene for another eleven years). Even so, my drive-the-dozer daydream felt like a pretty radical step. Teenage dropouts with sobriety issues simply weren't supposed to be spending time on taking out their city's commercial building stock.

But if that were true, then why was it starting to feel like the only choice?

With the front door once again reading "Open," I put Spirit's *Twelve Dreams of Dr. Sardonicus* on the turntable, and carefully dropped the needle onto the band between the first and second tracks. Nothing wrong with the opener, the song that not so very long ago had first started me talking to Karl, but what I wanted in that moment was the second song, "Nature's Way."

Now, I'll be happy to admit that some of Spirit's songs were completely opaque to me (frankly, some of them still are), but "Nature's Way" was clear enough. That tune is about death, and death's approach. It's a song about how any of a billion symptoms or situations could be signaling that something is fatally wrong.

Now, I would have just stood there, see, listening, absorbing the song's message and thinking about Karl and my mother and everyone else I'd ever heard of who'd died and moved on, but just as the first chorus was ending, the shop's front door opened, and in came Judy Treviso. She was flushed and red-cheeked, but whether that was from the cold or because she was two inches from a crying jag, I couldn't tell.

"Oh!" she said, as if seeing me was completely beyond expectation. "It's you."

I nodded at her, but mostly I was still lost in the music, which I'd turned up pretty loud.

"Just as well!" she said, half-shouting. "Fate!"

Since she clearly wasn't going away, I turned the volume down and said, "What's that?"

"You know, fate. That you're here again. Because you were here before, and, um, I need to go back inside. Through that tunnel."

Hearing that kind of made my stomach go sour.

"What?" she said. "What's wrong?"

"Why exactly," I said, "do you need to go back?"

Judy Treviso drew herself up and got a better grip on her purse, which was slipping off her shoulder. She said, "I don't need to answer that. How old are you, anyway?"

Her question made me feel ornery on top of sour. Not exactly a winning combination. "Doesn't matter how old I am," I said. "You're old enough to be my mother twice over, at least."

Judy had an open, sunny sort of face, but my crack about her age brought out a whole thunderstorm's worth of clouds. "You're right," she said. "I'm old enough to be your mother, and thank God I'm not, because if my own child behaved the way you do? I mean, do you even listen to yourself? If I were your actual mother, I'd be ashamed."

I had my mouth open long before she finished, ready to sling back the nastiest reply I could think of, but somehow, after she got to the part about being ashamed, nothing came out. Was it possible that my mother, if she were still around, would also be ashamed?

Well, Judy Treviso must have understood that she'd landed a serious punch, if only because I hadn't mustered a response, but what she said next flat-out blew me away.

"Oh," she said. "You don't have a mother."

How she made that leap so quickly, and with so little context—well, it amazes me to this day, but some people have that talent, and most of those who do are, in my experience, women. There's also no question that I confirmed her guess, and in spades, too, by completely losing control of my voice. That left me unable to explain, defend myself, or demand that she get lost. All I could do was stand there, mute and staring, with one of my hands clenching and unclenching, hand to fist, fist to hand.

"Wow," she said. "I didn't realize. I'm sorry. I have kids, they're just a little younger than you, and I can't, I can't imagine…"

As if my trauma somehow stabilized her, she got a fresh grip on her purse and strode over to me. She came close enough that I thought she was going to give my arm a reassuring pat, but at the last moment, she seemed to lose her nerve, and she let her arm fall back to her side.

She said, meaning my name, "It's Karl, right?"

"No," I said. "Brendan."

It sounds a little crazy now, but in the moment, that simple confession felt tidal, earth-shattering. It was all I could do just to breathe.

Judy said, "So, when you told me before that you were Karl…?"

"He's the one who's supposed to be here. To help people like you."

"People like me?"

I gave up speaking and gestured hopelessly toward Elvis.

Judy took a deep, patient breath. "You have a lot riding on your shoulders."

I halfway laughed at that, but it was the kind of laugh that was a hair's breadth away from a storm surge of tears, and to be so close to breaking down wasn't just infuriating, it was unacceptable. I was not going to cry in front of this woman, this stranger, this mother to kids I'd never met and never would. I simply was not going to sink to that level.

"Okay," Judy said. "I guess if I were guarding that door, I'd be a little on edge, too." As she spoke, she reached into her purse, scrabbled around for a moment, and drew out a roll of mixed-flavor Life Savers. "Want one?"

Now, candy wasn't my thing; I'd never really craved sugar. But, for the sake of keeping myself anchored, and to make sure that my mind didn't crack, egg-like, right down the middle, I nodded and held out my hand, and Judy used her thumb to push the next candy out of its foil packaging until it dropped soundlessly into my palm. It was bright yellow, which meant lemon, and lemon was my least favorite flavor, but I popped it in my mouth anyway.

"Thanks," I said. And I meant it.

Judy took a moment to look around, as if she were noticing for the first time that she was standing in a dingy used record shop, the sort of place where women her age—mothers—never ventured. She said, after her gaze settled on Elvis, "Should I come back another day?"

I should have said either "No" or "Yes." Instead, I said, "I'm going to destroy it."

Judy took this in by pursing her lips and rocking back on her heels. "Okay," she said, "Are you going to destroy it before or after you let me in?"

This time, my laugh was quick but genuine, and the lemon Life Saver was starting to taste, well, not quite as awful as I'd expected. "Look," I said, "if you're hell-bent on going, I won't stop you. But I think you should know that I've explored some on my own in there, and I've talked to a few people like you—not, you know, *like* you, but people who went in for what they thought was the right reason, but I'm here to tell you, there is no winning on the far side of that door. None."

The smile on Judy's face looked as if it had been molded in plastic, and I got the sense that underneath, she carried the kind of wounds that Life Savers don't ever help. She said, "I'm not naïve enough to think I'll win. But I wouldn't mind breaking even."

That sounded like the closest thing to realistic expectations that I'd encountered in a while, so I pulled my keys out of my pocket and walked over to Elvis. As I moved him out of the way, I said, "The King says you get to go through, and I don't argue with the King."

Judy accepted this without comment, and she waited patiently while I unlocked the door. When I had it open, she thanked me, avoided meeting my eye, and walked inside as if doing so were no more remarkable than getting an oil change or shopping for sweaters at Lazarus.

"Good luck," I said, once she was out of earshot, and then I did my duty and called October and let her know who was on the way.

October sounded pleased. "This one," she said, "will be fun."

I feared for Judy Treviso when October said that, and for a moment, I considered going after her, but I stayed put, reasoning that I'd have zero chance of finding her, especially if October didn't want her found. No, for better or for worse, Judy's lot was already cast.

The door, however, and the wasteland overall? That was another story. The mayor wasn't going to help. Fair enough. But I thought I knew someone who might.

It was time to pay a visit to the one and only Jonesy Davis.

Chapter Twenty-One

THE TRICK TO VISITING JONESY was figuring out where to find him. I'd long since lost his phone number, because back when random scraps of paper were the primary method by which phone numbers got passed around, that happened a lot, and I didn't know where he lived. Plus, there were hundreds of Davises listed in the phone book. Far too many had the first name John, or simply J. Was Jonesy even the man's real name? I had my doubts.

In warm weather, I would have had a decent shot of spotting Jonesy at the Park of Roses, but now that we were in the depths of winter, checking the gardens would be a guaranteed dead-end. Luckily, I had three additional clues, the first being that the man loved to drink, the second that he refused to drive, and the third that he was old and slow. I figured he couldn't possibly live very far from the Park of Roses; if he did, then he and his geriatric bike would never have been able to make it there. Logical deduction insisted that he lived somewhere near the park.

It was Sunday night, and I'd let Judy Treviso out from the tunnel about fifteen minutes before closing. Whatever she'd brought home, I couldn't see it; presumably, it must have been small enough to fit in a pocket. When I'd asked her if she found what she went in for, she blushed ten shades of scarlet and told me to mind my own business. Then she surprised me by giving me a peck on the cheek.

"You're all right," she said. "Don't forget that."

And without another word, she left.

Once I'd closed up Vinyl Wonderland, I drove north on High Street, and as I got close to the turnoff for the Park of Roses, I kept my eye out for local watering holes. I passed three, but only one that seemed like the sort of place Jonesy might cotton to, an old, brick, dark-looking building with neon beer lights in the window and a sign out front that would have spelled "Tavern," except that the "T" had fallen sideways, making it look a bit like a letter "C." I had a hunch that drinking in a "Cavern" would suit Jonesy Davis to a T.

Now, the fact of my being seventeen was not the most convenient thing in the world, see, and actually walking into a bar was not something I'd ever done. In Ohio back then, nineteen was the cut-off for beer, with wine and the hard stuff at twenty-one. Either way, my presence would not be something the owners and operators were likely to appreciate. It wasn't illegal, per se, but they knew they could get closed down for serving minors, and while I was a big guy, I couldn't really grow a beard, which made it hard to pass for being much older than I actually was.

But I knew I had to give it a shot, so I walked in like I owned the place and tried to ignore the sting and stink of cigarette smoke. Neither of my parents smoked, and while I'd lit up at parties plenty of times, the bar scene back in 1984 was all about mixing nicotine with the alcohol, and in that room, especially compared to the crisp, December air outside, it was like I'd walked into a sauna made entirely of second-hand smoke.

As for the bartender, well, he took one look at me and said, "Kid, you'd better have some really impressive fake I.D."

Knowing I had only moments before he tossed me out, I got right the point. "I'm not here to cause trouble. I'm looking for a guy named Jonesy Davis."

The bartender was using a pure white towel to dry off a sparkling glass mug, and he looked as if I'd just ruined his day or maybe insulted his mother, but he called out, "Jonesy! Kid here to see you!" and from the back of the room, a whole table full of old men looked around, and the smallest of them, Jonesy, detached himself from the rest, peered at me, and gave a little salute of recognition. I waved, and Jonesy headed my way, caroming off a table as if he were a confused, slow-moving bumper car at the fair. When he got close enough to be heard over the juke box (pure country, Reba McEntire), he said, "Brendan, you should be proud of me. I was just telling my buddies over there all my best Helen Keller jokes."

Well, it took some wheedling on Jonesy's part, but the bartender grudgingly allowed me to stay, provided we sat at a table in plain sight, and provided also that Jonesy promised not to slip me anything stronger than a 7-Up, which is what I ordered. I certainly wanted something stronger—anything, really—but I wanted information even more, so I nipped that urge in the bud and concentrated on corralling Jonesy.

Was the man in a mood to be corralled? No, he was not.

In all my previous encounters with Jonesy, we'd met in public, and mostly, except for the odd soccer match, in daylight. Without exception, Jonesy had been pleasant, daffy, amenable. Now, with a few extra drinks in his system, he was still affable enough, but his mind wouldn't fix on a target. Every time I tried to get him to listen to what I was saying, he'd veer off on a topic that only he could follow.

Well, I rolled with the punches until I was just about out of 7-Up. Jonesy was mumbling his way through a passionate re-telling of a "Kojak" episode that he'd seen some time back in 1975, but when he reached for his beer, I put my hand flat across the top of the mug and said, "Hey, I'm trying to ask for your help."

Jonesy blinked several times in a slow but accelerating sequence, and then he looked down at my offending hand. He said, sounding concerned, "Is this the sort of help where I have to sober up?"

"I don't know. Can you talk? Think?"

Jonesy beamed happily. "We both know I can talk. Not so sure about the thinking part."

"Okay, listen. I know you were in the Navy."

"Was I?"

"Wait, you weren't?"

"No, I was. Long time ago. Where else would I learn to drink like this?"

"Jonesy," I said, voice low. "I need to blow up a building. Or maybe not blow it up but destroy it. What's the best way to do that?"

"Riddles!" said Jonesy. "I love riddles."

"I'm not asking a riddle."

"What's big and red and eats rocks?"

"A big red rock-eater. Not what I'm talking about."

"Why?"

"Why what?"

"Why is that not what we're talking about?"

By this point, he'd pushed my hand away from his mug and was all set to slurp another mouthful of beer.

"Look," I said, "I'm not asking you to do anything illegal."

"That's good."

"I'm just looking for advice."

"Like Lucy."

That stumped me. "Lucy? Who's Lucy?"

"Peanuts. 'The Doctor is In.' She gives advice for five cents. So, I tell you what. You got a nickel?"

I dug in my pockets and found a dime, but no nickels. I plunked the dime on the tabletop and said, "Here, double your money. Now, you cough up the advice."

Jonesy narrowed his eyes, which took some doing on his part, a feat of real concentration, and he said, very slowly, "You're more fun when you've been drinking."

"Yeah, no. You're the one that told me I'm a mean drunk."

He looked perplexed. "I said that?"

"You did."

"Well, I'm never wrong, so. Must be true." He drained the last of his beer and slid my dime off the table and into his trouser pocket. As he set the empty mug down, he said, "Here's my advice. Which you have paid for. Don't take any wooden nickels."

Jonesy was in Seventh Heaven over his own joke, but I wasn't in the mood to spectate while he drowned in a sea of beery giggles—and of his own making, too. "Come on," I said. "You were in the military. I have no experience, and I need to take down a building. It's not exactly something that's safe to ask about, right? I can't just go to a library and beg the woman at the reference desk for books on homemade explosives.”

That was, in fact, a scenario I'd considered, and I knew through friends about various "army manuals" that might be available if I looked in the right places, but I'd also heard that most of those titles were about how to survive in the desert, or how to build a pontoon bridge—stuff like that. This was long years before the internet, and for whatever reason, my bad-boy self hadn't bumped into *The Anarchist's Cookbook*, which is why I'd settled on Jonesy as a possible fount of information. He'd been in two major wars, for crying out loud, or so he'd claimed, so it stood to reason—or that's how it seemed to my seventeen-year-old self—that he must have had extensive experience with bombs, dynamite, and fuses.

Turns out, he didn't. It took another half hour of prying and coddling, plus another frothy mug of Michelob, to get him to provide any kind of useful information. Along the way, he told a hilarious, X-rated joke about how not to have sex with a polar bear, and then he launched into a long-winded reverie, full of burps, about how he and his ex-wife still got together once a year in June to trap fireflies in glass jars and make wishes.

"But," he said, elbows on the table, one finger waggling in the air, "when it comes to blowing things up—munitions—explosives—I was a radio operator. Communications, that was my wheelhouse. Biggest thing I ever blew up was a firecracker."

"Huh," I said.

"Hey, don't look so sad. I didn't say I couldn't help. Plus, with firecrackers, if you get enough of them together, they can make a pretty big bang."

"Okay, but Jonesy, you just said you don't know the first thing about explosives."

He rolled his head from side to side and said, "True, not true. I had a bunkmate named Steve who loved Crackerjacks."

"Jonesy…"

"That man ate those things every chance he got, and after the war—the big one, not Korea—he went and got hitched to a girl from Nebraska who wore these real short skirts, like a pin-up. Remember pin-ups? Betty Grable, Rita Hayworth? All those ads? You know, back in the day, every crime novel, every magazine, not to mention all the beer ads, cigarettes…hey, you don't happen to have a smoke, do you?"

"Jonesy, man. Focus. Why did you bring up Steve?"

For a second, I thought he was going to say, "Steve who?" but instead, he tapped at the rim of his mug and said, "Steve was a gunner's mate. A true-blue powder monkey. Never really saw him at work, but we'd talk a fair bit, because our bunks were so close, and two things stuck. The first is that if you know how to set it off, fertilizer will blow sky high. The second is that all explosives follow the path of least resistance."

"What's that mean?"

Jonesy grinned sleepily. "Let's say you want to blow up a bridge. You can put all the explosives you want on top of the bridge, light the fuse, ka-boom! But all that force, it's going straight up in the air. Harmless. Maybe leave you with a pothole for your trouble. So, what you do is, see, you either look for weak points, or you tamp it down."

"Tamp what down?"

"Whatever you're using. You put sandbags on top. Or maybe cement. You direct the force toward where you want it to go. And as for the fertilizer, it has to be the right kind. Has to have—hang on, I'll think of it. I know sometimes on the bag it'll say 'chemical fertilizer,' but that's not the important part. It's gotta have nitrate. That's it. Ammonium nitrate."

He smiled, pleased with himself, and then he slapped one hand on the tabletop and said, "Now, I have absolutely got to go to the head, or I'm going to be the one having an explosion, and if that happens, we're going to have a very wet floor."

Listing a bit, he stood, got hold of the back of his chair for support, and smiled. "The head," he said, again, relishing the sound. "The head, the can, the john. A rose by any other name."

Then he staggered away, and he aimed for the men's room, but he missed and wound up fumbling his way through the women's room door instead. I thought about getting up and redirecting him, but then figured, what the hell. It was late, the place was nearly empty, and, so far as I could see, the remaining clientele were all men.

I wondered if my father would like this place, and decided he wouldn't. Too much smoke. I'd have some laundry to do when I got home, that and a shower. If I didn't, by morning, my clothes were going to smell like stale ashes, and my hair would be worse.

Now, I wasn't too excited about hanging around on my own in that bar, waiting for Jonesy to come back—and he sure was taking his sweet time—but there's no getting around it, inspiration strikes at the oddest moments, and as I sat there, debating whether I should get up and make tracks, I realized that I'd been thinking about Vinyl Wonderland all wrong. It wasn't the building that needed to be taken down. It was the tunnel.

And that felt a whole lot more feasible than taking out the building itself.

It also felt safer, a project I could legitimately tackle.

As for fertilizer, that wasn't something I knew a damn thing about. My parents' version of gardening came down to mowing the lawn, trimming what few shrubs had come with the property, and (once) putting in tulip and hyacinth bulbs for what my mother had optimistically predicted would be "our personal Easter parade." That hadn't really come to pass, in part because Easter kept moving around, and also because the weather never seemed to cooperate. We got blooms, yes, but they were spread out over a five-week span, with no one moment providing a particular explosion of color—a phrase that now felt newly apt. No point, I thought, in setting up whatever demolition scheme I came up with if it only went off in fits and starts. No, my future plans for a Big Bang would have to go off the way the tulips were supposed to: all at once. Boom.

Just when I was ready to head for the door (I'd already stood, leaving money on the table to cover my soda), Jonesy wandered out of the restroom. The table of old men tried to call him over, but he waved them off and managed a pretty direct path back to me.

"Brendan!" he said, as if he hadn't seen me in years. "What's black and white and red all over?"

"A newspaper."

"Wrong!" he crowed. "A sunburned zebra!"

He insisted on walking me to my car, and once we were outside, he showed me where he'd parked his bicycle (he gave the seat a loving pat) and told me that he never minded falling off his bike when drunk because the landing was always soft. "Skidded on gravel once," he said, smiling happily at the memory. "Wiped out pretty good but didn't get so much as a cut."

I was all set to go, ensconced behind the wheel and ready to close the driver's door, but Jonesy put his hand out and stopped me from shutting it. "Brendan," he said, "you're in a pretty dark place."

That wasn't a sentiment I wanted to hear, so of course I denied it, but Jonesy was like a dog with a bone. Maybe the cold had sobered him up?

"I've watched you," he said. "At your soccer games, I took a good look around, and you were the only player with no parents in the stands. No mother, no father, no relatives of any kind. Not once. That must be lonely."

"Gotta go," I said. "Getting late."

"And now," he went on, looking past me, over the roof of the car, "you show up here, asking about how to blow up a building. Which is a serious crime. Probably federal. I have to say, as a military man and a loyal citizen of these mostly United States, under any normal circumstances, I think I might have a duty to report a fellow who goes around asking that kind of question."

I craned my neck and stared at him, and he looked down with a sad, patient smile. After a long moment of locking eyes, I said, "I'd appreciate it if you didn't go telling anyone else about tonight."

"Because," he said, "you have a very good reason for what you're doing."

"That's right. I do."

"Tell me this much. Tell me you're not talking about your school. Former school. Whetstone."

Swearing to that was a cinch. "No," I said. "Nothing to do with school."

"And this building you're fixed on, is it empty?"

"It will be."

"Swear it."

"I swear."

He nodded, and looked around again, at the night, the dark, the streets. "Okay, then. You sure you don't want to tell me about your folks?"

The funny thing was, I'd assumed that I'd long ago spilled the beans about my mother being dead, and about my father being lost at the bottom of a bottle. Was it possible that Jonesy didn't know? I wasn't sure that I would have flat-out intended to tell him, but we'd spent enough hours together that I just figured it had already come up. Apparently not. Apparently, my memory was once again proving to be a very suspect piece of equipment.

"Maybe next time," I said.

"All right. You clearly know where to find me. And Brendan, I wasn't kidding, before. Don't take any wooden nickels."

He moved away from the door, and I tugged it shut, started the engine, and drove off, yawning. It was late, and I'd had a long day. The next day was looking to be even longer, with a rapidly growing to-do list that included visiting a garden center and figuring out where to get sandbags.

Yes, indeed. It was starting to look as if December 24th, 1984, was going to be my strangest Christmas Eve ever.

Chapter Twenty-Two

AS IT TURNED OUT, THE Christmas Eve workday bordered on routine. There wasn't a garden center open anywhere in the city, so I decided to cool my jets and stick to the basics: selling last-minute gifts to used record connoisseurs. To my surprise, we had a good crowd. In fact, we got so much foot traffic that I couldn't break away for lunch—that was a first—which meant that by the time I drove home, Karl's till was stuffed, and I was starving to the point where I was shaking slightly from low blood sugar. Christmas lights were on at almost every house (except ours), but the city wasn't the Winter Wonderland it could have been, since once again, the snow we'd had had melted, and the nearest White Christmas was somewhere in Canada.

Inside, my father was nowhere to be seen, but I could hear water running, so I figured he was taking a rare shower. That seemed like a good sign, since hygiene hadn't been a big priority with him for quite a while.

After moving two beer cans and an empty bottle of Johnny Walker to the trash, I heated up a frozen pot pie, and I wolfed it down as soon as it was cool enough that it didn't burn my tongue. Only then did I register that the water was *still* running. One thing about my dad, he had a phobia about not "wasting time" in the shower, so the ongoing hiss of all that gurgling water struck me as being about ten shades of peculiar.

I padded down the hall, turning on lights as I went. The bathroom I used was empty and dark, so I kept on until I got to what had once been my parents' bedroom and was now just my dad's. The bathroom was wide open, and the lights were off, and I didn't hear the shower. In fact, the sounds of running water were fainter now.

"Dad?" I called.

No response.

Back down the hall I went. The mud room was where we kept the washer and drier, but they weren't running. That left only one significant water source: the back-yard hose.

It wasn't a wrenchingly cold night, maybe high thirties, but it was chilly enough that I pulled on my coat before heading through the mud room door and outside. Now I clearly heard water running, a splashing, chugging sound, and I nearly tripped over a loop in the garden hose, which, the last time I'd seen it, had been neatly coiled and hung on the wall for winter. A week ago, it would have been frozen solid, too full of ice to propel water, but now it was running full-tilt, and its heavy brass nozzle was lying in the deep end of the swimming pool. The pool's winter cover had been pulled off and left to flounder like a dead thing on the grass, and while the darkness made it tough to be exactly certain, it looked as if the pool's eight-foot end was at least hip-deep in swirling, chilly water.

"I know what you're thinking," my father said, from a distant lounge chair, one that he'd set up near the diving board. He was huddled under a crazy array of blankets and winter layers, and he was looking downward, into the pool, presumably tracking the progress of the slowly rising water.

I'd expected that my father would go on to actually tell me what I was thinking, since he claimed to know, but he seemed to have forgotten that he'd spoken. I walked over to where the outside tap poked out of the wall, and I turned the faucet handle until the water flow shut off.

"Hey!" said my father. "What are you doing?"

"It's winter."

"But it's been getting warmer."

"It won't stay warm. We've still got January, February, March, and if that water down there freezes, we get cracks in the lining."

"Brendan. That's a myth."

"You're the one that told me that's what would happen. It's why we drain the pool, remember?"

My father stood up. "No," he said, "we drain it so it can be cleaned." As he stood, he tried to keep all his warm layers on, but one blanket immediately got away and slithered to the ground at his feet. "Sorry," he said, "but it's taken hours just to get this far, and I want it ready for Christmas."

"What? Man, you can't be serious."

He strode toward me, shedding blankets and shawls and scarfs like old skins. He said, "This is my house, I don't need your approval, and I am going swimming for Christmas."

"Uh, no. You'll get, like, hypothermia and die."

"Turn the water on. Turn it on now."

"No."

Now, I've mentioned that I'm a big guy. Not Andre the Giant big, but hefty enough that the football coaches were always buzzing around, wanting me to gear up in pads and a helmet and hit the grid-iron. As for my dad, I'd topped him height-wise in ninth grade, and weight-wise one year later. Whatever stature I have didn't come from him.

All that said, I really wasn't sure I could take him in a fight. He was a grown-up, for crying out loud, and my father to boot, plus, he was bearing down on me like a blanket-covered earthmover, and it was clear that he was going to do whatever it took to get that hose running.

So, I protested a few more times, but when he got close and started pushing at me, I put up my hands and got out of the way.

"Dad," I said, as he twisted the faucet handle, "this is nuts. You can't be doing this."

"Not your call," he muttered, and he pulled the last of his blankets tighter over his shoulders.

A six-pack of awful scenarios raced into my head, beginning with a damaged swimming pool but ending with my father, floating face-down in the rising water come Christmas morning, whether by accident or suicide, leaving me with his death as my one and only present.

That was not an option I could live with.

"Okay," I said. "Fill the pool. Do what you gotta do, but you have to promise me something."

My dad gave me a look like I was trying to sell him bad life insurance. "Fathers," he said, "don't have to make promises."

I ignored him. "You need to stay back from the edge, okay?"

He frowned as if that was the most ridiculous worry he'd ever heard. "I'm not going to fall in. How drunk do you think I am?"

To answer his question, I stepped up close and gave him a soft, two-handed shove in the chest. He went over in perfect slow motion and landed on his ass with his legs sticking out, like a doll. The answer of whether I could take him in a fight was now answered.

I said, "Dad, you didn't even try to catch yourself. So, promise. We're gonna back your chair up to where you can still watch the water filling, but you can't possibly fall in. Got it?"

As he tried to pick himself up, my father murmured something caustic about "Drill Sergeant Brendan," but he didn't argue, and when I moved the lounge chair he'd been using a good two yards back from the lip of the pool, he didn't protest or try to reposition it. He simply sat and allowed me to arrange his various layers over top of him again, as if I were preparing him for hibernation, or maybe embalming, like a pharaoh.

When I finished adding the last blanket, my dad gave me a lemony look and said, "You worry too much."

But he was wrong about that. The galling truth, as I was finally learning, was that I hadn't been worried enough.

So, I gave him a kiss on the top of his head—not, I hoped, a Judas kiss—and told him I had to go, and that I'd be back as soon as I could. He didn't ask where I was going. Just as well. I didn't want to tell him. In fact, I didn't even want to say it out loud, to in any way admit that my next stop, instead of a Christmas Eve workout session with my weight set, would be Vinyl Wonderland.

But even that wasn't accurate. Vinyl Wonderland didn't carry what I needed, and never had. No, what I needed lay somewhere well past those quiet, well-behaved bins of jettisoned records. What I needed was waiting for me—calling, even—in the junk-pile wasteland run by October Roberta.

What prep I did was short and sweet: water bottles, filled and then stuffed in my pack, along with a granola bar. The drive was short, the traffic light. I spotted a cluster of carolers warbling away on someone's doorstep, but otherwise, just about everyone had melted into their homes, ready, I figured, for a long winter's nap. I wouldn't have minded doing the same, but instead I splashed the Cutlass through the back alley and parked behind the shop.

For a long time, that's as far as I got. Unfolding myself from the driver's seat took some serious determination, and I wasn't quite sure why. I knew where I was going, after all; I'd survived the Elvis door before, and more than once, too. Maybe I was just getting smarter, wising up. This time out, even with my backpack and supplies, I knew more than enough to be afraid.

But eventually I screwed up the courage to let myself in to the shop, and I did it quietly, furtively, as if I were a burglar.

The lights were off. I debated turning them on, but again, that whole fishbowl problem of being on display to anyone in the darkened world out on the street made me hesitate. Just get on with it, I told myself. Shift the King out of the way, open up the Elvis door, and get cracking.

And that really is what I was about to do when the telephone rang.

In the dark.

At ten p.m.

On Christmas Eve.

I didn't have to pick up the receiver to know who was calling.

The phone rang again, the noise of it filling the shop, jangling my nerves, but I didn't move. I remained poised between the Elvis door and the back-alley hallway, frozen in place. If there'd been a medic standing next to me, they'd have had to check to see if my heart had stopped.

The third ring was so loud that I jumped. It was insistent, jarring, twice the volume of any phone I'd ever heard. I gritted my teeth, glared at the phone, and willed it to shut up.

But it didn't, and the fourth ring was louder still.

"Stop it!" I yelled. "Go away!"

Dear God in Heaven, I had just told my mother, my dead mother, the person I wanted to see more than anyone else in the world, to get lost.

The fifth ring wasn't loud at all. In fact, it was the opposite, almost soft, plaintive. Like it was crying and wanted my help.

I almost took a step toward it. But I didn't. I stood my ground.

The sixth ring was softer still, and it cut off halfway through.

Well, I wasn't waiting around to see who or what would reach out next. I got Elvis shifted and fitted the skeleton key into the lock as fast as the dim light would allow, and when it didn't immediately turn, I swore at it and gave the door a kick and got a good front row seat for just how on edge I really was. Only after a series of deep breaths and a quick circuit through Showtunes and Classical did I try again, and this time, of course, the mechanism gave way with no resistance at all.

In I went, and the corridor shifted into its tunnel form right on schedule, but it was darker than usual. Once I'd rounded the first bend, the light spilling in from October's end was muted, barely enough to guide me. I had to feel my way along, my hands tracing the side walls from wooden support to wooden support, each of the old braces tinder-dry and sharp with splinters.

Good, I thought. If the brace-work was halfway to powder already, it would be that much easier to detonate.

I turned the second corner and walked the final few yards until I stood at the end of the tunnel and could look out at the sprawling world of cast-offs. For once, I didn't have to shade my eyes or shrug off my coat; for once, I didn't feel beads of sweat rising like hot liquid pinpricks all over my skin. And no wonder. Low-hanging clouds covered the sky, and a steady fall of gentle snowflakes were drifting down to cover the endless junk in a perfect coat of fluffy white.

"I should have known," said October. She was sitting on top of the desk, legs dangling, facing me and the tunnel rock, and she had bundled herself up in at least as many blankets and coverings as my father had been draped in at home. Her sunglasses were nowhere to be seen, and from the look of things, she'd been sitting in the exact same position for a good long while. There was almost as much snow on her as there was on the desktop.

I left the tunnel, got my pack comfortably over one shoulder, and walked toward her desk. I said, as I closed the gap, "What's going on?"

October spread out her arms, which made the blankets bulge. "I'm guessing somebody ordered up a White Christmas."

"How about you be real for once," I said, as I dug out my gloves and put them on. "You're the one in control, not me."

October laughed, but as usual, there wasn't any warmth in the sound. "Me," she said at last. "In control."

"You're the one makes up the rules."

She gave her head an emphatic shake, and rivulets of snow tumbled off her hair. "Brendan, when it comes to rules, I enforce my share, but I have nothing to do with making them up, and for goodness' sake, please don't ask me who does."

I looked around at the white, half-lit world. I said, "If you're not in charge…"

"Don't even try," she said. "I'm just a humble custodian, not so different, really, from Karl. Here to do my time."

"Wait," I said, "so this is like jail for you?"

She bent her head, as if I were about to bless or knight her. "If this were church, you might call it penance—and someday, if I'm lucky and do my job, I'll get to go home."

"What on earth did you do to get stuck with this?"

Rather than answer, she said, without looking up, "You're kind of a rule-breaker, you know that?"

I didn't feel qualified to argue the point, so I said nothing, and the snow fell around me as I shivered inside my coat.

When October spoke next, I could see her teeth flash, white like the snow. She said, "Just to be clear. Did anyone recommend you come here?"

"No."

"But you came anyway."

Shrugging, I said, "How 'bout you tell me which road to take?"

"Last time," she said, "you came with someone. That's not allowed, either."

I said, "Yeah, yeah, and then I really got your goat, because I didn't take anything home."

Her smile had turned coy, like she was flirting with me. "That's right. And now, like you haven't thumbed your nose at this place enough, you show up all over again. Who do you think you are, the mayor?"

This was getting old in a hurry, and I shifted around, trying to figure out which road I'd take if I didn't get any help. "Come on," I said, "tell me what path."

"Depends."

"On?"

"Depends on what you want."

But I knew that wasn't it. I knew what I wanted, and I'd already passed it up—twice, in two different flavors. I was here for one thing and one thing only: what I needed.

October pointed, and just like that, I was on my way, tramping through four inches of ever-deepening snow in my totally inadequate sneakers, and forcing myself to keep going by thinking dark thoughts of my father, huddled like October as he watched the swimming pool, by night, filling at an agonizingly slow pace. The pathway I followed was a solid white trench leading between hillocks and mounds of who knew what on either side; the smaller items, especially, were snow-covered enough to be indistinguishable. Only the bigger objects were still easy to identify: mufflers, phone booths, milk crates.

My feet were freezing off, and, because my coat didn't have a hood, the snow was going down my neck. My hair got wet, then icy. Given the weather where I'd started, I hadn't thought to bring a hat. It occurred to me that maybe I should be keeping my eyes peeled, that there could be a pile-up of hats ripe and ready for the taking, but then I started hoping I wouldn't find any such thing. What if I took one? Did borrowing count?

Keep your eye on the ball, I told myself. Just like soccer. Keep your eye on the ball.

In a literal sense, this was getting trickier to manage. It was snowing harder now, and the flakes were batting into my eyes, so I was mostly walking with my head down, just trudging along, humping a backpack full of water that now felt totally useless, and hoping I'd bump into one particular nightstand, the one with a diploma on top. I wasn't optimistic. Besides the fact that I could barely see where I was going, I had to assume that at least a few basic rules still applied. Snow, for example, was snow. When wet snow met dry paper, the paper got ruined. What kind of condition would my father's AA diploma be in if it was sitting out, exposed to this godawful snowstorm?

After a while, I realized I'd been trekking steadily uphill, and I was getting seriously winded. The snow was getting deeper, maybe six inches, and my feet were wet and heavy to the point where every step was an effort. The slope wasn't steep, but even so, it felt like I was mountaineering, slogging my way up the side of something big and eternally arctic: an alp, maybe. Mt. McKinley. The Himalayas.

The summit leveled off. I'd reached a plateau. The snow, though far from stopping, lessened, thinned out. I took a breather and dared to look around.

I had arrived at a five-way intersection. Was it the same one that I'd been to before? Or was this one different? I had no way of knowing. What I was sure of was that on each of the other four branching paths, a figure stood at a distance, facing me, watching me. Thanks to the curtains of snow, none were close enough to make out easily, plus they were bundled up for winter, which only made them that much more anonymous. Even so, as I studied them, certain small markers gave them away, little oddities of stance and height and bulk.

To my left was my mother, and she was blowing on her hands—she didn't have gloves or mittens—trying to keep her fingers warm. When she saw me looking, she gave a little wave.

On the next path over stood my father. As I watched, he pulled a bottle from under his coat and tipped it up to his mouth. He took a long swig, then looked back at me, as if daring me to stop him.

More or less straight ahead, Celine waited. As soon as she was sure I was looking her way, she began, very deliberately, to unzip the front of her parka, and while the snow made it impossible to prove, I knew for a fact that she wasn't wearing anything underneath.

After wrenching my eyes away from Celine, I looked to the right. It took me a second to figure out who I was peering at. A guy, for sure, and pretty big. He had gloves, but he wasn't wearing a hat.

A fresh gust of flakes swirled around my face, and, as if on command, all four of the figures turned and began walking away. The wind picked up, and I looked down and put up a hand to hold the wind off of my face. By the time I looked up, it was snowing harder than ever, and each of the four figures was receding into the storm like phantoms, darkish blots in an otherwise white-on-white landscape.

Just to be sure, I checked behind me, and sure enough, the road that had brought me to this intersection had vanished, replaced by a cliff-like wall of rubber boots.

So. There it was, my four options. I was supposed to go after my father, but I wanted to follow my mother. The temptation of Celine nearly overwhelmed them both. But October had been right in her assessment of me. I was a rule-breaker, and because that was the rock-bottom truth, I ignored both my parents and closed my mind to Celine.

Only one choice remained. I turned to the right and followed myself.

Chapter Twenty-Three

UNLIKE ALL THE OTHER TRASH-LAND roads I'd traveled, this one didn't run straight. Oh, it did at first, just long enough for me to get comfortable, but then it bent slowly left, then back to the right, and after that, it was one rattlesnake bend after another, until I had no idea whatsoever of where I was in relation to October and the tunnel rock.

The one major comfort was that the snow let up, and then the sun came out, and pretty soon it was warm enough that the snow started melting. The tiny sounds of dripping water sounded from every direction, every mound of junk. All the pips and plinks, especially from the trash heaps that were mostly metal, were mesmerizing, musical, and for a moment, I paused, listening.

That's when I realized I'd lost sight of my other self, the one I'd been following. Ahead, the path looped to the left, and I hurried forward, jogging, thinking to catch up. It was no use. No matter how fast I went, there was no one ahead of me, no one left to follow. I was, again, on my own.

I stopped. I took a good look around. When I'd discovered my father filling up the pool, coming here had seemed like a solid plan, maybe the only plan. The man needed help, and I had the power to get that party started. Now? Now I was wondering how on earth I'd gotten myself into this. Only a couple of hours before, I'd been one hundred percent convinced that not only would I never set foot in this wasteland again, but I was going to take active steps to destroy the access point. Was it humanly possible to be any more inconsistent?

The sun blazed overhead, straight up as usual, and I could all but see the snow around me shrinking away, wilting in the sudden heat. I sighed and wiped a puff of snow from the seat of a nearby tricycle. The poor thing was missing a handlebar (it looked like it had been cut away with a hacksaw), but the seat was undamaged, so I plunked down, thinking I'd rest up while I checked over my options, none of which were attractive. One was, stay put, but I couldn't see why I'd just sit down and stop. Road-wise, I could go back the way I'd come, or I could go forward. Given how the junk piles seemed capable of rearranging themselves, I was pretty sure that it didn't matter which of those options I chose.

A third possibility, the rule-breaker's choice, was to go overland, to pick my way across the junk piles themselves in search of a high point, a place where I could scan the horizon for the jutting tunnel rock and hopefully find my way back.

That third option clearly had my name on it, but it also sounded exhausting. Why hadn't I thought to bring more food? Annoyed with my poor planning, I unslung my pack and rummaged for the granola bar, thinking I might as well eat what I had.

Once I'd finished off the granola, I let the foil wrapper drop from my fingers. Littering wasn't something I did a lot of, but in here, I really couldn't see the harm—except that as soon as I let that wrapper go, the breeze, which had mostly taken a break during the snowstorm, started up again and it took that foil on a joy ride, zigging it this way, then that, before dancing it around in a tight little cyclone of twists and turns.

It hit me then that all my original options were out the window. The foil was what I was supposed to follow next.

Sure enough, when I got up from the tricycle and took a few steps toward the foil, it skittered away, bouncing over the patchy snow and leading me into an open cove with dictionaries on one side and rust-stained porcelain toilet tanks on the other. I reached out to grab the wrapper, but every time I caught up a little, the foil rushed out of reach. It was like trying to coax a newly freed puppy back to its leash, but I kept at it, getting closer, closer, close enough to snatch at it but never quite pinning it down. At one point, just when I thought I had it backed against the dictionaries, it darted underneath me, through my legs.

Cursing, I spun around and charged after it, but I was brought up short by a massive crunching, pouring, rolling sound, and I stopped, stunned, as walls of trash and garbage rose up around me on all sides, each piece tumbling over the next until I was at the bottom of a pit, fully surrounded. The noise was appalling, ear-shattering, and still the walls kept rising: ten vertical feet, then twenty, up and up, and now it wasn't separated by type, it was one horrible mishmash, like a landfill, but without the dirt. Forks and radios and soup cans, barbed wire and boxing gloves, spare tires and alligator purses, Topps baseball cards, ceramic pastry dishes, Weebles, macramé plant hangers, shattered light bulbs, costume jewelry, ploughshares, medical charts, dolls from "The Sunshine Family," arrowheads—there was no end to the variety, and every last item had a little white paper tag, either tied on with string or attached with tape.

At last, the garbage stopped moving. At the same time, the breeze faltered, and the foil wrapper rolled over and lay still in a puddle of snow melt—not that I was paying it any attention, not anymore. I was much more concerned with all those white paper tags. I was pretty sure I knew what I'd find, but I had to check, so I headed toward a brass lamp that had gotten entangled with a pair of snowshoes and a jackelope (stuffed and mounted on a wooden placard), and when I got close enough, I held the tag between my thumb and forefinger and read, of course, my name. Same thing for the snowshoes, the jackelope, everything.

I stood back and turned in a slow circle, newly hesitant.

All this trash was mine.

A lifetime's worth, presumably. But was I looking at actual objects I'd meet in the future, or were these just possibilities? Choices I could make. Items I could reject, or cling to, make use of, or perhaps exchange in place of what I'd come for.

But I didn't want any of it, see, and if I was supposed to choose something, well, how was I supposed to narrow the field? What kind of criteria was I supposed to be working with?

I walked to the center of the pit again, and from there, I scanned the walls of junk as best I could, mostly in hopes that I'd spot the Alcoholics Anonymous diploma. If it was here, if I could get at it, I still thought that was what I'd take. Made sense, right? It was what I'd set out to capture in the first place. But I couldn't see it anywhere, and I didn't spot a telephone, either. I did pick out a pair of women's underwear, but I didn't get close enough to decide whether they belonged to Celine. I told myself that I didn't want to know.

It was a stand-off, I guess. Or at least, that's what it felt like. Me versus the cast-offs of my life so far, or perhaps the life that was coming up. No way to tell, and no one to ask.

I was supposed to choose something, that was clear. I was pretty sure that once I did, the trash would rearrange itself and let me out. Until then, I wasn't going anywhere. The walls were too steep to climb, and unstable besides. If I tried scrambling up, I'd bring down the house, and the last thing I wanted to do was get buried alive by junk.

So. Choices. If I wanted to get away, I'd have to pick something, and then, presumably, I'd have to live with the consequences.

But was that really what a rule-breaker would do? No, not in a million years.

And so, I did the one thing that took the whole notion of choice right off the table. It wasn't hard, either. In fact, it was simple.

I closed my eyes.

Then I spun in a slow circle, taking steady breaths to keep myself calm, and I kept on spinning until I had no idea whatsoever about which direction I was facing. That done, I stopped, faintly dizzy, and extended both arms in front of me, like a sleepwalker in a comic book, or maybe Frankenstein.

Eyes shut, I advanced carefully, fingers extended. My plan was to find, by feel, one of the little white tags, at which point I would choose the tag rather than the object it was attached to.

The first thing my fingers encountered was hard and planar, like a refrigerator door, so I worked away from that, past something that crinkled, and something else that felt like nasty old jelly, and then I worked my way to my left, touching, sensing, begging my fingers to do the work of my eyes until, having passed over an object that might have been a stuffed animal and another that I was pretty sure was the wire mesh from a screen door, I found, dangling from something above, a paper tag.

I pinched the tag, held it in my fingers, and drew a breath. What was it that I'd latched on to? A soccer ball, maybe. That would be great; it would be a sign that I was going to be welcomed back onto the team. Or what about a diploma, not for my father, but for me? A suggestion that I'd graduate after all, eventually. Even a G.E.D. prep book would have been welcome. Better yet, perhaps I'd stumbled on the keys to a car—preferably a '66 Mustang. A checkbook, that would have been perfect, or a credit card, something that might signal wealth, or even just plain old getting by. What about a fancy ring, a wedding ring, an omen that someday, I'd be lucky in love? I'd get married to a wonderful partner, and life, and from there, would be one long red carpet of happily ever after.

Was that even possible?

Hardly daring to hope, I opened my eyes.

The tag I held was attached by the usual twist of white string to an object I could only partly see, since it was buried in the pile, and it took some tugging to pull it out—and then, once I did wriggle it free, I strongly considered putting it back, because I wasn't honestly sure what I'd latched on to. It was some sort of metal decorative piece, with a finish like aged copper, and made in the shape of a cubicle house or hut, but hollow, with a pyramidal roof on top. One of the little house's four walls opened like a door and was held in place in with a little clasp. On the floor inside was a tiny spike, quite sharp, set in the center and aiming at the top of the roof. The walls and even the triangular pieces of the roof had been cut away in complicated floral patterns, leaving gaps, some of them wide enough to insert a finger. All in all, it felt sort of like an overgrown Christmas ornament, but I was pretty sure that wasn't quite right. The fact that I'd arrived at that comparison was just a function of the season.

"All right," I said to no one in particular, and, after double-checking the tag to make sure it bore my name, I got a better grip on the metal hut and turned around. I had made my selection.

With a resounding crash, the walls of junk around me tumbled backward. The noise was like twenty trash trucks all tipping up Dumpsters simultaneously, and I blinked and squinted and tried to shut it out, but not with much success. When the storm of falling objects finally ended, a new pathway had opened up, leading straight toward—in the near distance—the tunnel rock.

"Okay," I said, again to myself, and as soon as I realized I was speaking out loud, I put a sock in it, and fast. Back in the eighties, see, schools were still actively promoting the idea that people who talked to themselves were mentally unstable. It took at least another two decades for folks to come around to the idea that talking to oneself was perfectly normal (or at least not abnormal). Lately, I've even heard people claiming (maybe a little too loudly) that it can be a sign of creativity.

Off I went, walking at a fast clip toward the rock and October. I knew that I couldn't afford to take my good view and my straight course for granted. I figured October (or something) could change the deal pretty much any second, and the last thing I wanted was to push through another blizzard.

I won't say that for once, luck was with me, because I was learning not to trust to luck or, really, anything else, but I made it back to October's desk without incident. The snow was entirely gone, and even the leftover damp spots were evaporating at a crazy pace. October had donned her wraparound sunglasses, and all her extra layers were nowhere to be seen. The various newsprint and paperwork on her desktop looked dry as a bone.

"You," said October, once I was close enough, "are exactly what I said before."

"And that was?"

"A puzzle. Honestly, I don't understand you. You came here for something very specific, and now you've got…that." She pointed to the little coppery hut, which I'd been carrying with one finger looped through a metal ring attached to the tip of the roof. "I really don't understand."

Neither did I, but I wasn't about to admit it. Besides which, October had a point. I'd come here to save my dad, and instead, I'd hared off in some completely different direction, and wound up with an object that I supposed would have looked okay hanging in a garden, the kind my family didn't keep or know how to plant.

October drew a long, I'm-learning-to-be-patient breath and shook her head as if I'd let her down, personally. She said, "Bring it over here, so I can sign you out."

I handed her the little house, and she took off the tag, wrote something on her ledger, and put the tag in the top right desk drawer.

"There you go," she said. "Good luck."

"You, too," I said, out of habit, then immediately wished I'd kept my big mouth shut. Did October Roberta need luck? Or deserve it?

Ten minutes later, I was back in my car, with the little house sitting at a steep tilt on the passenger seat. Once I had the Olds started, I turned on the radio to Q-FM, my usually reliable rock station, and of course the first thing I heard was "Feed the World," the Bob Geldoff Christmas song that had taken the airwaves by storm starting at Thanksgiving. Ethiopia, I'd heard, was mired in a famine, and thousands were dying. Maybe more than thousands. Geldoff and his co-writer, some guy with the crazy name of Midge Ure, seemed to think that a pop song could help.

For a moment, I sat there listening. To me, "Feed the World" had always sounded more like a commercial than a radio-worthy song, but for once, I wasn't bothered. Instead, I found myself wondering if it would be possible to contact Bob Geldoff directly, and tell him about Vinyl Wonderland, the Elvis door.

"I can help," I'd tell him. "I've got a way to save Ethiopia."

Next to me, the little copper hut sat still and quiet, condemning my fantasy as nothing more than a hopeless joke. Save Ethiopia? Hell, I hadn't even been able to stay focused long enough to save my father, and as for Bob Geldoff, well. I didn't have the man's phone number.

It was late, past midnight, which meant it was now officially Christmas, and I drove home slowly, dreading what I'd find when I walked in the door.

Chapter Twenty-Four

MY FATHER SPENT CHRISTMAS DAY supervising the hose, but since it takes a garden hose a good long while to fill a swimming pool, he alternated between bouts of sleeping, binge cooking (he made brownies, a salad, and garlic bread), and, of course, drinking. He also made wild proclamations about how, in the New Year, everything was going to change. More than once, he broke down sobbing that this was the first Christmas he'd spent in twenty years without my mother.

As for me, I put the little coppery house on my bed-stand, and tried not to waste the day wondering what the damn thing was for, how it worked, or what it might alleviate.

In the evening, with the pool still a good ten inches below its fill line, my father and I exchanged gifts. I'd taken the time to wrap mine, using proper gift paper that I'd found in my mother's supply closet. My father, however, had placed my present in a paper sack from Benny's Liquor Mart, which I guess fit with the general chaos of dirty dishes, slumped piles of unsorted mail, rampant dust bunnies, crumpled laundry, and unmade beds. As for my father's attempts at being seasonal, all the lights on the Christmas tree were on one side, in a clumped-up mass, and they looked so off-kilter that we quickly agreed to switch them off.

"Sorry," said my dad.

"Don't sweat it," I said. "It's not like I did anything to help." Which was true. I hadn't draped a single strand of tinsel or hung so much as one ornament. Nearly every decoration we owned remained in boxes, and we'd piled these boxes loosely under the tree as a way of pretending we had more gifts than we actually did.

"You first," he said. "Open something."

Cousin Doris had sent along a Hickory Farms sampler box of pasteurized cheese balls, crackers, and hard sausage. My dad's cousin in Alaska provided an ashtray shaped and painted to look like a sockeye salmon. My one remaining grandparent, my father's dad, from Rhode Island, sent a reindeer card full of platitudes about how important it is to let go and move on. As a previous, less morose version of my father would have pointed out, these sentiments came from a man who'd lost his wife eighteen years ago and hadn't stopped talking about her since.

Only our two presents remained, and my dad insisted I open his first. Fair enough. I lifted the paper bag by its handles, brought it close, and reached inside. To my surprise, it was something I actually wanted, a Sony Walkman with Dolby noise reduction, a telescoping case, and auto reverse, all brand new in the box.

I should have been grateful. Instead, I felt a surge of anger. Sure, purchasing a holiday Walkman wasn't like buying a car, but even so, this wasn't something we could afford.

"I know," my father sighed. "Don't say it."

So, I didn't, and for a long moment, we sat there together, musing on how even a well-chosen gift can be oh-so-easily tainted. No two ways about it, every time I used that Walkman, I'd be thinking about the expense, and that thought would forever drown out whatever song was playing.

Was I about to admit this to my father? Hell, no.

"Hey," I said, as I gamely tore off the shrink-wrap, "did you get batteries?"

My father started to laugh.

"What?" I said. "What's so funny?"

"No!" he said. "I couldn't get batteries! I spent the last cash I had on the damn Walkman!"

That got me laughing, too. It was just too awful. There we were, snug and warm in a nice house on Christmas, and we didn't have the money for two triple-A batteries. Mrs. Felsen would have cited O. Henry.

"That's okay," I said. "Who needs batteries when we've got a swimming pool?"

That sent us both right over the edge, howling with laughter, rocking back and forth, cackling until our jaws hurt. It was hilarious and perfect and awful.

"Dad," I said, once we'd finally settled. "You need to open mine."

My dad picked up his present. It was boxy, an almost perfect cube, about seven inches on a side. The wrapping paper I'd found had a bright red background and lots of little dogs wearing Santa hats. It was charming and stupid, and my dad ripped into that paper with both hands, like my present was wild game, prey, and he couldn't wait to gnaw on the heart.

"Oh," he said, once he'd pulled enough of the gift wrap away to realize what was underneath. "Huh."

What I'd given him was a Magic Eight Ball. I'd picked it up at K-mart a few days back, after work. Getting the man what he really needed—a therapist—was totally beyond me (at least in the real world), and also a couple thousand miles outside our budget, but with a toy oracle, I figured he could ask in-the-moment questions and get quick answers. Magic Eight Balls, see, were seriously popular back then. The outside looked like an oversized eight ball from a pool table, but it was hollow inside and filled with inky liquid. Floating around in all that murk was a polyhedron die with messages printed on it. When you flipped the Magic Eight Ball upside down, you could look through a clear porthole on the base as one message at random floated to the top.

"Go on," I said. "Ask it a question."

My dad smiled, and said, "Do I say it out loud?"

I shrugged. "You can, if you want."

He gave the ball a shake, held it up, and addressed it. "O Magic Eight Ball, will the pool be filled by midnight?"

Then he flipped it over and waited for the message to appear. When it did, he read it out: "You may rely on it." This made him inordinately happy. "Oh, good!" he said. "I like that answer."

I encouraged him to ask it something else, and this time he wanted to know how we were going to afford groceries for next week, but this was open-ended, so the Magic Eight Ball's response of "As I see it, yes" didn't make a whole lot of sense.

"You gotta turn it into yes or no questions," I said.

"Fine. Magic Eight Ball, will we have money for groceries for next week?"

The Magic Eight Ball replied, "My sources say no."

Well, my father thought that was hilarious. Me, not so much.

"I wonder," said my dad, "what its sources are?"

"Probably Walter Mondale's campaign team."

My father ignored that crack and gave the eight ball a fresh shake. "Dear Magic Eight Ball, will I have money for drinks next week?"

The Magic Eight Ball replied, "Very doubtful."

My father considered this answer quietly for a moment, and then he reared back and hurled the Magic Eight Ball at the Christmas tree. It spun through the branches, smacked off the wall, and dropped to the floor with a broken crunch. I jumped up, ready to rescue the carpet from whatever the liquid was inside, but after I'd shimmied around behind the tree, I was amazed to find that while the ball's outer shell had cracked like an egg, the inner layer was intact.

"Stupid thing," muttered my dad, as he got up. "I'll be outside."

I wormed my way out from behind the tree's plastic needles and watched him go, picking up blankets and his hat as he went. Being outside that day had been no picnic; the last time I'd checked the thermometer, it was twenty-four degrees and falling.

"Hey," I said to the eight ball, as I gave it a back-and-forth shake that I hoped wouldn't break it. "Is this the worst Christmas ever?"

The porthole plastic had a jagged new crack running across it, so that it looked like winter ice on a solidly frozen pond, but the die inside floated up right on cue. It read, "Better not to tell you now."

Which was most definitely not the answer I was looking for.

I put the ball on the kitchen counter and followed my father outside, intending to make the offer of a lifetime. That's right: my goal in that moment was to offer my father the ultimate referral, and to turn him loose on the world beyond the Elvis door.

And why not? I hadn't been able to provide any serious help, whether from innate selfishness, or some lack of clear purpose, or maybe just a flat-out lack of funds. But maybe, if given a push or a shard of opportunity, my father could save himself.

In retrospect, that decision sounds pretty simple, the kind of choice that fits neatly inside a sentence. The truth is, I was feeling seriously disoriented, almost physically dizzy. In the past forty-eight hours, I'd gone from convincing myself to destroy the Vinyl Wonderland tunnel to venturing in myself, in search of some sort of cure, and now I stood ready to send my father into a world that had come fairly close to killing me at least twice. At best, it had left me with nothing to show for my efforts except a miniature metal hut with no apparent purpose. The whiplash was putting a serious crick in my neck.

So, there I was, crossing the back deck on a cold Christmas night and walking toward my father. The water at his feet was swirling slightly. Bits of debris were floating in circles, mostly leaves and twigs that my father hadn't bothered to net, and the water was cloudier than it ever was after a proper late-spring cleaning. It really didn't look inviting, but there was my dad, standing at the edge and lit from below by the soft blue glow of the pool lights. He was wearing so many layers that he'd pretty much doubled in size.

He didn't look up as I approached, but he knew perfectly well that I was there. He said, "Pathetic, I know. I'm so sorry, Brendan. You deserve better."

I said, "Come on, man. Remember what I said about staying back from the edge?"

He kept his eyes on the lapping water. "I want to get better, I do. I *need* to get better. It's just that right now, if you really push it to the wall, the only thing I want? The only thing I want is to go for a swim."

I watched him lift his left foot, and as he started to sway, I cried out a warning, but he knew what he was doing, or he thought he did, and having me yelling at him to get back wasn't going to help.

So, I raced toward him as he tipped, like a tall tree being timbered, straight into the water. The splash when he hit was tremendous, and thanks to the ten thousand layers he'd draped himself with, he sank like he was wearing lead weights. A stream of rowdy bubbles rose behind him, tracing his path to the bottom in wobbling silver.

Now, it's a stone-cold fact that I'd finished up my Red Cross swimming lessons way back in eighth grade, and I'd even done the capstone life-saving class, so I knew enough not to simply dive in. No, what I did instead was to kick off my shoes and shuck off my coat, and then I struggled out of my jeans in what I'd like to think was something like world-record speed. Then and only then, with the worst of my dead weight gone, did I step to the edge, draw in the biggest breath I could possibly hold, and dive like a rocket for the bottom.

It was a good thing my dad had switched on the pool lights. If I'd had to wrestle that ball of coats and blankets only by touch, my father would have drowned—and he very nearly did anyway, because I couldn't get a solid grip on him. Everything I grabbed came away in my hand, as if I were my pawing my way through thick, sodden layers of shedding snakeskin.

Well, I was working as fast as I could, trying not to panic, and trying, also, to keep my head away from my father's flailing arms—first rule, said my Red Cross instructor: never let whoever you're trying to save hit you in the head—and all the while I was keeping a running count, a mental clock of ten seconds, fifteen, twenty. If I got to thirty and we were still at the bottom, I knew we were in trouble.

But with twenty-five seconds gone, I finally got my arms under his, and I swept my feet around so that I was standing, and then I gave a mighty push and launched us both toward the sky. We surfaced, gasping, then sank again, but I adjusted my grip, kicked for all I was worth, and resurfaced a moment later in reach of the side wall.

"Swim, damn it!" I said, once I could speak. "Kick your damn legs!"

He didn't, although I do think he tried. That water wasn't actually icy—it hadn't had time to get there—but it was plenty cold, and I don't think he had much command over his muscles. As for me, I was rapidly losing what control I had, and since I couldn't get my father up and over the side, not in the deep end, I concentrated on towing us along the wall until we reached the shallows. Once I could touch bottom, things got easier. I pulled my dad along on his back, as if he was a barge and I was a tugboat, and when we got to the steps, I hauled him out and started dragging him toward the deck and the back door.

Now, it's true that the pool hadn't been ice-water frigid, but the air? Man, the air felt like it was mounting an active attack, biting its way into each and every pore. It was like it was begging me to just accept that I was a human icicle, born to freeze up and stop moving.

I even listened for a moment—my dad was so waterlogged, so heavy— but in the end, I kept going, and at last I made it inside, alternately towing and rolling my father behind me, and we collapsed in the mudroom.

I gave myself three seconds to lie there and feel sorry for myself, and then I forced my body into action all over again. I began stripping the rest of my clothes off, and as I did, I stumbled to the hallway Thermostat, and I jacked the temperature as high as it would go. In the bowels of the house, the furnace responded with a gratifying rumble, and I staggered back to the mudroom, naked except for my underwear, to get my father out of his wet things.

The details on that don't need to be written down. Let's just say that putting my mostly nude ice block of a father under a hot steaming shower is not an experience that I want to repeat. Ever.

Plus, he wouldn't talk to me afterward, not even after I dragged him into bed. Shame, I guess. Was he mortified because I'd had to step in and save him, or because he'd actually intended to drown himself, and he'd botched the job?

Either answer sounded pretty sickening in my book, and once I had him properly tucked in and lights out, I found dry clothes and went back outside to turn off the faucet. That done, I came in, heated up a frozen platter of "steak" and potatoes, and sat at the kitchen table to review my options. As bad as things were, I figured I had a few. After all, before the near-drowning, I'd been a heartbeat away from telling my father about the Elvis door.

Now, with a moment to myself, I went through my plan with a little more of what my Whetstone teachers would have called rigor, and this is what I came up with: the next day, after my father had enjoyed a major snooze, I'd load him into the car, and we'd drive to Vinyl Wonderland. I'd help him through the tunnel. I'd even introduce him to October Roberta. And then—because this was the only way this plan could possibly work out, or so I told myself—my father would venture forth like a knight from the days of

King Arthur, and he'd explore that trash-land waste until it gave up its last, best secrets, and then he'd march back in triumph, clutching his personal holy grail.

There were two flaws with this plan. First, it might not work. Second, for it to have any chance of working, I knew I'd need help. I'd need Celine DeLapp.

Chapter Twenty-Six

I SLEPT LATE THE NEXT morning, but I moved fast once I was awake. Step one was to pull the cover over the pool. Not foolproof, but I figured it would make my father think twice about a second swimming trip to Davy Jones' Locker. After that came breakfast, bacon and eggs, and a deep dive into the back of my closet, where I'd long ago hidden a whole sack of firecrackers, a stash I'd been saving to play who knows what awful prank. Now I had a more practical use for them, and the firecrackers came with me when I set off in the car.

My roundabout trip to work that morning involved picking up a whole series of supplies, including eight bags of "chemical" fertilizer from Frank's Nursery (which, on the day after Christmas, didn't open until noon), fifteen bags of pure white "sandbox sand" from the Linworth Lumber Company, and four full cans of gasoline from four different service stations.

Regarding the gasoline, it would have been five cans, not four, but at the fifth station, my dad's credit card finally gave up the ghost and stopped working. My stomach rumbled right on cue. I figured my income from Vinyl Wonderland could stave off actual starvation, but not with much left over, and once we got evicted, well. What then?

The car, sagging a bit on its rear axle from all that extra weight, complained every step of the way to Vinyl Wonderland, and loading all that crap into the back hall had me sagging and complaining, too. There's no getting around the fact that sandbags are heavy, and so are sacks of fertilizer.

That work done, I called home to see if my dad was awake, or at least willing to answer, but he didn't pick up, so I had to trust that at least for now, he was safe. I hung up and dialed Celine.

Wouldn't you know it, her husband answered, and because I was so focused on my rush of planning, I wasn't ready with my practiced fib about Celine's special order having finally come in. That's the way it is with wishful thinking; you think you'll get your wish, and then you don't.

So, I stumbled and hemmed and hawed, but eventually I convinced good old Stan DeLapp that this wasn't a crank call, and that Celine really did have a record to pick up at Vinyl Wonderland, and he grudgingly promised to relay the message. He did, too, because not one hour later, Celine walked in, boots and leather jacket on full display, and I knew without having to ask that she had plenty of clothes layered underneath, just the way any normal person would, especially in winter, or when they weren't in any way trying to be seductive.

"Don't ever," she began, "call me at home again."

I held up both hands in surrender and said, "I won't. Promise."

Celine, still looking seriously pissed, glanced around the shop; she looked even less happy when she discovered that we didn't have the place to ourselves. Two random customers were browsing through bins toward the back, so I went over to the stereo, where Otis Redding was gliding around and around on the turntable, and I raised the volume several notches higher. Celine came closer, and she leaned across the counter, whispering.

"I don't want to be here," she said. "You should know that. Every time I even drive by, it's a temptation."

Nodding, I said, "I get that. How's your sister?"

"Better. The prognosis is still ugly, but yeah, for now, she's on an upswing."

I was about to say something polite and appropriate about how that was great news, but Celine slapped a palm on the counter and interrupted. "Don't," she said. "Just tell me why you dragged me down here."

Relenting, I admitted that what I needed was a referral. For my father.

Celine made a face like I'd just told her that the grass and the sky had changed places. "You couldn't do that yourself?"

"I don't know for sure, but I'm thinking not. The rules for whoever runs the desk—'custodians'—it's different from everybody else. October's made that clear more than once."

"Okay, but why ask me?"

"I don't know how to reach most of the people I've let in. It was either you or the mayor."

Her eyes widened at that, which I appreciated. It meant I could really see the color, a cool, gemstone green.

She said, "The mayor comes in here? Accardi?"

"Don't tell, okay?"

She pretended to zip her lips shut, and then she tossed an imaginary key over her shoulder. "My lips? Sealed."

"So?" I asked. "Will you do it?"

Celine sighed and stared at the counter, where Karl had taped a little paper note reading, "Returns Must Be Accompanied by Receipt."

At last, she said, "I don't know what's going on with your dad. Never met the man. Obviously. But, speaking as the voice of experience, to go through that door and expect something good to come out of it, you've gotta be on your last throw of the dice."

After glancing at my other two customers to make sure they weren't eavesdropping, I told Celine the quick version of what had happened the night before, about how my father had tried to drown himself in the pool. That got both her attention and her sympathies, exactly as intended.

"Okay," she said. "Does this mean I have to meet him?"

I nodded. "Pretty sure, yeah. Maybe we could do it over the phone, but I'm not positive, so why chance it?"

"And you've never told him about this place? The Elvis door?"

"When he's sober, he remembers I work at a record shop, but he can't even keep the name straight. And no, I've never said word one about a magical garbage dump guarded by the King of Rock and Roll."

She smiled, which made my heart do a little flip, and left me with a definite case of goosebumps. The notion that something I'd said had put a smile on the face of Celine DeLapp was just too wonderful for words.

"When you put it like that," she said, "I guess it does sound pretty preposterous."

"Next up, dogs and cats living together. Mass hysteria."

That might have seemed like a random response, but the movie *Ghostbusters* had come out the previous summer, and quoting it had become a sport on the Whetstone soccer team. As a general rule, if Bill Murray said it, we thought it was hysterical.

Would Celine get the reference? Apparently yes. Her response was to ask me if I was the key-master, which, frankly, floored me.

"Please don't," I said.

"Don't what?"

"Don't flirt unless you mean it."

This was where she should have backed off, but Celine had a mischievous streak, and her smile only grew. "Brendan," she said. "You just asked me to meet your parents. I'm pretty sure I hear wedding bells."

Well, if there were a quicker way to knock my mood out of the sky, I don't know what it would have been. "Not my parents," I said. "Just my dad."

She did her best to roll with this new information. She apologized, allowed that divorce isn't any fun, and went on to inform me that her folks had split when she was twelve.

I could and should have been merciful. I didn't have to explain how far wrong she'd gone with her assumptions, but I wanted her to be smarter, quicker, faster on the draw, to live up to my fantasy of her as perfect, and so of course I had to punish her for getting it wrong.

"My mom's dead," I said, "and that's why my father's trying to off himself."

Timing is everything, and because life is life, I spit that out at the exact moment that the record tracked between two different Otis songs, with the result that the guys at the back of the store got an earful of my family history, and the one guy kept his cool and went right on thumbing through the albums, but the other man's head snapped up, and he looked around like somebody had hit him from behind with a snowball. Only as the next song started did he get back to assessing Rock, Letter B, featuring the Beatles, Boston, and Badfinger. He was in the right place, although I didn't know it at the time. If you want a rock 'n' roll take on death and suicide, Badfinger is a fine place to start.

As for Celine, she took a moment to compose herself, and then she said, "I'm sorry. I didn't know. When do you want me to meet your dad?"

Well, she had to work during my "lunch break" and for most of the day afterward, so we arranged to meet at seven, and I scribbled down my address on an old receipt.

"Remember," I said, "you don't have to convince him of anything. You just have to make the invite. I'll do the rest."

"Am I telling the whole truth, and nothing but the truth?"

"I was thinking we keep it general if we can. See where that gets us."

Celine turned her attention to the record bins. "Time for a recommendation," she said, "because if there's one thing I'm not doing, it's walking back into the house without my Vinyl Wonderland special order. Not after that chat you had with my husband."

"Okay. What do you like? What kind of music?"

"Loud and fast."

That sounded like a challenge, and on multiple levels, too, but that might have just been me, my brain set to "crush." Doing my best to keep my cool, I led Celine to the bin marked Rock – J. I flipped through the covers for a few moments, then withdrew Joe Jackson's *Look Sharp!*, an LP I'd only just discovered the week before.

"This," I said, as I handed it over. "The last song, especially."

Celine took the record as if it were the oldest news in the world. "'No such thing as tomorrow,'" she said, and I could tell right away that she was quoting. "'Only one, two, three, go.'"

Damn that girl. Woman. Whatever. She really was the coolest act in town.

"Don't panic," she said. "It's only four bucks, right? And my copy, it's pretty much worn out."

After she left, the other customers finished their shopping in quick succession. The second guy, as I finished ringing up his purchases, said, "So, you know that woman? The one in the leather jacket?"

"Sure," I said, smooth as silk. "Friend of mine."

"Lucky," he said. "She is drop-dead spectacular."

What could I do but agree? Which I did, and then I spent the rest of the afternoon trying not to be too smug about the fact that I was friends—sort of, maybe—with a woman like Celine.

Or, not *like* Celine. With Celine herself.

And in just a few hours, she'd be at my doorstep. She'd be at, and then in, my house.

Assuming my father didn't mess it all up, I figured there was an outside chance that my evening would be a dream come true.

Chapter Twenty-Seven

IN HIS WAY, MY FATHER messed things up plenty, but I'm confident that what ultimately happened wasn't really his fault. How could it have been? I was the one that set all the wheels in motion.

As it turned out, my father had spent his day hauling whatever he considered to be junk out to the curb, without even bothering to put it in a trash barrel. This included the Christmas tree, all our Christmas decorations, most of my mother's clothes, and (for the second time) his queen mattress and box spring.

"Haven't you ever heard of Boxing Day?" he said, once I'd tracked him to my mother's bedroom closet, where he was loading up an armload of her shoes. "On Boxing Day, you throw out your holiday boxes. And everything else."

It was tempting to get into a serious fight, but I decided I needed him to be in a good mood when Celine showed up (which I knew could happen at any minute), and if worst came to worst, I'd spend the middle of the night moving all the worthwhile stuff back inside.

At least it wasn't raining, or snowing. Given where life had been dragging me of late, these weren't blessings to be taken lightly.

Celine pulled up five minutes later, driving a VW Beetle the exact color of Grape Crush. Was I surprised that the cool girl came with an ultra-cool car? Not a bit. I wondered what her husband drove. Probably a hatchback Honda.

He'd be a Yuppie, the useless kind that wore his sport coat without a tie. If the temperature was anything less than seventy, he'd add a plaid wool scarf over top, and on the weekends, he'd play golf, but only to be seen. Whatever it was that he did for Celine, I was certain that he didn't do it well enough.

Celine started to park in the driveway, but thanks to the mess my father had made, she had to go curbside, instead. I met her at the door, and she indicated the growing junk pile in the drive. "Yard sale?" she asked.

I said, "I wish. We could use the money."

Her eyes flicked over the property, no doubt gauging how much it must have cost.

"I know," I said, "but looks can be deceiving. Come on in. Meet the man of the house."

We found my father on his knees, rummaging through the hall closet, the one where I'd found the Christmas wrapping a few days before. The closet was narrow but deep, and we (my mother, really) stored luggage in there, along with seasonal items like winter boots, plus an enormous quantity of scrap book and craft supplies. Every time I had cause to open that door, I caught a whiff of something that I could only describe as an elementary school art room, a tantalizing mix of Elmer's glue, construction paper, and unloved modeling clay—all of which, taken together, smelled exactly like my mother.

"Dad," I said, as I led Celine down the hall. "Someone here to see you."

My father pulled his head out from the depths of the closet and squinted at me. "Who?"

"Her name's Celine," and I made room so that Celine could peek around me and give a little wave.

My father sat back with his arms draped on his kneecaps. His hair was a tangle, and he was wearing a light blue button-down with the buttons done wrong, which left the shirt hanging lopsided on his body. Did I have to ask if he'd been drinking? No, I did not.

"Don't know any Celine," he said at last.

I rolled with his objection and said, "You do now. And she can help you."

"Help!" My father made no attempt to disguise his contempt. "If she wants to help, she can start by helping me haul all this stuff out of the house."

I really wasn't sure how I was going to direct this conversation or steer it toward an invite from Celine to tour the innards of Vinyl Wonderland, but in the end, I didn't have to. Celine took the wheel.

"Mr. Purcell," she said. "I'm not here to help directly. And I'm definitely not here to help with lifting and hauling, or cleaning house. But I know a place where you can find what you need, and Brendan's going to take you there, later today."

"Brendan," my father repeated, with acid disbelief, "is going to take me to a place where I can find what I need."

"Right. And once you're inside, once you get there, you tell them I sent you. Okay?"

My father chewed on this for a moment, then said, "Inside. Inside what?"

"You'll see. I promise."

"Maybe later. Got work to do." And, having said that, my father stuck his head back in the closet and started digging like a gopher, flinging random items that reminded him of my mother into the hall. A couple of shoes smacked off the opposite wall, followed by fuzzy deerskin slippers and an old wooden tennis racket.

At my shoulder, Celine whispered, "Is that it? All I have to do?"

That was it, so far as either of us knew, but I didn't want to admit it, because as soon as I did, I knew Celine would get away. So, I asked her if she wanted a sandwich, or maybe a drink. I wasn't a hundred percent certain that we had sandwich fixings, not anymore, but drink—alcohol—that was something I felt very confident that we had on offer.

"Brendan," she said, in that way that girls—women—have when they feel they need to let you down gently, but I brushed past her and led the way to the kitchen, because I wasn't ready to hear that kind of rejection, not with everything in my life swinging so perilously out of control.

"This way," I said. "Let's see what's cooking."

But Celine, she was wily. She kept her distance and hung back, and she planted herself in the hall instead of the kitchen, with the front door looming behind her like a bolt hole.

"Brendan," she said, again. "I have to go home. Have supper with my husband."

Spurned, I glared at her and asked what he'd cooked.

"Pot roast, with all the trimmings."

"Wow," I said. "You've got him on a nice short leash."

Celine brushed her bangs out of her eyes and tried to act as though what I'd said hadn't hurt, but it wasn't the kind of performance that wins Oscars. "We take turns," she said. "Tonight's his night."

"Great," I said. "Better go, then. No point in eating cold pot roast."

She actually stamped her foot in response. "You could make this easy."

I had one hand on the fridge door, intending to pull out mustard and mayo, assuming we had any, but when I hauled the door open, I reached for a beer, instead. "Go on, now," I said, without looking up from the dirty, crumb-lined, mostly empty refrigerator. "Run on home to the pot roast."

Giving up, she marched to the front door, opened it, and paused in the gap. "I did what you asked. Don't forget that."

When I finally pulled my head out of the refrigerator, she was gone, but I had to give her credit. Even when riled, and even when I'd behaved like a jerk, she had too much class to fall back on cheap theatrics like door-slamming.

In the meantime, I looked down at my left hand and was surprised to find that I really had gotten hold of a longneck beer bottle. What the hell, I thought. Why not? My first in months. I popped off the cap with the Coca-Cola opener that my dad, back when I was in diapers, had screwed to the wall, but as I raised the bottle to my lips, ears pricked to catch the hum of Celine's accelerating engine, it came to me that I was lying to myself, and that I'd been lying for quite some time. My first beer in months? Hardly—although it had pleased and flattered me to think so.

Maybe I hadn't been drinking as much, or as steadily, over the past week or so, but the notion that I'd stopped, or even made a serious effort to try? Total fiction. Once again, the story I told of myself, my life, was proving to be highly unreliable.

A sandwich really would have hit the spot, but we were out of bread, we didn't have lettuce or tomato, and the only deli meat remaining was pepperoni, which didn't count. On the plus side, I knew that pepperoni had a ton of preservatives, so unlike a lot of the other aging scraps lurking in the refrigerator, I was pretty sure it was safe to eat. With that in mind, I scooped up the whole bag (what was left of it) and headed down the hallway, nibbling as I went.

"Dad," I said. "Hey. We gotta go."

"Go?" said my father, who was still busy littering the floor with junk from the closet. "Where do we need to go?"

"Someplace special," I said, as I flipped another piece of pepperoni onto my tongue. "What Celine was talking about, the thing she invited you to. Come on. I'll drive."

He sat back and gave me a long once-over. "You sober?"

"Sober enough."

"All right, fine. We'll go. Father and son adventure."

I smiled, feeling expansive, pleased as punch that I wasn't going to have to wrestle him into the car. "Exactly," I said. "A father and son adventure."

The drive to Vinyl Wonderland was quick and easy, and my dad chatted all the way, gesturing at the world beyond the Cutlass as if he hadn't been outside of the house for years. After I parked in the back alley, he got out of the car and inspected the puddles as if they were deeply important. "So," he said, "this is where you work!"

"No," I said, from where I was unlocking the back door. "This is the alley behind where I work. Come on, it's cold out here."

His infatuation with the alley faded fast once we were inside the shop itself (and yes, this time, I switched on the lights, so he could see where we were). "Outstanding!" he said, and he did his best to let out a wolf whistle. "I had no idea. All this is yours?"

"Not exactly. I'm like the babysitter."

He nodded, profoundly impressed. "So many records, all in one place. Do you have any Burl Ives? That man's voice gets me every time."

Karl had a well-stocked section of forties and fifties crooners, so I fished out a Burl Ives disc and, as my dad wandered around, oohing and ahhing— which, frankly, was incredibly gratifying, even if it was the alcohol that was doing the talking—I fired up the amplifier and the turntable. When the first notes of "Lavender Blue" drifted out of the speakers, my dad looked up, enraptured. It was like he was seeing the Northern Lights, indoors, playing across the ceiling.

"Perfect," he said. "This was your mother's favorite."

If so, this was news to me. I couldn't honestly recall my mother having ever mentioned Burl Ives, much less listened to his music, but my dad looked so happy, standing there in the middle of the shop with his arms out, mock conducting, that I didn't have the heart to contradict him. Like a lot of other things, I guess nostalgia doesn't play by the rules.

While my father bobbed along to "Lavender Blue," I moved Elvis clear of the Elvis door, and I got the door unlocked. My father went right on leading his unseen orchestra, happy as a clam in a clam bed.

As the song wound down, I got on the phone and dialed October, who sounded sleepy when I picked up. "What?" she said. "It's late."

"Incoming," I said. "Sorry."

"Now?" I could imagine her checking her watch, although to the best of my knowledge, she didn't wear one. "Who is it?"

"Frank Purcell."

Her objection was immediate. "No, no, no. Not your job, kid. You don't get to send people in, especially family."

I grinned, pleased to have outsmarted the system. "Oh, I'm not sending him. Celine made the overtures. All I'm doing is opening the door—which is, as you like to tell me, my job."

On the turntable, "Lavender Blue" segued to the next track, and my father leaned against the bins of jazz albums and let out a tremendous, cathartic sigh.

"Brendan," said October, "you're up to something."

"Look," I said, "can't you for once just be helpful?"

I hung up before she could argue the point or talk me out of my plan, although in retrospect—hindsight being twenty-twenty and all—I pretty much constantly wish that she had.

"Ready?" I said to my father, and he drew himself up, tried to straighten his lopsided shirt, and gave me a faux military salute that I'm sure Jonesy would have said was sloppy to the point of being offensive.

"Ready!" he said. Then he paused, confused. "What am I ready for?"

Herding my father over to the Elvis door was no trick but getting him inside the tunnel took some doing. His reasons weren't clear cut, like Judy Treviso's, but he sure was skittish.

"In there?" he said. "I don't know, Brendan. It smells funny."

If there'd ever been a particular smell in the tunnel, it had never struck me before, much less bothered me. "It's nothing," I said. "Just walk in, easy-peasy. And when you get to the end, remember: tell them Celine sent you."

He took a few steps, then balked all over again. "You're not coming?"

"I'll be right behind you."

This was a bald-faced lie. I had long since concluded that it would be best if he tackled October and the scrap-yard solo, according to its rules. I figured that if I did go along, I'd knock something out of whack, wreck whatever good might come out of this.

"And where, exactly," asked my dad, "am I going?"

I told him that the "where" part didn't matter. "It'll help," I said, and I believed that, one hundred percent, because I needed to. Out of options, out of aces, October was all I had left to offer.

"Well," said my father, and he turned toward the tunnel and let his eyes adjust to the dim light. "I guess I don't have anything better to do."

And he walked inside. In short order, he reached the bend, turned the corner, and disappeared. His footsteps, scuffing a bit, echoed their way into the distance until at last, all I heard was their absence.

For once, I didn't close the Elvis door. I figured that since the shop wasn't open for business, who else could possibly go in? Besides, I had about five tons of supplies stashed in the back hallway, and given that I had no idea how long it would take for my father to find what he needed, I decided to make good use of the time.

So, once again, I got started hauling sandbags, and fertilizer, and heavy, sloshing cans of gasoline. At first, I just wanted to get it all out of the shop and into the tunnel, but then I got to thinking that there couldn't possibly be a better time to get it all stowed than when October was distracted by a visitor. So, bag by bag and can by can, I moved everything into the mine-shaft portion of the tunnel, and I began propping the fertilizer bags against the wooden braces and ceiling supports. That done, I separated the firecrackers into a couple of fat handfuls, like wrapped sticks of dynamite in miniature, and I went around taping these to the sides of the fertilizer bags. Making sure to leave at least some of each fuse line showing, I arranged the sandbags over the top of the fertilizer, then changed my mind and placed a can of gasoline on top of the fertilizer first, and then draped the sandbags over top of that.

Every so often, I checked down the tunnel to see if I'd attracted any attention, but even though I kept expecting October Roberta to poke her head in and say, "Brendan, what the hell do you think you're doing?" she never did. I'm pretty sure she had no idea I was there.

It was while I was hauling in the last of the sandbags that I caught a scent of something acrid and chemical, kind of like paint thinner. I was pretty sure the tunnel had never smelled like that before, so I paused, wrinkling my nose, and got a second whiff. Was this what my father had paused over? No, because this particular odor hadn't been in the tunnel when he passed through it. What I was smelling was gasoline.

After setting the last sandbag down, I went around and inspected the gas cans, one by one. Two were brand new plastic jugs, purchased from the service stations where I'd pumped the gas. The other two were my father's. They'd lived in our garage since before I was born, and they were much older, made of metal. They even had warnings on the lids about being careful not to strike sparks with the pump nozzle while filling up. One of these cans, I realized now, had corroded badly around its base, and the gasoline inside was slowly leaking out, slicking its way down the plastic sides of the fertilizer bags and staining the gravel underfoot with a liquid film of fuel.

Had it been doing this in the car? Surely not—I would have smelled it—which meant that this rupture was recent. Maybe I'd banged it on the tunnel walls, and the gas can's metal seams had given way? Whatever the case, the leak wasn't exactly a flood, so I thought that maybe I could plug it with something. Karl kept a toolbox, and I was pretty sure that I'd seen both duct tape and a caulking gun. Thanks to a summer job the year before, one that I'd spent working with a local handy-man contractor, I knew how to work with caulk, so off I went, headed for the supplies closet.

Unfortunately, I never got there.

As I stepped from the tunnel back into Vinyl Wonderland, I heard a knocking sound from the front of the shop, the fleshy clump of a fist thudding on thick glass. I looked up, and sure enough, there was a man pounding on the front window, clearly asking to be let in. I thought at first that it had to be Tony Accardi, because who else other than the mayor of the city would have the gall to demand entrance to a clearly shuttered business well after closing time? But it wasn't the mayor. It was the scruffy guy with the missing tooth.

My first impulse was to ignore him, but as soon as I turned away, bound for the toolbox, he started knocking even louder, to the point where I wasn't sure the old plate window would stand up to his fist. I started making traffic-cop gestures designed to tell him, "Sorry, we're closed!" but he didn't like that answer, not one bit, and he went right back to hammering on the window, with occasional pauses to jab a pointed finger toward the front door, which he clearly wanted me to open.

No way, I thought. Not in a million years.

"Get lost!" I yelled, and I headed for the storage closet, thinking that was the end of that.

Next thing I knew, there was a tremendous, glassy crash. It was so loud that I ducked. When I spun around, I saw the man with the missing tooth in the act of throwing Karl's second doorstop brick through the window, which of course brought down a fresh rain of shards.

"Ha!" the man cried, as if what he'd achieved was some major victory, and not the world's biggest clean-up catastrophe. "You should've opened up when I asked. You really shoulda opened up!"

He started kicking a few last sections of glass out from the base of the window, and was clearly all set to clamber in. I thought about marching over, picking him up, and shoving him right back out, but I wasn't anywhere near drunk enough to be quite that stupid. I'd cut myself on broken glass before, and tackling a guy surrounded by that many jagged shards was clearly a suicidal choice. So, I stood my ground and waited for him to come to me.

"Roger sent me here," the man said, as he stepped over the sill and crunched a foot onto Vinyl Wonderland's glass-covered floorboards. "Roger!" he crowed, as if that name were a suit of armor, the most important fact going. "Roger sent me because I need an advance, another loan, and I need it *now*."

I said, "Mister, we're closed, and if you don't turn yourself around, I'm about two seconds from calling the police." This seemed like an even better plan than attacking the guy, and I was already edging toward the phone. Sure, I could deal with this idiot all on my own, but for once, I was inclined to do things by the book.

The man with the missing tooth reached into the folds of his coat, and for a second, I was sure he was going to pull a gun or a knife, but all he withdrew was a pack of smokes. He grinned as I started to protest, and he fumbled a cigarette into his mouth.

"Yeah, yeah," he said. "You and your 'No Smoking' policy."

Having reached the phone, I made a show of lifting the receiver. "You see what I'm doing, right? I'm calling the cops."

He swayed on his feet, the same way I did when I'd had a few too many, and I realized that talking to this guy wasn't going to get me anywhere. He was sloshed, totally hammered, and there wasn't a threat in the world that was going to hold him back.

"Call away," he said. "Maybe those peckerwoods'll do something about all this glass."

Disgusted, I spun the phone around so I could reach the dial, and then I got busy with the nine in 9-1-1. In the moment, that felt like the absolute right move, but what I probably should have been doing was paying more attention to my visitor, because the next thing I knew, he'd made a wobbly beeline for the Elvis door.

"Later!" he called. "Have fun with the clean-up!"

I could have caught up and intercepted him. It wouldn't have been hard, and it wasn't like the guy with the missing tooth was sprinting. The thing of it was, I'd started dialing, and it felt like I should finish, because that's how 9-1-1 works, right? You start the call, you make the call.

My witless hesitation gave the man the time to reach the door and disappear through it, and I decided that I really couldn't allow that. So, just as the phone connected, I dropped the receiver and gave chase. In the background, I could hear a tinny voice on the phone saying, "Hello? What is the nature of your emergency?"

Which frankly would have been very difficult to explain.

I got to the door just as the man with the missing tooth reached the first bend in the tunnel. For a second, he turned back to look at me, and as he did, he smiled, pulled out a lighter, and lit up his cigarette.

"Thanks," he said. "See you 'round."

"No!" I shouted, as my eyes went wide. "Put that out!"

Too late. I'd made one too many wrong decisions that night, and now there was nothing to stop the man with the missing tooth from disappearing around the corner, which he promptly did.

In his wake, my nose caught the distinct, unmistakable smell of evaporating gasoline.

And that meant there was only one choice left.

Instead of charging inside to catch the man with the missing tooth, I did the opposite. I slammed the Elvis door as fast as I could, locked it, put my back to it, and, legs braced, squeezed my eyes shut.

I know: trying to brace the door was monumentally stupid. But, in the interest of telling the truth, I'm here to report that that's what I did, and all of one second later, I felt more than heard a terrific *whump* of an explosion, followed by a second concussion, much louder and deeper than the first. The door at my back punched like a fist and sent me sprawling, but it didn't break or burst into flame. Amazingly, it held, and as I crashed bodily into the record bins, Elvis and I heard the sounds of falling rock and tumbling stone as the tunnel gave way and collapsed.

Long after the final pebbles fell, long after the last of the dust settled, I lay there, frozen in place and sprawled in a kind of crocodile position, like I was halfway doing a pushup. Only after there'd been total silence for a full minute did I very gingerly get to my feet. Outside, the usual High Street traffic flowed past, a car here, a car there. None of the drivers seemed to have noticed that Vinyl Wonderland's front window had gone the way of the dinosaurs, and if anyone cared that the lights were on, they certainly weren't slowing down to comment. Those were busy people out there, with lives in no way related to mine, and I guess they had more important places to be.

The phone rang, sharp and sudden, which was nuts, because the handset was off the hook, dangling over the edge of the counter from when I'd abandoned my 9-1-1 call, but the sound served a good purpose: it woke me up. The full extent of what had just happened finally hit home. The man with the missing tooth had brought the roof down on the tunnel, the one that led to October's scrapyard, which meant that my father was now trapped on the far side.

I grabbed for my keys, unlocked the Elvis door, and flung it open, only to be met with a billow of gray dust and a wall of broken, fractured rock packed so densely that a mouse couldn't have gotten through.

The phone rang again, insistent and demanding, and I staggered away from the cave-in that only minutes ago had been a useful, open, between-the-worlds portal, and I made my way through the silent, pleasantly lit shop to the counter. I took a breath and picked up the still-ringing telephone.

"Hello?" I said.

I guess I was expecting that this would be 9-1-1, calling me back. That they'd traced the call and wanted to know if I was all right. But it wasn't the emergency response team. It was October, and she said precisely two words: "Thank you."

The line went dead. There wasn't even a dial tone. It was more like wind in a desert, constant and lonely, the kind that never once gets to where it's going, and I had to assume that somewhere in October's trash-filled wasteland, that wind was whistling past my father, and he was wandering, searching, maybe even enjoying his adventure, unaware for the moment, for now, that his one road home was gone.

Chapter Twenty-Eight

THIS MIGHT BE A GOOD moment to take a long time out and admit that I've been telling a barrel full of lies, especially about my sobriety over the back half of my Vinyl Wonderland adventures. Remember when I said I poured out all of my dad's liquor stash? Well, that was true enough, but once he re-stocked, I didn't have the spine—what my English teachers might have called "fortitude"—to stay on the wagon. So, while it's true that I was very skilled at skimming, at never plunging too far into my cups, it would be untrue, in a major way, to suggest that I got myself through Christmas week sober.

I didn't.

I wasn't.

It's also true that there were a number of times that I shouldn't have been driving, and I did it anyway. On that score, I let Jonesy down, not to mention myself. There's no excuse. I don't expect you to forgive me.

I do think it's possible that I fooled a few people along the way, but certainly not my father, and probably not Celine or Tony Accardi. I do hope that I didn't come off as drunk in front of the mayor's kids, but I'm sure I'll never know. What those three saw, what they perceived, well, it's anybody's guess.

It's also true that I drank more, not less, in the hours and days immediately after I lost my father—and please don't think that I'm using that term "lost" out of some kind of loyalty to basic Midwestern politeness. A lot of people I know, when loved ones die, they like to say that that person has "passed on," or "passed away," or "gone to a better place." They've "lost" their spouse, or maybe their brother or their favorite golden retriever. Don't get me wrong. People have a right to describe death and loss in any way that they wish. To each their own, right? But my father didn't die or pass away, at least not then, not so far as I know. My father got lost. For real. And I'm the one that lost him.

A few details that I'm pretty sure are true: on the night of the tunnel collapse, I had a third of a bottle of very cheap, off-brand whiskey stowed below the turntable, so after trying to dig my way in—first by hand, then with Karl's rusty old snow shovel—and getting absolutely nowhere, I fetched that bottle and I put on some music and I sat down in a corner with the bottle in my lap, and I waited for the police to arrive.

They never did. Apparently, the operators at 9-1-1 weren't big on tracing calls, or maybe October's final words had effectively cut them off. Or maybe they'd simply hung up and moved on, fingers crossed, hoping for the best. As for the idea that the police might respond to the lights being on all night, well, the cobbler next door managed to make that mistake about once a week, and there were other hole-in-the-wall shops all through the neighborhood that left their lights on intentionally to ward off burglars, so I guess that from the outside looking in, having Vinyl Wonderland lit up by night wasn't in any way remarkable.

Now, if there'd been a beat cop on foot, I'm sure he would have noticed the shattered window, and from there, they'd have found me, and maybe had questions about all that fallen rock behind the wide-open Elvis door, but there wasn't a neighborhood beat cop making the rounds, so none of that happened.

Instead, the night dragged on, and I drank and fell asleep and woke a few times, and eventually I got up and wandered over to the Elvis door, which I closed and locked, more out of habit than anything else. I thought about starting the search for another door—a door to the place where I'd lost my father—but I had no idea where to begin.

Next, I thought about driving home, but I was pretty far gone, and I didn't want Jonesy to read in the newspaper that I'd caused an accident and maybe sent some stranger to the hospital, so I stayed off the roads. I did go out to the car, though, and I slept the rest of the night bundled up in my coat and sprawled across the Cutlass's back seat, fighting to find a position where the seat belt buckles weren't digging a trench through my hip bone. It was a losing battle, but that felt appropriate. Hadn't everything, that day, been a losing battle?

At my size, sleeping in the back seat of any car makes for an early wake-up call, and besides, it was freezing cold, so I was up before six, shivering, and I made my way back into Vinyl Wonderland, which was just as cold as the outside world, thanks to the wrecked front window. My initial goals were to clean up, get oriented, and find some coffee. After that, I intended to ring Mayor Accardi's bell one more time and insist that he bring whatever excavation crew the city had to offer, so we could dig our way through the tunnel and rescue my father.

That didn't happen, and the reason it didn't is that overnight, the Elvis door had vanished. In its place were bricks, the same kind that made up the rest of Vinyl Wonderland's perfectly ordinary back wall.

I remember walking over to where the door had been and putting my hands flat on the wall and pressing them into the rough, gritty brickwork to see if they'd give way. They didn't, not even a little, and when I searched for a join, some kind of seam, there was nothing. It was for all the world as if this wall had always been exactly this way: unremarkable, fixed, solid.

What exactly happened next, and the order in which it all took place, has gotten increasingly jumbled down the years. I know I went for coffee, and I know that eventually, I called the police to report a break-in, and somewhere in there, I admitted to the responding officers that I thought my father might be missing, too, and that led to full-scale search of my house, and from there, I think it's fair to say that my life spun totally out of control.

One thing for sure, a lot of people I'd never heard of wormed their way into my orbit. Police, health inspectors, social workers—a lot of social workers. The amount of energy all these people used in trying to figure out what to do with me could have powered a good-sized generator for a year. They asked *so* many questions. I answered the ones I could, and I lied whenever there wasn't any point to telling the truth. Mostly, I lied about my dad, his whereabouts. Everybody wanted to know where he'd gone, and did I have any ideas? I said no, and I said that over and over and over again, until even I halfway believed it. He'd wandered off. How was I supposed to know where?

I do have a clear memory of being attacked by Tony Accardi. That was interesting, and it's a matter of historical record. It was caught on camera, so it made the papers, and believe me, I'm not using the word "attacked" lightly.

What happened was this: I was at Vinyl Wonderland, supervising (uselessly) the installation of several plywood sheets over the broken front window, and it must have been the afternoon of the day after the tunnel explosion, and I'd just finished another round of questioning from the police, who clearly thought I was guilty of something (up to and including killing my father), when in walked the mayor. He made straight for the Elvis door, which was now the Elvis wall, and he stared at it, hard, and then he whipped around to face me.

"What did you do?" he demanded. "What in God's name did you do?"

His voice was shrill, out of control, and I knew he wasn't worried about votes or budgets, not this time. No, the only thing he had on his mind now was Michael.

It's important to understand that when the mayor charged in, Vinyl Wonderland wasn't empty. Not even close. The two police officers, plain-clothes, hadn't left yet, plus there were workmen dealing with the window, and one of them was inside, fussing with a stepladder. On top of that, the State Farm agent from next door had stopped by in the interests of "professional curiosity," and as if that wasn't enough, both the *Dispatch* and the *Lantern* had sent junior reporters to sniff around and see if they could rustle up a human-interest story for their respective papers. One of them, the kid from the *Lantern*, not much older than me, had his camera out when Mayor Accardi bull-rushed me, screaming bloody murder and doing his best to beat me senseless.

I'm ashamed to say that even though I was a head taller and a whole lot stronger, I lost that fight big-time. Why? Well, for starters, I didn't fight back. I just didn't have it in me, not that day. I felt wrung-out, limp, like I was coming out of a three-day fever, and I was just now at the soda-crackers-and-ginger-ale phase. Plus, I understood the man's fury. Let's face it, I'd done exactly what I'd threatened to do—not in the right order, not at the right moment—and as a result, I'd condemned his only son to die young.

Sure, I understand that in theory, it wasn't that clean-cut. It's possible that no matter what the mayor did, and no matter what he eventually selected from October's trash, Michael's muscular dystrophy would have stolen him anyway—and on top of that, it's not as if the fact of Michael's illness was in any way my fault. But, for better or for worse, I've never cut myself that kind of slack. I knew what I was doing when I purchased my bomb-making supplies. I knew it, and I went ahead anyway.

On paper, my actions were a simple case of how the needs of the many outweighed the needs of the one, a concept I'd cribbed from *Star Trek II* a couple of summers before. And in my situation, the logic of that scenario made perfect sense. Closing the Elvis door was an action that Mrs. Felsen, back in English class, would have identified as a clear moral imperative. That said, I could understand why Tony Accardi felt it wasn't my call to make, and because he felt that way so strongly, he tried to batter my head through the floor. I definitely came away with some serious bruises, and as anyone who's ever been beaten up knows, head wounds bleed. A lot.

Anyway, the police pulled the mayor off of me, and the *Lantern* photographer caught it all on film, and then there were more questions, beginning with how on earth did I know the mayor, and how did he know me? Suffice it to say that none of these questions were ever answered to anyone's satisfaction. It's also true that in my mind's eye, I can still see Tony Accardi's agonized, bereft expression as he knocked me over, then pinned me from above and raised his fist to drive it as hard as he could into my jaw.

At some point later that day, I must have made it home. I feel pretty clear on this point, because I hadn't cried, not yet, and I was really starting to think that I might never cry again—that I'd grown up overnight, and despite all evidence to the contrary, I still harbored the ridiculous notion that adults had no use for tears—but then I spotted my father's curbside trash-pile, and all the taps let loose. All that stuff, see, most of it my mother's, plus the mattresses and the Christmas tree, with a corn-yellow sundress stretched on top, and the whole mess of it just left for dead on the shoulder of our perfectly well-to-do road. It reminded me of October's wasteland in miniature, and I thought of my father, wandering those radiating paths and looking for salvation, or maybe an exit, until he just plain ran out of energy, and that was it: I was a human waterworks for the next hour at least.

But, for an adult to officially go missing requires at least twenty-four hours, so that first day, I'm pretty sure that when the authorities went through my house, they didn't actually turn it upside down. Did I stay there on my own the night after the explosion? I suppose I did, only because I can't think where else I would have gone, and I'm sure I only spent one night in the Oldsmobile. (One was enough.) Also, I'm pretty sure that I remember waking up that next morning with my face stuck to the pillowcase, thanks to the oozing blood from the cuts and bruises left behind, like bad get-well cards, from Tony Accardi's fists.

Over the next few days, my house became ground zero for a whole slew of detectives, none of whom looked at me as anything but a suspect. I didn't blame them, and I spent a fair amount of time fantasizing about offering up a come-to-Jesus confession, laying it all out the way I've tried to do here, just to see what they'd make of it.

With no better theory to fall back on, the more charitable detectives were inclined to label my father's absence a "probable suicide," and they made me go over the details of my pool rescue so many times that it started to feel like something I'd invented rather than a specific event that I'd personally survived. The lawmen were especially interested in the various articles of clothing still floating in the pool, and my explanation that I'd simply forgotten to go and fish them out didn't impress. Mostly, I had social workers present for these in-house interrogations, but not always. Sometimes, see, the police decided it was question-and-answer time in the middle of the night, or two minutes after any given social worker had just left.

To be fair, these weren't Hollywood cops, the corrupt kind who happen to be wearing a badge and maybe brass knuckles. These officers were conscientious, hard-working, and genuinely mystified by the crash-and-burn arc of both my life and my father's.

"Sheet metal?" said one, after getting confirmation from the Guernsey County coroner about what had happened to my mother. He scratched at the back of his buzz-cut scalp. "Jeez, kid. I'm sorry."

Whetstone High got in on the act, of course. They made it clear that I hadn't dropped out, and I have to say, I kind of appreciated the clarification. The truth was that I'd been suspended, then kicked out for good, first for starting fights in general, but most specifically for assaulting my assistant soccer coach, an ex-Army guy who deflected the blows I tried to land, then twisted me into a human pretzel and sat on me until he had enough help, including from Alan Geryk and Derek Glasscock, to keep me immobilized. When the police asked the soccer assistant why I'd gone haywire like that, the guy said, and I quote, "How should I know? Some kids are bad apples."

By the time the cops quizzed me about "the soccer incident," I'd internalized that answer, made it my own. When asked why I'd gone after my coach, I explained that that was what bad apples do. "They snap," I said. "They hurt people."

"Brendan," said the investigator who happened to be on point that day, "you do realize that your coaches didn't know anything about your mom."

I told the cop that that was ridiculous. The whole school knew. But, as it turned out, that wasn't true, either. According to the school's front office staff and the various forms they kept on file, my father had never officially informed anyone of my mother's death, and neither had I. I guess we'd both assumed that the news of her death had made the rounds, but my mother wasn't a celebrity, and her friends, with the major exception of the Glasscocks, hadn't been connected to Whetstone High. It turns out that gossip and rumors are like echoes; they only travel just so far.

That left Whetstone in a bind, because they were a public school, and now my expulsion came gift-wrapped with "mitigating circumstances." As one of the social workers put it, "Brendan, the school would be happy to have you back—or maybe not happy, but at least willing, and this time, there'd be a counselor for you to talk to. Before, they truly didn't understand what they were dealing with. Or what you were dealing with."

There were a lot of moments like that, attempts at sincerity. Some of them, I even believed.

Three days passed, maybe more, and the bruises on my face turned purple and the twin questions of what do with me and what to do with Vinyl Wonderland still hadn't been settled. Karl Wickett had been verified as Vinyl Wonderland's owner, but his speech was so sluggish, still, that he was barely able to communicate. Nor could he write anything down. At one point, I visited Karl, flanked by a police officer (presumably to make sure I didn't cause bad-apple problems for the patients or staff). The same social worker who'd explained about Whetstone also made the trip, and her prognosis for Karl wasn't optimistic. "Knitting," she said, in disbelief, as we left. "He can barely find his thumbs."

A different social worker (there must have been five, and two of them looked almost exactly the same) spent her energies trying to "grease the rails of society," with the goal of making sure I could get a decent job, if need be. "In case," she explained, delicately clarifying, "in case school ultimately isn't a good fit." For her, that meant collecting references, but Whetstone (surprise) wasn't any help on that front, and at Vinyl Wonderland, I'd been a solo act, with no one available to tell the world what a faultless worker I'd been. Probably Karl would have written a recommendation, but writing, for him, was a thing of the past—or perhaps the very distant future.

That left Big Bear, but the management there was very clear. I'd been fired after showing up to work both late and inebriated for the better part of one week straight. According to them, I'd threatened two of my fellow stock-room employees with physical harm if they didn't buy me beer, so the last thing in the world I was going to get out of Big Bear was a good reference. I suggested the social worker try to contact Lani Bell, but she'd moved out of state, no one quite knew where. I was relieved, not to discover she was gone, but to find out from an unbiased third party that she really existed. I'd begun to worry that Lani (not to mention sex with Lani) was just one more thing I'd made up.

Eventually, somebody made some sort of decision, and that involved removing me from the house I'd grown up in and installing me, instead, with Doris and Fitch Arnold in Guernsey County. I would live with them (unless by some miracle my father turned up), and I would attend the local high school. After three years, more or less, as a Whetstone Brave, the plan was that I would graduate high school as a Meadowbrook Colt.

I didn't fight it. Whatever reserves I had left, they weren't up for that particular battle. Besides, what better plan did I have? I'd gotten to know myself well enough, over the past several months, to be very clear on the fact that I had no wish to live alone.

The keys to Vinyl Wonderland went back to Karl's mother, but not before I'd let myself in to the shop one last time, where I helped myself to a milk crate's worth of records, the basics of what I believed then to be essential listening. I didn't think of this as stealing, and really, it wasn't, because I left my back pay behind, figuring Karl and his mother would need it more than I would. As for the albums, I have long since forgotten most of my choices, but I most definitely took Spirit's *Twelve Dreams of Dr. Sardonicus.* It was time, at last, to wake up.

As for Elvis, I left him where he stood, even though I briefly entertained a corny idea that he might liven up my Guernsey County bedroom. I'm sure that eventually, Elvis left the building, but he didn't do it with me.

From home, I took more than I thought I would. Surrendering to a new life with nothing but the clothes on my back felt heroic in the abstract, but in practice, it made zero sense. So, when Doris and Fitch came to pick me up (an event that involved signing a lot of papers), I loaded up pretty much everything that would fit in their pickup, which was a considerable amount, because Fitch had a camper shell on top, and it's amazing how much space there is in one of those if you really push and shove.

The most important item of all traveled in the center of a suitcase filled with soft clothes, and that was the little copper hut. I had considered leaving it as a way of closing the book on Vinyl Wonderland, but I still didn't know what exactly the hut was, or how I was supposed to put it to use. The idea of leaving that mystery unsolved when so much of my life had been cracked wide open, well, that just wasn't an option.

Later, once we got to Guensey County, and after Doris showed me the very plain upstairs bedroom I'd be sleeping in, that copper hut was the first thing I unpacked, and I set it on the top of a tall bureau that stood opposite my bed, as if it were a beacon, a lighthouse.

I also unpacked my Christmas-gift Walkman, and I set it carefully on the bedside table, on top of the two books Doris had left out for me. Thoughtful choices, I guess, but nothing I wanted to actually read. One was a yellowed hardback copy of *When Bad Things Happen to Good People,* and the other was a picture book, *The Fall of Freddy the Leaf.*

Doris was five years older than my mother, and Fitch was at least a decade older than Doris. He wore his gray hair in a greased pompadour, and for dinner, he'd dress up by adding a shoestring tie to his checked work shirt. At least once a week, he'd take Doris out dancing, and on those nights, he had a spring in his step and a sparkle in his eye, but the rest of the time, he was a hard-bitten, hard-working farmer, a man of few words. I think it must have cost him a great deal to say as much as he did, that first night that I joined them at their dinner table, but I'll give him full credit. He made every word count.

The meal began with passing around Doris's heaping platters of mashed potatoes, salted lima beans, and meatloaf, and I was so lost in myself that it was all I could do to say please and thank you. I had my fork halfway to my mouth when Fitch cleared his throat, closed his eyes, and upturned his palms.

"For food that stays our hunger,
For rest that gives us ease,
For memories that linger,
Lord, we give our thanks for these."

Fitch opened his eyes, spread out his cloth napkin, and gave me a patient frown. "Go ahead, son. Eat up."

Halfway through his meatloaf, after Doris had explained where to find useful things like towels and soap and can openers, Fitch said, "Here's the thing. We thought we were done raising kids."

This made sense. Even the youngest of the Arnold's three children, Delaney, had been out of the house for years. She was married, getting ready to start a family one county over, on a farm of her own.

"Because of that," Fitch went on, "you're coming into a home where we have certain routines. Habits. We do things in a certain way, and in a certain order. I recognize that this might not be the easiest household for a young man of your age to join. You'll have to bend to fit, and I suppose we'll have to bend a certain amount for you."

To my surprise, he was having trouble speaking. Before he could continue, he had to reach a hand across the table to Doris, and she put down her cutlery and placed her hand over his.

Fitch focused his gaze on the cooling dish of lima beans and said, "This is a working farm, and on a farm, you earn your keep. You'll have chores on top of schoolwork, but I promise never to give you a job without teaching you how to do it. Also, we go to church when we can, and when we do, you come, too. Beyond that…"

He paused and looked out the window. Doris gave his hand a squeeze and said, "Our older two children don't speak to us anymore. We did better by Delaney, and we'd like to do better by you. So, yes, we have some expectations, but you get to have the same. We'd like to hear what you need from us."

This was so entirely unexpected that for a minute, I was just as tongue-tied as Fitch. When had my father last asked me, in a serious way, what I wanted, much less what I needed?

Testing the waters, I said, "Well, maybe this is putting the cart before the horse, because I don't even know if you'll let me use a car, but I've been told that I'm kind of a rule-breaker, and it's been a long time since I've had a curfew, and I think, if that's okay, I'd like to continue not having one."

Doris and Fitch shared a look, and Fitch, looking infinitely tired, nodded. He said, "I don't know what I'd say if you were a girl, but seeing as you aren't, all right. Deal. What else?"

I went for broke and said, "I want to know that it's okay to have my turntable in my room. I won't wake anyone up, and I've got headphones for late at night, but I want to know it's okay to listen to what I want."

Again, Fitch nodded in that incredibly deliberate way he had. "Anything else?"

"I think, if it's all right—because I've never seen—I don't know even exactly where it happened—I'd like to see the place my mother died. And I think I'd like to do that right now."

Fitch hesitated. He said, "Brendan, we treat mealtimes as sacred. Once we sit down to break our bread…"

"But in this case," said Doris, as she scooted back her chair. "Come on. I should have offered right out of the gate."

We all three went outside, through the kitchen door and down three concrete steps, white-painted. The sun was down, and I couldn't see much, but Doris switched on an outside floodlight, and the darkness retreated enough that I had a good view of the lawn, two sets of clotheslines, and a midwinter flower bed blossoming with clods of dirt.

"It's here," said Doris, and she led the way to a non-descript spot just past the first laundry line.

I walked over. I stood on the spot where Doris pointed. There wasn't anything to see. No outline, no imprint, no bloodstains. It was just grass.

Well, maybe it was just grass, but I knelt down, and I curled my hands and fingers into the roots, and I let the cold from the muddy, half-frozen earth seep into my fingertips. I stayed very still and very quiet and I think I imagined that I was listening for a sound I could almost but not quite hear. I know this: I stayed there for a long time.

None of us had brought coats, and there was a mean west wind, so we were all three shivering by the time I finally stood up. I looked first at Doris, then at Fitch. I said, "I want to be able to come out here any time I want, and if I sit here for an hour, or five hours, I need you to not worry about me. Okay? Can you do that?"

Doris was hugging herself pretty hard, and she wasn't really up for talking, but Fitch gave a single nod and said, "Absolutely."

"One last thing," I said, and I know to this day that if I hadn't been standing right where I was, the rest wouldn't have come out—maybe ever, which would have been a tragedy, for me at least and probably for a whole lot of other folks, too. Call it luck or call it fate, it doesn't matter a hill of beans to me. What matters is that those two near-strangers, Doris and Fitch, got to hear what I'd never been able to say to anyone else, myself included.

Of course, even on a good day, courage takes its sweet time, and as I paused and wrestled with my tongue, Fitch stepped in to prompt me. "Say your peace, son. Go on."

I looked that man in the eye, and I said what needed saying most: "I'm an alcoholic. If I'm moving in here, are you sure you're ready to help with that?"

Chapter Twenty-Nine

IT'S A SAD FACT THAT I never saw Jonesy Davis again. Whatever finally killed him, whether it was liver failure or a bike accident or who knows what, I hope it was quick, and not too painful. That man, in his addled, bleary-eyed way, was the best.

Most people wouldn't get that. To most folks, Jonesy was dismissible. Maybe even despicable. They're wrong.

If I really count it up, of all the people I interacted with during my time at Vinyl Wonderland, I only saw three of them ever again in any capacity once I moved away. The least remarkable of these was a social worker, who showed up at the Arnold's farm long enough to introduce me to another social worker who was more local, based in Cambridge. I remember a great deal of handshaking, and a lot of good will.

As for Tony Accardi, well, technically I never saw him again, either. At least, not in the flesh. I saw his photo a few times, usually in the context of "former mayor," and I think he might have made a run for governor, although I'd have to look that up to be sure. That's not to say that he didn't make his presence felt. He did that in spades. Beginning in April of 1985, he made sure to be in touch once a year, by sending me a birthday card.

It wasn't my birthday he was celebrating. It was Michael's.

That's right. For eleven long years, see, no matter where I moved or lived, Tony Accardi made certain that I received a card acknowledging that his son had survived to go 'round the sun one more time. Most years, he included a photo of Michael. Sometimes it was a school head shot, and other times a candid. I got to watch that boy grow up, long-distance, and it was wonderful, in its way, to see his features change and harden as he slipped away from being a child and passed by degrees into adulthood.

But in the spring of 1996, June ninth came and went, and I didn't receive a card. For a day or so, I told myself that the mail was slow, or that Tony was late getting to the post office. But when June twelfth rolled around and still no card, I knew. Michael Accardi was dead.

I was pretty sure I could discover the Accardi's street address, and I thought about sending condolences via Hallmark, but I didn't. What could I possibly say?

And that takes me to the most remarkable of my post-Vinyl Wonderland encounters, which was (of course) Celine DeLapp.

A fact of life for most rural folks is that once in a while, like it or not, you make a pilgrimage to the great big city. Things come up. Things get broken. Certain specialties only exist in a major metropolitan area. In the case of Doris and Fitch Arnold, my parents' house dragged us back into Columbus on a semi-regular basis. There was some question, apparently, of who owned the house, who would inherit. What we discovered, to our collective surprise, was that the house was paid off. My dad and I had been poor as starving church mice, sure, but not because of the mortgage. That had been reduced to zero just after the life insurance kicked in for my mom. They'd paid for a good policy, and the result was that he owned the house outright. If only he'd done an equally solid job updating his will, I would have inherited a three-bedroom suburban home, complete with in-ground pool, on the day I turned eighteen.

Unfortunately, my parents had last updated their will back in 1971, and at the time, given that neither one had any siblings, they'd left the house to my mother's parents, both of whom had long since passed away. Fitch and Doris had hired a lawyer to see what could be done, and eventually, with the calendar reading 1986, a probate judge reached a decision: the house would be held in trust by the Arnolds until I turned twenty-one, provided everybody was willing to show up to a fancy downtown office and sign a truckload of documents.

Now, when the country mice visit the big city, see, it's never a one-and-done sort of trip. Excursions like this involve a whole laundry list of errands that just can't be done anywhere else, and you "make a day of it." I asked to come along, because I'd developed a sweet spot for my home city, and since it was a Saturday, permission was granted. For what it's worth, permission of all kinds, from Fitch and Doris, usually was granted. Apparently, they'd been proper tight-ass drill sergeants for their own kids, and I was the surprise beneficiary of their newly reformed thinking.

The trip overall went off without a hitch. We left on time, the weather was decent (early April in Ohio means forsythia, daffodils, and tulips), and the fancy downtown office was exactly as expected, and then some. We had lunch at the French Market, and then it was on to Colonial Music, where Doris and Fitch intended to drop me off while they went to a nearby fabric store, searching for just the right pattern to sew new kitchen curtains.

I'd never been to Colonial Music, and the trumpet I'd been playing (not very well) with the Meadowbrook band didn't need any help, but I'd also discovered Doris's mostly neglected mandolin. I'd been experimenting with that in the evenings, inspired, mostly, by the coda to Rod Stewart's "Maggie May." Fitch had proclaimed that my playing was "coming along," but Doris was firm that if I had any hope of continuing to "come along," I'd need new strings.

Colonial Music had two people on staff that afternoon, and one of them was Celine.

We spotted each other at the same moment, and I just about fell over. Celine managed to get halfway through her basic customer service greeting of, "Hello, how can I…?" before trailing away.

She looked exactly the same, but also completely different thanks to a conservative skirt and a white blouse with a lightweight, button-down sweater, forest-green cashmere, over top. Except for the haircut, she looked like a Norman Rockwell school teacher.

Now, I'd love to report that I said something smart and clever, the kind of thing that greases the wheels of an awkward conversation and makes everyone involved feel at ease. Instead, I said, "Wow. I didn't know you worked here."

Proof that Celine was still Celine, she tilted up her chin as if I'd offered this as a challenge. "One day a week. The rest is still instrument repair."

"Got it," I said, and then we stood there, facing each other but thinking private thoughts, and not saying a damn thing.

Celine found her tongue first. "What are you doing here?"

I pointed to a row of guitars and ukuleles hanging from the wall. At the end of the row was a mandolin. "Strings," I said. "I've started playing mandolin."

She laughed, then cut herself off. "Sorry," she said. "You're serious."

"What's wrong with the mandolin?"

"Nothing," she said, and then she caught hold of my arm and steered me toward the back of the shop. "Beth!" she called to the other woman on duty. "I need a minute!"

Once we were in a corner, surrounded by cream-colored filing cabinets stuffed with music books, Celine jabbed a finger into my sternum and hissed, "You need to tell me *everything*."

Well, I had no intention of doing that. I hadn't told anyone "everything," and how would my life have been any better if I had? Besides, the longer I'd lived in the shoes of my current life, the faster my escapades at Vinyl Wonderland slipped into the gentle chaos of memory. My time there hadn't made much sense while I was living it, and it made considerably less sense now.

As for Celine, maybe she really did want to know everything, but what she needed was something that would satisfy her curiosity, a tale to explain both the disappearance of the Elvis door and my sudden relocation.

But I truly had no idea how to compress all that into something short, or even sensible. My life wasn't an elevator speech. On top of that, I'd done a lot less boasting since arriving at Meadowbrook—thank you, sobriety—so when it came to making things up on the fly, I was frankly kind of rusty.

"October closed up," I said, with a shrug that I hoped would convey that I didn't know much more than that. "One day I came in for work, and the Elvis door was just gone."

She looked at me sidelong, searchingly, knowing (I'm sure) that even if my statement was factual, it wasn't even close to what mattered.

"You know the whole place is gone now," she said. "It's flowers, a flower shop."

I told her I hadn't heard that, and then I asked after her sister. Celine said she was better, enjoying a good spell, and they were all learning to enjoy it while it lasted.

"But," she said, "what about your dad? Did he go through?"

This was a line of thought that I never allowed myself to dwell on except very late at night, when keeping the drift of my thoughts in line, especially lying in bed, was hard to the point of impossible. It was kind of a shock, standing there in Colonial Music, faced with Celine, to realize that I'd never said a word to anyone about what actually happened to my father.

"Brendan?"

"Sorry," I said, "it's just…"

"Brendan, what happened?"

I was about to answer that I lost him, but I couldn't say it. Not because I was casting around for a euphemism for his death, or because I was suddenly emotional, which I most certainly was, but because it wasn't true. I hadn't lost my father, I'd marooned him. And even if I took the low road and laid the blame at the feet of the man with the missing tooth, I was the one who'd prepped the tunnel with explosives, and I was the one who'd convinced Celine to extend the initial invite.

So much for my career as a consummate liar.

Celine blew out a breath and got a good look at me, top to bottom. "You're a mess," she said.

Until bumping into her, I'd have said I was doing more than a fair job of keeping things together, but now I wasn't so sure. The know-it-alls that run the world added "repression" to the dictionary for a reason, and I was starting to think that maybe I was reason number one. After all, I had long since stopped making any effort to look for my father. True, I had the best excuse in the world, because I didn't know where to look. Sure, maybe if I'd tried harder—maybe if I'd been desperate, which October had once suggested was the key—maybe then, I would have found another way in. But the fact was that I had lost interest in the whole project, and while the guilt of my inactivity had wrapped long, painful tendrils through every inch of my body,

I was long since done with taking active steps to recover my father.

Celine brushed away her bangs, folded her arms, and said, as if this settled something important, "You've grown."

I hadn't grown, at least not upward. But I was filling out. In the sixteen months since I'd last laid eyes on Celine, I'd gained twenty pounds. Plus, my beard had come in, which Doris and my various teachers hated, so I was shaving daily.

"Thanks," I said. "And you've given up on the boots-and-leather look."

"Dress code," she replied. "But like I said, I'm only in here once a week. A little extra cash, for home."

"So," I said, "some big project? A trip? A baby?"

That last part just slipped out. I didn't mean to fire off such a direct question and I didn't mean for it to matter, but I could tell at once that I'd landed a gut-punch.

"No baby," she said. She opened her mouth to say more, then shut it again, and got a look on her face as if I were the central variable in an enormously complex equation, and she was half a heartbeat away from solving it.

"Brendan," she said, "if I told you…"

"If you told me what?"

She reached out, grabbed not my arm but the front of my shirt, and tugged me toward the back door. I followed, pulled along in her wake, and looked back once to see that Beth was chatting away with a couple of other customers, and then I was outside, at the back of the service entrance, flanked by a Dumpster, cinderblock walls, and a dilapidated wooden fence.

Celine steered me to the wall, pushed me lightly against it, and said, "Don't make me repeat this."

"Don't make you repeat what?"

She drew a steadying breath and said, "This is a good time of the month."

I shook my head, lost. "What are you talking about?"

She held my eye, ignoring my question. "You can say no. Maybe you should."

"Say no to what?"

The hand she'd been using to grip my shirt unclasped, and she slid her palm up my midriff until it was resting flat on my chest. She didn't move it away, and at last, in a flash, I understood.

I reached out—slowly, gently, as if she were made of thin blown glass, like an ornament—and I let my fingers stray across the side of her face.

"If we do this," she whispered, "you will never contact me again. Are we clear?"

I didn't want that to be in any way true, but I said, "I understand," or I tried to; the words came out so softly that I could barely hear myself, and then I leaned down and she stretched up, and we kissed. It was intense, but over in a flash. She got hold of my belt and used it to spin us both around so that she was the one up against the wall.

Whatever we do, we do it together.

"Quick," she said. "Before I change my mind."

Her fingers worked frantically to get my belt unbuckled and my jeans unzipped. At the same time, I hiked up her skirt so that it rode above her hips, and then I got hold of her underwear and peeled them down her thighs until they dropped to her ankles, and she kicked them off. They were black satin, a perfect match, an *exact* match for the pair I'd found in the trash-land.

"Lift me," she said, and I hoisted her against the wall until she was high enough to press against her, and then we kissed again, so hard that the back of her head banked off the cinder block, and then—well, that was the end of the erotic portion of the program.

See, the girls in Guernsey County, both in school and out, had pretty much avoided me, and even though the braver ones were curious and thought that I was dangerous in some kind of exotic, big-city way, I was equally guilty of avoiding them. I hadn't been near a girl since leaving Columbus, and in all honesty, I have to say I wasn't unhappy about that. I'd become willing, for once, to bide my time.

But with Celine, none of that worked in my favor. We were over and done inside of thirty seconds, and I have to say, that encounter made all the bad sex I'd had with Lani Bell feel like paradise by comparison. Celine hadn't let me into her pants for fun, or because her marriage didn't rock her world. She wanted one thing, and one thing only, and from me, she got it.

Down the many years since, I have always honored her request: I left her and her family alone. In that sense, her grand statement of "Whatever we do, we do it together," turned out to be—well, not a lie. That was just me making a mountain out of something she'd intended as a molehill, temporary and specific. All that said, of the two of us, she's the one who broke our deal, and she did it only once, by mail. I'm pretty sure it was the one thing that she and Tony Accardi ever did in common.

It was ten years later, see, and I was living in Seattle. Doris forwarded me an unopened envelope with a return address from Colonial Music. I tore that letter open and fished out the note inside, a folded sheet that enclosed a second piece of paper, a yellow carbon that turned out to be a generic receipt, the kind you fill out by hand. I had it upside down at first, but when I flipped it over, I realized that Celine had mailed me a work order for a damaged clarinet, an instrument brought to her for repair. The items that needed work were hand-written and listed as "Fix lever action on register key" and "Replace all cork." Total charge, $88.50.

Near the bottom, Celine had added her signature, stating that the work had been completed. The signature on the next line down, to indicate that the bill for the refurbished clarinet had been paid, read "Lauren Purcell."

Celine DeLapp and my mother. Briefly, oddly, together.

The accompanying note was short and blunt, pretty much an amalgam of Celine herself. It read:

Brendan,

I was clearing out old files and found this. I thought you should have it.

Your daughter's name is Caroline. She started playing soccer last year, and she's got talent. Maybe she gets that from you.

Yours, once,
Celine

Later that day, I went out and bought an inexpensive but handsome frame, black-bordered and glass-fronted, and I put the receipt in the frame and hung it on the wall in my kitchen. Before I sealed it up, I tucked Celine's note into the cardboard backing. It's been hiding there ever since, and we ignore each other, that note and me. I. Whatever.

And that's about it, right? The adventure concluded. Except, of course, for the little copper hut, my one physical memento from the scrap-yard world beyond the Elvis door. For a long time, I still didn't know what it was or what it was for, but a year or so after Celine wrote to me, I met Marjorie, who it turns out is exactly the woman I'd been looking for since, well, pretty much forever. What's truly astonishing is that she feels the exact same way, in reverse, about me.

Anyway, the first time she stayed over at my place, she spotted that little house, and she asked me why I was keeping such a cleverly designed candle holder if I didn't ever put it to use. Well, I had to laugh, because now that I looked at it, of course it was a candle holder, and the spike in the middle, which I'd regarded as a profound mystery for so many years, was simply a way to anchor any given candle in place.

We found a short, half-used candle, impaled its base on the spike, and set the copper hut on the table as a centerpiece. Once the candle was lit, the flame guttered and danced as I poured wine for Marjorie, then sparkling water for me.

"Oh," she said, "I didn't realize you don't drink."

I smiled, wanting to reassure her. "There's a lot you don't know, but I think you're the person I might want to tell. You might even be the person I need to tell."

Marjorie raised her glass in a toast. She said, "I've known that you have secrets since the day we met, secrets and—I'm not sure what exactly. Reserves. But I have secrets, too. Maybe we can share."

We clinked glasses and drank, and then I stared at the candle through the cut-outs in the hut's copper walls, and I watched the shadows flickering over the tablecloth.

That was twenty-three years ago. Marjorie and I have been married for so long that some years, our anniversary sneaks up on us, and we only manage to celebrate in a flustered rush, at the last possible minute. We come complete with two children and a dog, so life (as people are so quick to say now) is good. One thing for sure, I have never again bumped into a portal that functions in any way like the Elvis door. I consider that to be a very good thing.

Do I wonder about the fate of my father? Of course. I hope for the best, and I do what I can to prevent the unknowns from consuming me.

As for the little copper hut, either it has had absolutely no bearing on my life, or it is the essential glue that holds my marriage together. Marjorie teases me that if it weren't for my special candle holder, she'd have high-tailed it years ago, but even when we're laughing like that, poking fun, neither of us is inclined to take any chances. Even if that hut is nothing but a much-loved decoration, we keep it to this day on the dining room table, and at least once a week, without fail, my family and I turn down the overheads and make sure there's a lit candle burning inside. We hold hands all together, and then we eat and share the little details of our mostly unremarkable days. As we do, we watch the flame rising from the candle wick, and we note the shadows that spill across the table.

In these moments, I know that I should be at peace, but all too often, I find myself fretting that with each flickering shift in the light, a dry, questing wind is rising in a far-off wasteland of trash, junk, and unloved cast-offs. I suspect it of searching, this wind, stretching and rousing itself, seeking release, fresh victims, the one that got away. Change is coming, as it always does, and I hope that when it arrives, I'll be ready—not for my sake, but for the sake of those I love.

The End

CASTLE BRIDGE MEDIA RECOMMENDS...

If you liked this book, you might also enjoy reading the following titles from Castle Bridge Media available on Amazon or by order at your favorite book store:

Animal Charmer
By Rain Nox

Austinites
By In Churl Yo

Bloodsucker City
By Jim Towns

The Burning Gem
By Don Sawyer

THE CASTLE OF HORROR ANTHOLOGY SERIES
Volume 1
Volume 2: *Holiday Horrors*
Volume 3: *Scary Summer Stories*
Volume 4: *Women Running From Houses*
Volume 5: *Thinly Veiled: The 70s*
Volume 6: *Femme Fatales**
Volume 7: *Love Gone Wrong*
Volume 8: *Thinly Veiled: The 80s*
Volume 9: *Young Adult*
Volume 10: *Thinly Veiled: Saturday Mournings*
Volume 11: *Revenge*
Edited By Jason Henderson and In Churl Yo
*Edited By P.J. Hoover

Castle of Horror Podcast Book of Great Horror: Our Favorites, Top Tens and Bizarre Pleasures
Edited By Jason Henderson

Cherry Dark
By R.L. Wilburn

Dream State
By Martin Ott

Dominic
By Lee Guzman

FRENCH DECEPTION
A Forgery in Paris
By Janice Nagourney
A Forgery in Lyon
By Janice Nagourney

FuturePast Sci-Fi Anthology
Edited by In Churl Yo

GLAZIER'S GAP
Ghosts of the Forbidden
By Leanna Renee Hieber

Hellfall
By Jay Gould

Isonation
By In Churl Yo

JAYU CITY CHRONICLES
The Hermes Protocol
By Chris M. Arnone
Necropolis Alpha
By Chris M. Arnone

Junk Film: Why Bad Movies Matter
By Katharine Coldiron

MID-LIFE CRISIS THRILLERS
18 Miles From Town
By Jason Henderson
Lost Angel
By Sam Knight
Ties That Kill
By Deven Greene

Nightwalkers: Gothic Horror Movies
By Bruce Lanier Wright

THE PATH
The Blue-Spangled Blue
By David Bowles
The Deepest Green
By David Bowles

SURF MYSTIC
Night of the Book Man
By Peyton Douglas
Dark of the Curl
By Peyton Douglas

Vinyl Wonderland
By Mark Rigney

Yesterday's Tomorrows: The Golden Age of Science Fiction Movies
By Bruce Lanier Wright

Please remember to leave us your reviews on Amazon and Goodreads!

THANK YOU FOR SUPPORTING INDEPENDENT PUBLISHERS AND AUTHORS!
castlebridgemedia.com